*Coming soon from DAW Books

BOTTLE DEMON

STEPHEN BLACKMOORE

DAW BOOKS, INC.

DONALD A. WOLLHEIM, FOUNDER

1745 Broadway, New York, NY 10019

ELIZABETH R. WOLLHEIM
SHEILA E. GILBERT
PUBLISHERS

www.dawbooks.com

ACKNOWLEDGMENTS

As I write this the world is in the middle of a global pandemic that has killed over a quarter million people in the U.S., there's a tin-pot dictator in the White House desperately clinging to power in the most laughable and destructive ways possible, and the McRib is back.

God help us all.

2020 has been . . . let's call it challenging. Simply surviving it is a victory. Anything else is just frosting. I don't know about you, but I know I wouldn't have made it (provided I have—there's still a couple weeks left to go) without the support of my friends and family.

I'm going to keep this short because otherwise it would be longer than this book and I'd forget somebody and feel awful when I realize I missed a couple hundred people.

My wife, Kari, who calls me on my bullshit. My dog, Phryne, who is a goddamn holy terror, but she gets my ass out of my chair whether I like it or not. My agents, Al Guthrie, who made this whole journey possible, and Lisa Rodgers, who is helping me push it even further. And finally, Betsy Wollheim, Josh Starr, and the entire crew over at DAW, thank you for continuing to give a madman a forum for his lunatic ravings.

And to everyone who joked, made me think, helped me consider new possibilities or helped me crystallize the ones I already knew.

Thank you. I hope you enjoy the book and I hope you stick around for more. I've no intentions of hopping off this ride any time soon.

Chapter 1

Let me tell you about Belize.

Few years back I get hired by this burnt-out software millionaire who's convinced that the ghosts of his dead enemies are trying to murder him. All the normals he talks to think he's crazy, which he is. Totally batshit. Doesn't mean he's wrong. My line of work, things like this are an actual occupational hazard. I was in New York at the time and had just gone through a bad breakup where the girl I was seeing tried to eat my soul, and I figured getting out of town might not be a bad idea.

So I take his money, fly down to Belize, meet him at his compound. It's this weird Winchester House sort of thing with stairs that lead nowhere, doors that open onto windows, shit like that. Got a fifteen-foot-tall, razor-wire-topped wall surrounding the whole place. I'd have written him off as completely nuts except somebody's carved runes and sigils into the walls to ward against everything from demons to cockroaches. He might have been a normal, but he knew enough to hire real mages.

I do my thing. The only possibility is a Haunt of a murdered neighbor about five miles away who hated him, but more in a "Get off my lawn or I'll shoot you," paranoid sort of way, rather than a "I shall seek my vengeance from beyond the grave" sort of way. Guy's not a Wanderer, so he's not going anywhere. I reassure Mister Software Millionaire that if anybody is trying to kill him, they're not already dead.

Cue epic party. To be fair the epic party had started about a week before, and it was just finding its pace. He had like a hundred-and-fifty people in the place with him snorting, smoking, fucking. Real extroverted for a guy with an almost Howard Hughes level of paranoia. So, being a good guest, of course I joined in.

One morning as I'm staggering out of somebody's bedroom, he comes up to me and says, "Eric, do you want to see God?"

I can say from recent experience that when confronted with a question like that the best course of action is to say no, but at that point I'd never met a god. A few powerful spirits like the Voodoo Loa Baron Samedi and Maman Brigitte, but nothing you could really get behind on the whole divinity thing. But I figure he's talking metaphorically and grunt something that sounds like assent.

Guy hands me half a dozen pills of some shit he got from Singapore that's so new it doesn't even have a name yet. And before he tells me I should take half of one, I've already swallowed all six.

When I come back to myself it's two months later and I'm standing in the Belizean jungle, half-naked, covered in mud, waving a flaming machete around at some poor bastard who turns out to be my guide. He doesn't mind the machete so much, crazy fucking gringos are kind of a thing out here, but the fact that I'd cast a spell to wreath it in fire has him a little freaked out. I have no idea why I'm there, how I got there, or why the Belizean police are currently looking for me.

So when I wake up lying on my side, naked and

sweating, vomiting black bile onto a cold concrete floor, lights swimming around me, with no idea how I got here, where here is, or why I've got a hole in my memory so big I can barely see the edges, all I can think of is Belize.

Somebody hammers on my back, dislodging more of the black crap from my stomach, lungs, sinuses. I don't even want to know what's happening on the other end. The hacking and dry heaves subside, and I'm rolled onto my back, and someone wipes my face with a rough towel.

A face dips into my vision. Goggles, respirator, surgical cap. A hand gloved in purple nitrile comes up and waves. "Hello!" A woman's voice, British accent, muffled behind the mask.

She pulls the mask and goggles off. They catch a bit in the surgical cap, but eventually she gets it all off with a motion like she's slapping mosquitos off her face. Eventually I can see a woman with Indian features, black hair, a vibrant smile that says, "I'm bat-shit crazy, how are you?"

I have absolutely no idea who this person is.

"Sorry," she says. "I do hate those things. But, you know, fumes. Can you hear me? Oh. I probably should have started with that." I try to say something. Anything. But all I can do is twitch my fingers. She sees the twitch and amazingly her smile gets a little bit wider, like the Cheshire Cat on meth. I manage to make a vague sound that at a stretch could be considered speech.

"I haven't the foggiest idea what you just said," she says. "But you've gotten most of that crap out of your system and you have air in your lungs, and your larynx seems to work, so yay!"

My mind feels like it's been run across a belt-sander, my thoughts too smooth to get a grip on. Like

I'm looking at a shattered funhouse mirror, each piece reflecting back a distorted view of who I am. None of them quite sync up.

"Did it work?" A man's voice, deep, rough, like a rockslide. I can't move my head to see him, but the scorn in his voice and the disapproval on her face tell me these are not the best of friends.

"If it didn't, I wouldn't bloody well be talking to him, would I?"

"That's what you said last time."

"The fuck just happened?" I force the words out, straining not only to get the sounds, but simply to remember them. .

"Oh, nothing much," she says. The nonchalant tone disappears into bubbly excitement. "Just the most amazing piece of magic no one's done for a few thousand years. And it worked. Go me!"

"Yeah, this time," says the unseen man.

"Piss off, Joseph," she says over her shoulder. "Don't mind him, darling. He's just jealous that you're not dead and he is."

I hear the muffled pop of gunshots in the distance. "That was fast," says the man. I can hear metal on metal as he racks the slide on a gun.

"Of course it was fast," the woman says. "Everyone in a bloody thirty-mile radius knows something happened here, and at least a dozen know what it was. Now give me a hand getting him out of this circle."

"Not my job," he says. "I'm here to kill shit, not do manual labor. Exit plan's your department." I hear the metallic shred of a rusting door open and close.

"I swear that man is such a cunt," the woman says. "Now, where were we? Ah, yes. Escape. This is so exciting."

She grabs my wrists and begins to heave me across the room, grunting with the effort. I try to move my head to get a better idea of the space, but I can barely twitch my eyelids.

"If I had a pound for every dead-weight naked man I've had to drag across a room, I'd be richer than the Queen, let me tell you." She finally gets me where she wants me and lets my arms fall to the floor. I try to move but nothing's quite working. She stands over me, feet on either side of my chest, and crouches down to get a good look at me. Long black hair spilling over her shoulders, strands glued to her forehead with sweat. She's wearing one of those lab bunny suits with the hood down.

She listens to my heart with a stethoscope, pulls out a penlight, shines it into my eyes. Feels like my brain's being stabbed with an ice pick. I try to wince, but I just don't have the strength.

"Everything appears to be in order. All the things in all their right places. No extra limbs. None missing. Heart's beating. Now I must say the tattoos are a bit unexpected. You'll have to tell me about that, but right now darling, we're a bit pressed for time. If we both survive the next few hours, perhaps we can get together over tea and you can tell me all about it. If not, it was simply lovely to have met you. Ta!"

She touches my forehead with two fingers, the coolness a sharp contrast against my fevered skin, and everything goes black.

———

I dream of Nuestra Señora de las Sombras, Mictecacihuatl, Santa Muerte. She hasn't been more than a thought away for what feels like a thousand years, but I can't remember most of it.

I walk through the temple pyramid deep within the heart of Mictlan, the Aztec land of the dead. The home of Mictecacihuatl, a goddess who has adapted to the times and more often than not goes by Santa Muerte, Saint Death. I search through empty halls and silent rooms. When I reach the top where the altar stone sits, heavy, and dark with blood, I find her.

She pays me no attention—Santa Muerte, Mictecacihuatl, and a woman named Tabitha. A saint, a goddess, a mortal woman. Those three identities died by my hand, and became something new, something that had never existed before, and took up the name and the role as the protector of Mictlan.

But Mictlan cannot be ruled by only one. She needs a consort. She needs Mictlantecuhtli. At one point she wanted me to take that role. Insisted on it. But I don't remember what happened. And I don't understand why he's standing next to her.

Because I killed him. As completely as a god can be killed. I sacrificed myself, and in that moment, I broke his hold on me and shattered him into a thousand shards, a jeweled shotgun blast of deep green jade.

Yet here he is. Slowly I pull the knowledge from my mind, like hauling a truck out of mud, that he's supposed to be here. But I don't know why I would think that. He is powerful, immense. Frightening, but not in and of himself. Something else about him terrifies me.

He turns around, eyes black as midnight, the power of death radiating off him like the cold of a dying sun. He sees through me as if I'm beneath his awareness, and I realize why I'm so afraid.

He's wearing my face.

———

I snap awake in a motel room with a wet scream. Sweat soaked sheets, stink of Febreze, cigarette smoke, a thick chemical burn in my nose. Curtains drawn; a single dim lamp bolted to the wall fills the room with a fluorescent buzz. The room is too loud, too bright, too everything. My body feels wrong, like I've just been stuffed into a suit three times too small.

I have no memory of this place. I've lived the last several years out of motels like this one, and sure, they tend to blur together, but they all have something that stands out just a little bit, and I don't remember this one at all.

Blackouts are weird beasts. Sometimes, you don't remember anything's happened. Other times you can feel enough of the edges that you can tell you've got a big fucking hole in your memory.

After Belize, the worst blackout I had lasted a week and ended with me waking up naked and screaming in a burned-out cabin in the Mojave. I'm sensing a bit of a theme here.

The last thing I remember is landing on my back on a school blacktop after a demon by the name of, I shit you not, Hank beat the crap out of me. Hank was working for the djinn Darius, who's been trying to get out of the bottle he's been trapped in for thousands of years, and they knew I had it.

I thought I was safe in an extra-dimensional pocket that looks like a 1940s hotel room, but apparently, I was wrong. Hank got in, I got hammered, and I barely got out of there in one piece.

And then I'm lying on a concrete floor with an Indian woman and some guy named Joseph. There's a dream of Santa Muerte that's already fading. Did I dream the woman, too? The bunker? But what happened before all that?

My thoughts get shunted aside as my body decides that it really wants to throw up again. I peel the sheets off of me, roll myself out of the bed, and face-plant into the carpet. I grab the nightstand and slowly pull myself up, which turns out to be a really bad idea. Once my feet are on the floor everything inside me rebels. I vomit up more of that black gore, the heaving taking me to my knees. It goes on. And on, and on. I don't think I've puked this much since I drank three bottles of mescal in Tijuana and got in a bar fight.

Eventually, there's nothing left, and all I'm doing is dry heaving. The black liquid soaks into the rug and gives off a sharp, burning stink. My mouth tastes like the inside of a chemical toilet, my hands are covered in the stuff. But the vertigo is gone, the nausea is gone. My hands are steadier, the fatigue in my muscles I had just minutes ago is fading. But holy fuck are my abs sore.

I am covered in so much of this black filth I look like an oil worker at a pipeline break. And it burns. I am not going to do another goddamn thing until I have this shit off my body. I leave tar colored footprints into the bathroom. I flick on the lights, fluorescent tubes making everything look slightly green and far too bright. A stabbing pain shoots through my eyes and I close them tight against the assault.

The afterimages swim behind my eyes as I fumble for the shower and turn it on as hot as it will get. I crack an eye open and it's almost dim enough to not burn out my retinas before I have to close my eyes again. The scalding water washes the filth away, turning the bottom of the tub into the shower scene from *Psycho*. The sense of being crammed into my body like it's a sausage casing is beginning to fade. My head is clearing up. Even the pain in my eyes from the light is fading. All things considered, I feel okay. Nothing hurts.

Wait. Nothing hurts.

I can't remember the last time something didn't hurt. I've spent years popping Vicodin and OxyContin from the beatings I've taken, the bones I've broken, the cuts, the scrapes, the gunshots, the stabbings. I force both eyes open against the light and get a good look at myself.

I don't see scars that I should have. Tears, cuts, a set of three ugly puncture scars in my left hand where I got stuck to a table with a nail gun. Nothing. But that's not the weirdest bit.

Over the last twenty years or so I've been getting tattooed with protection and enhancement spells. I'm covered in tats from throat to wrists to ankles, a network of magic ink that covers every inch of skin with wards, tricks, traps. Healing spells and pain avoidance spells and spells to dodge bullets, knives, harsh language.

Our identities are made up of who we think we are, how we see ourselves. My tattoos are as much a part of me as my skin is. I can't imagine not having them. I don't even remember what I looked like without them. From what I can see, and what I can feel, they're all here.

Except they look freshly inked, like I just got out of the chair. And they're . . . colorful. All of my tattoos were done in blacks and grays over the course of twenty years, maybe some dull red here and there.

But now? Blues and greens, reds and yellows, all bright as sun-kissed gemstones. I am not a jewel-tone sort of guy. You see bright colors; I am not the first person that comes to mind. But every piece is almost painfully colorful. I look like tropical bird bukkake.

I have one tattoo that takes up most of my chest, a circle with birds inside it. The birds move, shifting position and pose. Watching them gives me a headache. I got that as a sort of last-ditch strike: triggering the spell releases the birds, raven-shaped bolts of magical energy.

At least they used to be. When I got the tattoo, the birds were ravens and the circle was Celtic knotwork. A while back, after I got mixed up with Santa Muerte and her crazy Aztec family, the tattoo changed from Celtic knotwork to an Aztec design. The ravens became stylized eagles. Before, it was just a spell I'd have to charge every time I used it, like loading a shotgun.

But the eagles are different. They have a mind of their own, and they don't always listen to me. Sometimes they'll come out, sometimes they'll protect me, but not always. Like they can't be bothered by trifles, the snotty little pricks. But they're intimidating as fuck to look at, and now that they're green as polished jade, they're downright terrifying.

I close my eyes against the hot water, center myself. I'm beginning to panic, and I don't have time for that shit. My mind snags on the Indian woman with the British accent. That wasn't a dream. Can't have been. She performed some ritual, in which I apparently played a starring role. But what was it, and why was she doing it? And what is all this black shit I've been puking out?

I'm not going to get answers standing in the shower. I've scrubbed as much of this gunk off me as I can and rinsed my mouth to get most of the burning chemical taste out of my throat and sinuses. I'm tempted to gargle with body wash, but that feels a bit much. Then I say fuck it and do it anyway. I shut off the water and get out.

The mirror's fogged. I almost leave it that way, but I really need to see. Tattoos have changed, scars are gone. What else is different? I wipe the mirror clean with my hand and see myself through streaked glass. My face disappears as steam covers the mirror.

In that short glimpse my face looks wrong. Not a lot wrong. It's like the way getting new glasses or a haircut feels wrong until you get used to it. Only I can't pin down exactly what's different. No scars, sure. Nose looks like it's never been broken before. But there's something else.

I towel off and plan out next steps. Okay, priorities.

Clothes would be good. I'm not crazy about walking around with a bedsheet wrapped around me like Caligula.

Get oriented. Where the fuck am I? How much time has passed since I blacked out? My mind is trying to grab onto something else, but it keeps slipping. Is anybody trying to kill me?

Get the hell out of here and on the move. I don't know what's happening. Staying in one place is just going to make me an easier target. Sure, you might think that's paranoia talking, but trust me, there's a reason I never stay anywhere for long.

I check the closet hoping somebody left behind at least a pair of shorts and am more than a little surprised to find my clothes hanging in there, or somebody's clothes, at least. Suit, socks, shoes, boxers. Did I stash all this here before whatever the hell happened to me happened? If I did, it's as lost in the crater of my memory as everything else.

My messenger bag is on the closet floor. I pick it up and empty it out onto the table on the other side of the room. Most of what I usually carry is still in there. Some useful, most not.

Ingredients for rituals, salt, powdered iron, grave dirt, ground-up bone, a Hand of Glory in a Zip-loc bag—that last after a hard-learned lesson that a desiccated hand covers all your shit in flakes of flesh and gristle if you don't wrap it up.

There's a straight razor, a couple Sharpies, some HI, MY NAME IS stickers to make the normals think I'm somebody I'm not. A ledger, thin, bound in leather, with more pages than should fit inside listing decades worth of magical garbage kept in storage, items ranging from the stupidly useless to the downright terrifying.

I find the key to the room at the Ambassador Hotel in the bag's outside flap, probably the only thing left of the hotel not made out of old memories and ecto-plasm.

Along with the key is a pocket watch, a gun, a lighter, all things that are more than they appear. The watch, a railroad grade Sangamo Special, keeps excellent time, and also twists it into pretzels in ways I still haven't figured out.

The gun is a Browning 9mm Hi-Power pistol my grandfather got off a Nazi in WWII. It's an ugly piece of hardware through and through. To most people it's just a cold hunk of metal. To a necromancer it's a hell of a lot more. There's so much death in this thing that my magic gets ahold of it and it wakes up. It has some awareness, more every time I fire it, and it's a raging asshole.

I get a vague sense of surprise from the gun. Holding it feels like I've stuck my hand in a bucket full of spiders, but it makes unusually large holes for a 9mm. I understand it does other things, too, but I haven't really let it off its leash. It feels expectant, like it's waiting for me to use it right. I'm told that I should be okay as long as it doesn't start talking to me.

And then there's the lighter. An old Zippo, brass, dented, scratched, an unrecognizable image on one side made of flakes of turquoise. It holds the power of Huitzilopochtli, a god of war and fire who wielded Xi-uhtecuhtli, the Turquoise Serpent, whose fires would burn everything it touched.

Quetzalcoatl killed Huitzilopochtli during the invasion of the Spanish and stole his power. The mad wind god stuck it in a lighter and gave it to me to burn down Mictlan. I refused, so he used it to burn Los Angeles to the ground instead.

But one thing is missing. And it's the most important one. A bottle. Old, multi-colored, Islamic glass with a rune-covered stopper held in place by pine tar and magic.

It holds an eight-thousand-year-old djinn named Darius. He's destroyed entire civilizations while bound to masters who kept him on a very short leash.

Wherever the bottle is, I hope it's in a really good hiding place. The last thing I remember I was holding onto it. After that it's all Blackout Central. The bottle was sealed by Mictlantecuhtli during a battle in Mictlan five hundred years ago that nobody walked away from unscathed. It ended up with Juan Cabrillo and stayed with him for the next twenty years until he died from an infected bone break.

There it sat in a hole on Catalina Island off the coast of Los Angeles while Darius tried to work out what to do about it. Eventually he figured out that though he couldn't get out of his pocket universe, he could let others in.

And that's what he did. He created doors all over the city. Some obvious, some hidden. To some he was a legend, an urban myth. Tales of the djinn's bottle brought people from all over to look for it. It was the Maltese Falcon, the Holy Grail, and a blowjob from Marilyn Monroe all rolled into one.

The people who found it, archaeologists digging on Catalina Island, had no idea what it was. But their security guy, a mage by the name of Robert Carter, did. He stole it, hid it in a place nobody was ever going to find, and laid clues that would eventually lead someone from his family to it.

Which is where I come in. See, our boy Robert was my grandfather. I followed his leads, got the bottle, and when I thought I had it safe and secure, I got jumped by Hank the Friendly Neighborhood Murder Demon.

There are a few scenarios I can think of right off the bat to explain why I don't have it. Scenario one: Darius has a new master and they figured out how to open the bottle and make Darius do what they want him to do. When Hernan Cortés, the Spanish conquistador, had control of him, he kicked the crap out of the Aztecs and managed to murder most of their gods.

Scenario two: There isn't a new master, Darius figured out how to get the bottle open himself. He's a free agent. He can do what he wants. After eight thousand years, I'm thinking he's built up quite an extensive shit list.

The third and most optimistic option is that neither of those happened and the bottle is, if not safe, at least not where Darius can do anything with it.

I'm not much of an optimist.

Chapter 2

The harder I try to remember where I put the bottle, or at the very least what happened to it once I blacked out, the more it slips by. I give up after a migraine threatens to settle in for the long haul. That's not normal blackout behavior, but then nothing about what's going on right now is particularly normal.

Technically, the only one who can open Darius's bottle is the one who sealed it, Mictlantecuhtli, who is way, way dead. But because of assorted and sundry cosmic fuckery I've been roped into taking his place. Last time I took a really good look at the bottle I could see all of the interlocking spells sealing it up. It was like suddenly understanding Greek while on vacation so you can't stop seeing all the SOCRATES ❤ PLATO porn on the Acropolis.

Not only did I know how the bindings were built, I knew how to take them down. Mictlantecuhtli might be dead, but apparently his shitty understudy is good enough to carry the show.

So as long as I didn't open it while I was blacked out, it's all good. Or mostly good. I'll take the lack of scars, and pain, and even the tattoos, but not knowing why makes me worry. But there really isn't a whole hell of a lot I can do about it right now, so I file it all away for later.

I put everything back into the messenger bag except for the Hand of Glory, which, true story, when I was a kid, I thought was a euphemism for a handjob. This one goes in the trash. I got it like ten years ago from a mortician in Portland. Maine, not Washington. It's seen better days, and I don't mean just at the end of the arm of the guy it came from. I doubt it even works anymore.

I pull the clothes out of the closet and take a good look at them. They're new, neatly pressed, shoes polished. That's a little unusual for me. I'm so hard on clothes that bothering to keep them in good shape is kind of pointless. But clothes are clothes and I can't go walking around with my dick hanging out. Everything fits perfectly. Also a little weird for me. I buy shit off estate sales if I buy it at all. Retail theft is easy with magic. So a good fit is a rare thing.

I slide the pocket watch and straight razor into a coat pocket, the Browning into its holster at the small of my back. The lighter stays in the bag. I don't trust myself enough not to burn everything down around me and I've had more than enough of that shit already.

Now what? Get my bearings. Talk to some people. Carefully. If Belize taught me anything, it's that though you can never be sure what you did during a blackout, you likely pissed off a few people. If you're me, that likelihood cranks up significantly. But I've got questions, like what the hell is going on?

The clock on the nightstand grabs my attention. It shows the day and month, and I know for a fact that it's wrong. But I can't remember what it should be. That's all lost in the blackout hole swirling in the center of my mind.

I don't have a chance to really think about it because that's when the room's phone rings. I don't have a good track record when it comes to motel telephones. Nobody wants to talk to you when you're holed up in some seedy shithole like this one, even if they know that you're there. No, not even that Vegas stripper you gave your number to after a drunk night full of lap-dances. No, you did not "share a moment."

The calls I've gotten on motel room phones have ranged from horrible family news to one from a pack of ghouls gunning for me in North Dakota, who wanted to make sure I was in the room before crashing a van through the wall. I got lucky. They hit the wrong room. That actually happened twice. The second time they used a semi.

I don't bother to answer the phone. Either it's going to be a van/wall sort of scenario, which includes anything from the van/wall category, truck/window, sedan/door, etc. Or it's going to be horrible news, like Darius has gotten out of his bottle, or the city's burning down. Again.

Of course, it could just be a wrong number, or some lonely soul wanting to chat.

Yeah, I crack myself up. Whoever it is, the message is clear. Time to bug out. I sling the messenger bag over one shoulder and across my chest, draw the Browning, chamber a round, and go outside.

I thought everything was off inside. It's worse out here. The smoke from the fires has reduced to the point where it just looks like any smoggy day in Los Angeles, but it's not a Los Angeles I completely recognize.

The Downtown skyline is off. For one, there is a skyline. Last time I saw it, more than half of the buildings were burnt-out shells or piles of rubble. Billions of dollars in commercial real estate went up like Kleenex in a fireplace.

But now? New buildings have sprung up like mushrooms. A lot of them are still under construction, but holy shit that was fast. You can measure the timeline of new construction in this city by geological epoch.

So, either these were all in the works way before the fires burned everything down, and they were ready to go up immediately, or everything moved really, really fast. Or—and much as I don't want to think about it, it's hard to ignore the possibility—maybe this blackout went on longer than I think it did. The more I consider it, the more I think that might be the truth.

My thoughts are interrupted by a high-end Mercedes peeling into the parking lot. I don't know who's in the car. I don't know if they're here for me, but let's be honest here. Much like my luck with motel telephones, waiting to find out who's speeding into an empty parking lot I happen to be standing in has rarely been a positive experience. If there's one thing I've learned, it's that there's a time to ask questions and a time to start shooting. This is not a time for questions.

I draw a bead with the Browning and fire, not really expecting to hit anything. Was a time when all the gun could do was make bigger-than-usual holes in things. But for a while now I've been feeling something inside it waking up, paying attention. My shot should have gone wide, but instead it punches into the windshield right in front of the driver.

Seems magic pistols are no match for modern ballistic glass and the shot does nothing more than spiderweb the windshield. I pick up a sense of burning hot rage coming from the gun.

Brakes screech, the car spins, smoke bubbles up from underneath. It comes to a halt, but three of the four people in it are out their doors before the car stops moving.

Two have guns, one an extendable security baton. I bring up a shield spell and the bullets ricochet off.

Guess they're not here for a friendly chat. The guy with the baton is luckier. It also helps that he's another mage. I feel a flare of magic as he triggers a spell and leaps impossibly high, coming down behind me in the blink of an eye, getting inside my guard because stupidly I had my shield blocking only one direction.

He swings, but he doesn't have good footing after that jump. Though the baton sails by, it's a little too close and it forces me back. The two guys behind me are still a threat, so I keep the shield up between us, bullets bouncing and sparking off it. It's splitting my attention and I almost get the baton in the face. Another swing of the baton, and I step back again. He's forcing me into the other two.

I need to get closer, but this guy's good and lightning-fast, his reflexes boosted with magic. Every time I step in, he pushes me back out again. I have an idea. It's an old trick, one I've gotten really good at the last few years. I scan around me for ghosts, and only find a couple of Echoes nearby, scratchy images of dead men and women who didn't leave anything behind except for the last moments of their lives played over and over again.

The ones I have to worry about are Haunts and Wanderers, ghosts with awareness and agency. Haunts are rooted near the spot they died, and they're only a problem if I'm close enough. Wanderers are what they sound like, ghosts that aren't stuck in place. They tend to be smarter, faster, far more dangerous. They have a lot more will than your typical Haunt.

It's easy to forget that ghosts aren't people. They're cast-off shells that look and act like, and even believe that they are, the person who died. Not everyone leaves a ghost. It takes trauma, and there's a whole lot of trauma in Los Angeles.

There are no Haunts nearby, but a couple of Wanderers across the street. I'll have to be quick, and though I feel fine now that I've puked up all that black crap, I don't know for sure that I can still do this. Something has happened to me. I have no idea what, but now would be a bad time to discover that I can't do something I should be able to.

I don't have a lot of choice, though. I can't back up far, the two guys behind me are pressing in forcing me to pull the shield closer to my back. Without enough space to bring up the gun, it might as well be a stapler for all the good it can do.

I step in as the baton swings toward my head. Right before it connects, I slide over to the other side of the veil. I can't stay here long. On the living side I can see the ghosts, and they see me, but we can't really do much to each other. But now I'm on their turf, they're gonna start looking at me like lunch. Ghosts eat life. Pretty soon those two Wanderers will catch my scent. If I'm over here too long, I'll have bigger problems than the guy with the baton.

It's so quiet over here I can hear my own heartbeat. It's not always like that. There's often a shrieking wind, or maybe it's the ghosts that are shrieking and causing the wind. All the colors here are drained until they're almost black and white. It's not just the ghosts but the place itself that will kill me. The whole environment is entropy. It wants life, sucks it out of you if you stick around too long.

So I don't stick around. From this side my opponent looks like a vaguely man-shaped blob of light, his baton barely an afterimage swinging through me, a cold trail like a finger of ice running through my face. I give it a second, duck down as he goes for a backswing, and then slide back to the jet-engine roar of life and sound and air all coming at me at once. The baton sails just over my head.

I stand up fast, shove the barrel of the gun up into

the crook between his jaw and his neck, and pull the trigger. The Browning doesn't disappoint. The top half of the mage's head explodes in a fountain of bone and meat, and he drops.

I hear car doors slamming shut. The two men who were behind me jump into the Mercedes, panic on their faces, the driver already slamming the car in reverse. I let loose with the Browning, and this time the bulletproof glass doesn't stop it. The round hits the guy in the passenger seat, going through his eye and clipping the forehead of the guy behind him, enough to run a furrow through his brain. I feel a sense of sick satisfaction from the Browning. I really need to get rid of this gun.

I don't shoot the driver. I have questions and he's going to have at least a couple answers for me. I don't want him to escape, but no worries on that front. Seeing as I've killed everyone else, he doesn't have much to lose. Not that you could tell from the look on his face. I don't think he's changed expression since I first laid eyes on him, blank-faced, apathetic. He throws the car back into gear and stomps on the gas to run me down. The whining of his transmission and the split second before the gears engage give me all the time I need to prepare.

I stand there, gun at my side, waiting for him to slam into me. At the last second, I slide back over to the dead side, feeling a cold wave pass through me as the car plows through where I was standing. I slide back a moment later to the sound of a hissing radiator and a horn that won't stop going off. He's rammed the car into the brick wall at the end of the parking lot, destroying its front end. I run over, hoping the airbags kicked in. They fired, the seatbelt is still locked in place. But he's not there. Instead of a driver there's a pile of what looks like soft clay covering the seat.

Huh. The other guys didn't disintegrate into clay.

I'd say the driver was a golem, but there are only a few types of those and none of the ways of destroying them include running them into a brick wall in a car with airbags.

I was hoping the driver would survive long enough to tell me who I pissed off, or at the very least would die relatively intact. I can work with dead, but I know fuck-all about what to do with clay.

Dead is easy. I can do dead in my sleep. If any of them had left a ghost, I could get some answers that way. Even without a ghost, I'd be able to reanimate them long enough to ask, except that I shot them all in the head. Hard to get anything out of a reanimated body with pulped brains.

It's probably just as well. The ritual I know to do that is long, complicated, and needs a lot of space and materials I don't have. Plus, time is a factor. Every second the brain rots a little more inside the skull.

Speaking of time, I catch sight of the motel manager through the office window with his phone to his ear, looking at me bug-eyed and panicked. I think time's just about up.

No great loss. I've learned that if someone wants to kill you badly enough, they'll be back. I'll bump into more of these guys soon.

I'm just glad it wasn't a kidnapping. Give me a straight-up pissed-off "I'm gonna kill a motherfucker"-type fight over that whole stick-a-bag-over-your-head and "go for a ride" shit. I am so over that. All it does is lead to some jackass threatening to kill me if I don't give them what they want. Half the time they don't even know what they want. I'll take cold-hearted murderers over kidnappers any day of the week. At least with an assassin you know where you stand.

Sirens getting closer. Thinking maybe it's time to hit the road. I pull out a HI, MY NAME IS sticker, write NOT THE DROID YOU'RE LOOKING

FOR on it in thick black Sharpie, slap it to the front of my jacket, and pump a little magic into it. I feel the magic take hold. That should keep the cops off me for a little while. But best to check.

I walk up to the office window and wave at the manager. He sees me, frowns, eyes glaze over. He waves back. Good enough for me. I'm on the sidewalk two buildings down by the time the black and whites show up. Nobody comes after me.

So, now what? Find someone who can tell me what the fuck is going on. Find some place to regroup, get my head together. Little flashes of memory snap into my head like bursting popcorn. Something about Mictlan. I can't remember. Maybe I should write a guidebook. After all, I did a fair bit of running for my life there. *Things To Do In Mictlan When You're Dead*. That triggers another fragmented memory. Cloaks made from the feathers of tropical birds. Standing at the top of a pyramid. I'm missing something, but for the life of me I can't figure out what.

From what I can see it looks like I'm on the east side of the river. The closest person who'll have information is about five minutes away. Gabriela Cortez. Gabriela is about twenty-five, five-foot-damn-near-nothing tall, cute as a button. She was a sorority girl at USC, Master's in Sociology. Honestly wants to make the world a better place. And she will murder anyone who gets in her way. She's one of the most dangerous people I've ever met, and that's saying something.

Gabriela's a mage. At least as powerful as I am and I'm no slouch. We threw down when I first met her. She thought I was somebody else. We beat the ever-loving shit out of each other. She likes to say it was a draw, but I'm the one who had a straight razor to her throat.

Not that I'd disagree with her, of course. Like I said, she's dangerous.

I find a Suburban nearby and a minute later I'm pulling away from the curb. I make a point of driving a circuitous route to Gabriela's warehouse. She used to own a converted single room occupancy hotel Downtown, before things went pear-shaped and she moved herself and her people to a warehouse on the other side of the river.

See, there are a lot of supernaturals in L.A. that can pass for human most of the time: lamiae, ebu gogo, aswang, vampires, naga, ghouls. You name it, we got at least half a dozen out here and probably two or three trying to get into the movies. We're very multicultural that way.

Problem is that they tend to be homeless. They can only blend in so well. Sometimes their appearance is a little off, or they have dietary requirements that get in the way of holding down a nine-to-five job. It's a rough life. Sometimes rougher for them than it is for humans. They can't out themselves. Forget what would happen if normals knew about them, mages would come down on them before the normals had any idea what's going on.

Gabriela thinks this is bullshit. And for the most part I agree with her. I don't have her trust of vampires, but then L.A. vampire society is kinda weird. I still haven't completely figured them out. But the rest? Absolutely. I've worked with ghouls. Hell, before she tried to eat my soul, I dated a lamia in New York for two years. That's actually a pretty good run, all things considered. My grandfather, though, he was with one for decades. Apparently caused some family disputes. Name's Miriam. Met her a while ago. She seemed on the up and up, but what do I know?

Point is, Gabriela doesn't sit back and just let shit happen. She *does* something about it. Not walking around with protest signs. She looks for solutions—

usually very violent solutions, but solutions. Which is what led to her buying the hotel Downtown and using it as a supernatural halfway house. All her residents could be open about who and what they were, and the real monsters, us humans, got shown the door.

And that's where things took a turn. Gabriela was so successful at helping out her people, giving them a place, some self-respect, that the ones who were drug addicts stopped using.

It cut into somebody's profits. Mexican Mafia, Armenian Power, 14K. Doesn't really matter. Gabriela looks less Morgan le Fay, more Manic Pixie Dream Girl. So they tried to take her out.

What's the worst that could happen?

They found out the hard way. But no matter how many enforcers she sent back headless, skinned and stuffed into beer coolers, they couldn't believe it. So they kept coming. And they kept dying.

Finally, Gabriela took a page from Baba Yaga and made up this ancient, withered hag called La Bruja. La Bruja carved a swath through the gangs and Mexican Mafia in her little corner of Downtown. Left calling cards, messages written in blood, heads in duffel bags, that sort of thing.

They weren't going to take Gabriela Cortez seriously, but an old witch who throws down the evil eye and fucking means it? Goddamn right they're gonna take her seriously. Got them to back off, and even got her a crew of humans who hung on her every word. Provided that those words came from La Bruja, through her "secretary."

From that point on, everybody's thinking they're dealing with a hundred-year-old monster witch. Even her own people. Until a bunch of Russian thugs followed me to the hotel and burned the place to the ground. And I kinda accidentally outed her.

Word that she was La Bruja got out fast. Things went south. Chunk of her army bailed, Mexican Mafia started sniffing around. A lot of boys who thought they were men had to be forcefully reminded that they weren't.

She had a backup place, a warehouse on the Eastside. Pulled up stakes, headed there and started over. But now she didn't have to hide herself. She'd made her point.

She is La Bruja and you do not fuck with La Bruja.

Not as much has changed during my blackout as I thought. More construction, a lot of rebuilds, a lot of teardowns. Vacant lots are choked with weeds, trash, and homeless encampments. But as to brand new buildings, not a lot. They probably rammed the Downtown work through as fast as they could and let everywhere else deal with the usual red tape.

Some things are different enough that I get turned around and end up on the other side of the river. I finally find the new Sixth Street bridge leading back across and immediately miss the old one. The utilitarian concrete and iron bridge was replaced before the fires by a sweeping modernized monstrosity made of massive looping struts holding it up. It survived the flames with nothing more than soot and some heat-cracked concrete, and now it's gotten a new coat of paint and looks like nothing happened.

But there's one change I was totally unprepared for. Gabriela's warehouse is gone.

Not abandoned, boarded up, in disrepair. Gone. The warehouse, parking lot, everything. The whole property has been bulldozed. It's nothing but a vacant lot of dry, packed dirt surrounded by a chain-link fence with signs that say PRIVATE PROPERTY—KEEP OUT at various points along it.

I check the location. Yeah, this is the place. How long did that blackout go on for? I try to remember anything that might have led to this, but I'm drawing a blank.

The last time I recall being here, I was getting patched up and learned I had multiple brain injuries I wasn't even aware of. Did I have a stroke? My last memory before waking up in a ritual circle was being at the Ambassador and taking a beating from Hank, Darius's pet demon. That must be what caused the blackout. I remember reading somewhere that brain injuries can cause problems weeks, even years, after the injury occurs.

The gate is chained, but it snaps with a spell. The dirt is hard-packed and furrowed from a bulldozer's scoop. Weeds poke up through the ground in clumps, amid previous years' dead grasses. This place has been like this for a long time.

Even with magic, bureaucracy is bureaucracy. This didn't all happen over a weekend. I'm actually starting to worry now. Between this and the skyline, I feel like I've stepped into a new world.

How long to bulldoze a site like this? How long before the city approved the demolition? How long before that did Gabriela and her crew leave? A year? No. Longer. Two, at least. Maybe more.

Goddammit. Something happened recently and I can't remember the last couple of years. Did my memory get erased in whatever the hell that ritual was the other night?

I close my eyes and feel around for any sign of magic. A good enough illusion can hide a building and trick you into thinking you just walked through where it should be. But I'm not feeling anything.

I am noticing some ghosts, though. A couple of Wanderers, some Haunts in nearby buildings along the street. A lot of Echoes. The fires didn't hit this area as badly. Gabriela's crew knew what to look for and was able to keep a lot of it from going up in flames. But that's just nearby. Further up the street, people burned to death working the night shift, or dancing at a warehouse rave, or otherwise being in the wrong place at the wrong time.

But nothing here.

So, scratch Gabriela off the list. Whether she's dead or just moved on, either way she's not an option. Who's next? Letitia or MacFee? I think maybe Letitia is a better bet. She can't be that hard to find, can she? As long as she's still with the LAPD and isn't dead, I've got a lead. Hell, if she were dead, I'd have an easier time getting hold of her and learning what the hell happened.

I'll have to talk to MacFee at some point, but not today. He's strictly South Bay and I'm not driving all the way down to Torrance on the off chance he'll be there. Letitia's probably closer.

It occurs to me that I'm a lot calmer than I should be. Weird days are sort of the norm for me, but today has been weirder than most. With the blackout, being totally spun about how much time must have gone by and wondering what the hell I did with it all, I feel like I've walked in on somebody telling an inside joke and have no idea what it means.

My best bet for finding out what's going on has taken off, I'm not really sure how to get hold of the second one, and the third one is down in Torrance if he's even still alive. I'd call one of them, but there are no payphones left in L.A. and I don't have a cell phone. Easy to rectify, I'll just go steal one, but for the life of me I can't remember anybody's goddamn number.

Also, somebody's trying to kill me, which is not a new thing, and some British Indian chick did . . . something . . . to me, which is.

Everything's different, and the blackout story is wearing thin, even for a guy who hangs on to a rationalization like it's a life preserver in shark-infested waters. I need some time to think and regroup.

There's only one place I know of where I can do that. And as long as it still doesn't want to eat me, I should be relatively safe while I figure out what the hell my next move is.

Chapter 3

Though it was demolished years ago, the Ambassador Hotel was such an enduring landmark with such a strong psychic footprint that it created a ghost of itself on the other side of the veil.

I've never seen another ghost that large, or even any ghost that isn't of a human being. Ghosts as I know them are just shells thrown off during great distress as someone dies, not a building with a strong enough connection to the world around it that it simply doesn't leave. And it's not just the hotel. It's the grounds, the rooms, the kitchens, the Cocoanut Grove, the people, the cars, the staff. They're all extensions of the Ambassador reliving its past glory days, when everybody who was anybody stayed there.

I'm honestly not sure if that's scary or just sad. The hotel could devour me and pretty much anything else if it wanted to, though apparently I have some sort of family deal with it set up by my grandfather. Everything in it is self-contained. How it's held onto its identity this long I don't know. Sometimes I feel sorry for the old place.

Granddad's deal with the hotel was to let him have access to a door. He tied that door to a room he created in—fuck, I don't even know what. A pocket uni-

verse? Another planet? Judging by the orange sky out
the window and the Lovecraftian abominations wandering across the landscape, I'm betting it's not Earth.

I don't know the details of the deal. I do know it
involved a lot of blood, a lot of life for the hotel to
feed on. Enough that the hotel was more than happy
to give him the door and allow him safe passage to it
for the foreseeable future. "Decades to come" is how
the hotel put it. That's a lot of blood.

I boost a car off the street, some junker Honda, and
head over to the Ambassador's former grounds on
Wilshire, halfway across town. The place has been
turned into a school named after Robert F. Kennedy,
the senator who was assassinated in the hotel's kitchen.
Seems odd to name them after a murder victim, but
who am I to judge?

The drive by the Downtown area is enlightening.
L.A. hasn't recovered from the firestorm, but it's well on
its way. New and restored buildings, repaved streets.
There's still a lot of construction happening. I pass a few
vacant lots that have been bulldozed, weeds knee-high.

The only thing that belies the veneer of success is
the traffic. I don't know what day it is, but there isn't
a day L.A. traffic doesn't suck. This looks like midnight in Tucson, not lunchtime in L.A.

I park the car about a block away from the school.
I need to get fairly close because there are a lot of
Wanderers on the other side of the veil. Pop over too
far away and I'll be ghost kibble. On the hotel grounds
I'll be fine. But it looks like the school has had some
upgrades since the last time I was here.

It's bigger now, for one. The blacktop area where
I'd usually go in, well beyond the grasp of the Wanderers, has been replaced with a building. I could get
in, but Christ, how long is that gonna take?

Fuck it. It's not like I've never run through a crowd
of pissed off Wanderers.

I get to one of the closed and locked gates. Is it Saturday? I really need to find out what day it is. All the clock in the motel room gave me was the date and month, which is less useful than you'd think.

I pop the lock and walk inside the school grounds, up to the new building. Wanderers pass by like sharks. Sliding over to the dead side this far out should, maybe, keep me in the hotel's sphere but only on the edge of it. Once I get deeper into the hotel's boundaries the Wanderers won't be a problem. But until then I'll be doing a lot of sprinting. I hope I kept up with my cardio.

A break opens in the river of Wanderers circling just past the gate. I slide over and run through the gap. They'll catch my scent in seconds. Holding off a ghost or two over here is easy enough. Holding off hundreds of starving dead? That's a little much.

Fortunately, the land of the dead doesn't quite reflect the side of the living. Cars and most buildings are too transient to leave much of a psychic footprint. It's the things that endure that end up on the dead side of the fence. Which means the school isn't over here. It's too new, giving me a straight shot to the Ambassador. Now I just need to get there without being eaten.

A piercing shriek sounds behind me. It starts a chain reaction until the void is filled with a cacophony of the dead. They bolt toward me as fast as they can, which is pretty goddamn fast. I only have a second or two of lead time and they're going to eat that up in a heartbeat.

A couple of things about getting tagged by ghosts. It feels like ice on fire. They dig furrows through your skin, into your soul, a thousand bites like piranha taking down a cow. I've been bit a few times. The scars looked like freezer-burned chicken. Hurt like a motherfucker. Eaten by ghosts is not a pleasant way to go.

I'm almost at the threshold and hope to hell the Ambassador remembers me. It thought I was my grandfather when I first showed up, and he'd died a long time back. With any luck my blackout didn't last quite that long.

I can feel the burning chill of a Wanderer bearing down on me. I throw out a repulsion spell that stops it in its tracks, but five more take its place. Problem with using magic over here is it's strictly BYOB. There's no connection to the magic on the living side, so you can't tap the local pool. Whatever power you walk in with is all the power you're going to get. You let the tank get too low and you won't have enough to leave.

The repulsion spell is pretty minor, and I push away the next wave riding my ass, but I can't keep it up forever. Fortunately, I don't have to. I hit the grounds of the hotel and the difference is like going from Kansas to Oz.

Almost everything over on this side is washed out blacks and bluish-grays that are more shadow than not. Most ghosts I'll see from either side are the same color. Only newer ones, ones that I have more of a connection to, or ones that are just powerful or plain stubborn enough will appear in full color and Dolby sound.

I hit a lawn of grass that's a sharp, overwhelming green. For the most part it looks and feels like grass, just slightly off. Closer to the hotel itself things become more concrete, more realistic. It's a good sign, but I'm not free and clear yet. The grass is just a marker, not the finish line.

But it is enough to let me slow down a bit. I get about twenty feet in, the shrieking Wanderers on my ass, when the lawn ripples like a sheet being shaken out. It catches the Wanderers that have followed me onto the grass, overwhelms them, pulls them into itself. Sometimes it's just a ghost-eat-ghost kind of world.

I hit the pavement of the short road leading to the

main entrance and fall to my knees. I glance over my shoulder and all those ghosts are gone. Good. The air over here, or whatever it is, is thin. Once I hit the boundary of the Ambassador the air thickens into something actually breathable, but I'm still panting like an overexcited Labrador.

I'm so focused on the ghosts that I don't see the car. It comes barreling up the road, headlights on, horn blaring. Yeah, it's a ghost—well, part of a ghost, anyway—and over here that shit's solid. I roll to the side as the car brakes, and I manage to avoid becoming road pizza by only a few inches.

The car's a white Cadillac. Coupe DeVille, maybe? Late fifties? It's weird the details you notice when you're about to become a smear on the street. The woman in the passenger seat, a platinum blonde who looks to be in her late thirties and trying to look a lot younger, rolls down her window and looks me up and down, an expression of stunned horror on her face.

"Oh, my dear! Are you all right?"

"Yes, thank you. And thanks for not running me over."

"Well, we wouldn't want to dirty the car," she says, her laughter like tinkling bells. She keeps looking at me while I dust myself off. "No, we definitely wouldn't want to dirty the car. Especially not with that pretty face. Are you a guest of the hotel? You look very familiar."

"Sort of an on-again, off-again resident."

"Oh. I didn't recognize you for a moment. Christophe, look who it is. I'm Maria, by the way." She puts out her hand and I shake it. The driver, a thin man with a shock of white hair, peers through the window at me and makes a *harrumph* sound.

"Oh, don't mind him. I saw you having a spot of trouble with the locals. Are you all right?"

Everything here, the building, the grounds, this

car, Maria, Christophe, they're all the same entity. Whether these two exist for my benefit or the Ambassador has them drive this circuit over and over again as part of the hotel's ongoing nostalgia play, I couldn't say. Either way, I'm having a conversation with the hotel, and these two are just puppets.

"Nothing really unexpected. How are things going here?"

"Oh, divine," she says. "Simply divine. Would you care for a ride? Perhaps join us for drinks?"

"Raincheck on the drink, but I'd love a ride." The back passenger door opens on its own with a pop, and I climb in.

"I'm so terrible at telling the time," she says, "but if I recall, you've been away for some while, haven't you?"

"Have I?" I say. "I honestly don't remember."

"That's fascinating! Don't you think that's fascinating, Christophe?" Christophe harrumphs. Maria waves it away with her gloved hand. "Oh, you must come to the club tonight and tell us all about your adventures. The girls will simply love you. Love you. Don't you think the girls will simply love him, Christophe?"

Harrumph.

"Appreciate the invitation," I say, "but I have some things I need to take care of tonight."

"Oh, that's fine," she says. "We come here at least twice a week, sometimes more. Oh, here we are!" The car glides into a spot at the hotel entrance and a valet runs up to take Christophe's key. We get out of the car.

"I appreciate the ride, Maria."

"My pleasure. And really, do come join us for drinks some time. Christophe is a dear but having someone else to talk to is so stimulating."

"I'll swing by."

"Marvelous." She takes Christophe's arm and the

two walk into the hotel. Is this how the Ambassador keeps itself sane? Or at least whole? Maybe that's why it puts on these little plays for itself, so it can always be reminded what it is.

"Any bags, sir?" A bellboy comes up to me. He looks like every other bellboy at the hotel. Literally. Same uniform, shoes, hat, gloves, face. It's the same guy over and over and over again. And before Maria back there, it was the only piece of the Ambassador I'd ever spoken with.

"I'm good."

"You certainly look it," he says. "For a moment I didn't recognize you. Thought you were your grandfather. Imagine that."

"Yeah, imagine that." Something about that is troubling, but I'm really not sure what it is. The hotel thought I was my grandfather the first time I met it, but this feels different. "How are things here?"

"You heard Miss Maria," he says, his face breaking into a grin. "Divine. Simply divine."

"Say, do you know what the date is?"

"I'm sad to say I don't, sir. I'm not very good at keeping track of the calendar on the other side."

"Fair enough. Do you remember when I was here last?"

"Yes, of course, sir. It's been some time, though I don't really know how long. It was during that unpleasantness with the demon."

Yes, that "unpleasantness" when Hank caught me off guard in a place I thought was safe and beat my ass back to the Stone Age. He got into my hotel room, which shouldn't have been possible. The only way in is through the front door.

But I'd gotten hold of a ring that allowed travel to pretty much anywhere, opening a hole in space that led to the new location. It was useful, but a setup.

Hank had made sure I got hold of that ring because he had its twin and they were keyed to each other. They both did the same thing, but if you had one, it could open a hole to wherever the other one was. Apparently even into pocket universes like the room.

I palmed his ring during the fight and left him on this side of the veil. I knew he could get back, but it bought me some time. I was pretty proud of snagging that ring. Pretty fuckin' clever, me. Now I'm not so sure it was, considering I can't remember a goddamn thing after that.

"Unfortunate business," the bellboy says. "I do hope you recovered swiftly, sir."

"Yeah. Me too."

"You sound uncertain."

"I feel a little uncertain." Something is hammering on the inside of my head demanding attention. What am I not seeing? Or is it something I just don't want to look at?

"Perhaps the gentleman in room 211 could help," the bellboy says.

"Excuse me?"

"Your visitor. He's in room 211. Not only did he attack a guest, but one whose family paid in advance for a very long time. I would be remiss if I hadn't done something. And since you'd taken his only method of rapid egress, I had plenty of time to get to him before he left my grounds. Plus, he hurt me." That last comes out like ice. I remember that. Hank had done . . . something. I'm not real clear on what, but it was definitely unpleasant for the Ambassador.

"So you stuck him in a room?"

"Oh, not like your room. Your room is a custom model that I had nothing to do with. Honestly, the only thing you're renting from me is the door. No, this is one I created myself. One of my guests had acted in a German expressionist film, which he would show to his friends every time he stayed. I modeled the room after that. I understand it's very off-putting."

My brain is not quite processing this. "Hank. The demon Hank."

"Yes, sir."

"He's been cooling his heels in a room in the ghost of the Ambassador Hotel that's modeled after a German expressionist film. Right now. And has been since I left?"

"He has indeed, sir," the bellboy says, a broad and feral smile with too many teeth plastered across his face. "Would you like to see him?"

"Oh, would I ever."

Chapter 4

The door to room 211 looks like every other room door in the hotel. I wonder if the rest have rooms behind them, too, and if the hotel plays out its puppet shows in them for its own amusement.

"It wouldn't be prudent for me to open the door," the bellboy says. "Obviously. However, I can make it transparent."

"Just looking into the shark tank works for me." The door disappears, showing the room behind it. When he said it was based on a German Expressionist film he wasn't kidding. Crazy angles, twisted perspectives, everything painted in shades of gray. Even the shadows are painted on. The only furniture is an open crate and a lantern hanging from the ceiling. This looks really familiar.

"This is from *The Cabinet of Dr. Caligari*, isn't it?"

"I considered something from *Nosferatu* but decided this would make him even more uncomfortable." Good choice. I'm uncomfortable just looking at it. And that's just the room. Hank looks even worse.

I ran into Hank when he was trailing me in his guise as a human. I thought he was a private eye working for Darius. He sort of was. He just didn't mention the whole demon thing for a while.

"He looks like twenty miles of rough road," I say. And then some. Hank is sitting on the floor, rocking back and forth, eyes closed, humming to himself. There are a few remnants of his human disguise. He's a little thick around the middle, with a bald head . . . but that's pretty much where it stops.

His hairless, scaled skin is colored a dark, rusty red. His fingers end in three-inch-long claws. He's wearing soiled pants and there are furrows in the walls where it looks like he's tried to claw his way out. From the jagged scars all over his face I'd say he tried to do the same thing to himself.

"He can't see me, can he?"

"No," the bellboy says. "Would you like him to?"

Not really. I mean, I've met worse demons, a lot worse, but still, this guy was an asshole. But I have questions he might be able to answer.

"Yeah." There's a slight shimmer in the doorway and the bellboy nods to me. "Hey, slugger," I say. "Long time no see."

Hank opens his eyes, revealing yellow irises and wide goat pupils. "Carter," he says. "You're looking better."

"You're not."

"Well, you caught me at a bad time. But really, you're looking a lot better." He squints at me. "Acid peel? Nose job? Whatever it is, you're looking good."

That's what was wrong with my reflection in the bathroom mirror. I've had my nose broken multiple times, my jaw at least once. But every feature looks like it's fresh off the factory floor.

"Laid off the salt and fatty foods," I say. "Went vegan."

"You don't say." He pats his belly. "Maybe I should try that. Souls can be so fattening, you know. So, what brings you here? Not that I'm not happy to see you, but you don't call, you don't write. You're not here to gloat, are you? Locked away the big, scary demon and now you want to mock him for it?"

"Oh, give it a rest. You've been in worse places for longer." He's a demon. Demons are next to immortal. Not that you can't kill them, but they won't die on their own. They don't need to eat or drink, they just happen to like it: blood, human meat, the occasional soul. Hank's probably a few thousand years old. Time isn't quite as much a concern for him as it is for humans.

"Oh, I have," he says. "Spent eighty years in Fresno. Man, that place. I don't know why nobody's gone and wiped it off the map. Nah, I'm just getting bored with this one." He turns his attention to the bellboy. "The least you could do is shake it up a little in here. Maybe something more Cubist? German Expressionism just gives me a headache."

"I'll take it under advisement," the bellboy says.

"So, why are you here?" Hank says to me.

"Filling in some gaps," I say.

"You don't say. And you came here to talk to me? I don't see what I could— Oh. You didn't. I just happened to be here when you popped by." He cocks his head and looks at me like I'm a particularly unusual bug. "Did you even know I was here?"

"Why do you think I stayed away?" I say. The last thing I need is to have this fucker think he's got one up on me, so telling him about the blackout's not a smart idea. He is so very not my friend.

"Can I ask you a question?" he says.

"Nine and a half inches."

"You need to get yourself a better ruler. No, seriously. What's the date?"

"Look, if you want to set up a date night, I gotta tell ya I'm really not looking for a relationship these days."

"You wish. There's not much sense of time in here, and I was thinking since you've been out there and I've been in here, you might be able to tell me."

"Forgot my calendar," I say. I don't like this. He's up to something, and I don't know what. "Sorry. I think it's a Tuesday."

"But the month? The season? Do you even know?" His mouth cracks open in a smile showing far too many teeth.

"What are you getting at?"

"You don't remember what happened after you left me here, do you? And you've got some biiiig holes in your memory you can't quite fill. Am I close?"

"What do you know about it?" I say.

"Not a goddamn thing, but I've seen people lose years of time for all sorts of reasons and they always have this vaguely stunned look in their eyes, like they just stepped into a new world. That, or like they're trying not to let anybody know they're high, but somehow I don't think you fall into that category."

"You are just as fucking boring as you were on the other side," I say. I make a throat-cutting motion and the door begins to fade back into its frame.

"You haven't had anything strange happen to you lately, have you?" Hank says as the door fades in. "Find yourself in any magic circles recently?" I put my hand up to stop the bellboy and the door disappears again.

"You're fishing," I say.

"And I'd say I hooked a big one just now. So, somebody wiped your memory of the last few, what, months? Years?"

"You ever get any visitors?" I say. "Any of your demon pals? Conjugal visits? Darius swinging by in your dreams to give you orders?" Being trapped in his bottle doesn't mean Darius can't interact with the outside world. He's set up doors into his little pocket universe and invites guests in to entertain or be entertained by. Last time I was there he'd done it all up like a 1940s jazz bar. And the time before that, he appeared in a dream I had while I was in Mictlan.

Which he shouldn't have been able to do, except that the bindings Mictlantecuhtli put on his bottle are wearing away. The warranty on god magic's running out. Seems that with a determined djinn pushing against the cork for five hundred years, something's gonna give.

"Nice lane change on the subject there," he says. "That's fine. Denial is a tried and true strategy for dealing with shit you don't understand. No Darius. Sorry. He wouldn't bother. I'm small fry. I don't have anything to give him. Just disposable muscle as far as he's concerned. Why? He talking to you?"

"Just curious."

"Why are you here, Carter?"

"Got a room upstairs if you'll recall. Needed to get away from it all for a bit. You know how it is."

"Right. And you decided to pop by and see the guy who beat you senseless, who you haven't come to see since. So I'm wondering, why now?"

"You're fishing again," I say.

"Blame a guy for trying? Say, any chance you could have a word with the management on the state of my accommodations? They're a little cramped. Maybe something more post-minimalist. I've always liked Hesse."

"I'll see what I can do." I nod to the bellboy and the door reappears, blocking him from view. Jesus. I know he's fucking with me, but how much, and is he actually lying? He can't know what happened during my blackout. How could he? He's been locked away in here and I've been—I don't know where I've been, but how the hell would he? I try to push the thought away, but it keeps gnawing at me.

"Thanks for letting me talk to him," I say.

"Of course, sir. Is there anything else? Do you need help with any luggage?"

"No, I'm good," I say. I hand him a fifty. He thanks me and walks away. I don't know what the hell he'll do with the money, but if the Ambassador is going to this much effort to puppet a bellboy, the least I can do is play along and tip him.

My room is on the fourth floor. When I fought Hank, we trashed the place. Reminds me, I should figure out where I stashed those portal rings. Put that on the list of Shit Eric Can't Remember.

On this side of the hotel door everything looks fine. When I open the door, I'm surprised to see that everything looks fine there, too. No sign of a fight. Everything's clean, just like it always is.

The room is a mid-forties-style suite with a kitchen, bedroom, living room, bathroom. The living room has a picture window looking out onto an alien world with the previously mentioned orange sky and creatures something like a cross between elephants and giant slugs lumbering and flopping their way across the landscape.

I've wondered sometimes what would happen if I smashed the window open. Is the air even breathable out there? I don't want to put too much thought into it. The fact that the air is breathable in here is mind-bending enough. You can do a lot with magic, but the scale and complexity of the spells needed to allow this place to exist go beyond anything I can imagine.

Every time I've come in here it's been clean. I tried to leave trash on the floor once, just to see what would happen after I left and came back. Gone. Same for spilled coffee in the rug. The bed's always made. There are clean towels in the bathroom. The whole place is a wonder. Running water, booze, food in the fridge, working gas range. It's got electricity, but it's all 1940s spec. I can't plug anything in, but I can get a cell phone signal.

I know my grandfather didn't build this place. He couldn't have. At least not on his own. I don't know what his knack was, that one thing that every mage does better than anything else, but I doubt it was trans-dimensional apartment construction.

I sit heavily into the leather club chair and watch the shoggoths go by outside the window. I don't know if that's really what they are, but they sure as hell look like it.

I should be safe enough from people trying to kidnap/kill me in here that I can do some thinking. What's next on the agenda? Same as before. Get answers. Hank was a dud, not that I expected he wouldn't be, or even that I'd run into him. So who can I talk to? I go down the list of people who didn't want to murder me the last time I was here. Santa Muerte? Kind of surprised I haven't heard from her already. Usually I can just think at her and I'll reach her. But now, it's like all I get is mental static.

Speaking of which, the wedding ring I've been sad-dled with since I met her isn't on my finger. With everything else going on, that was just one more weird sensation. New face, new body, new ink. A missing ring was not exactly high on my list of priorities. But now I'm wondering where it is.

If I can figure out a way to get her attention, I'll ask her. I think about going to one of her shrines, but that's a non-starter. She's not answering the direct line, she's not going to show up because I smoked some cigars and drank some tequila in front of a statue of her. It'd be like I was making a collect call from jail.

Who else? Vivian? Oh, hell no. I left things with my high school ex about as poorly as I could without one or both of us dead. Honestly, I'm amazed she hasn't murdered me already. So, not Vivian.

MacFee, possibly. But it's going to be a slog to get down to him, and there's no guarantee he's even around anymore.

Letitia. She's another person I went to the mage equivalent of high school with. She tried to kill me. Good instincts. Then she went on and became part of the Cleanup Crew, a loose grouping of mages who, instead of trying to kill each other, decided to work together, which is ridiculously rare. They help sweep the existence of magic under the rug and keep all of us as much out of the limelight as possible.

And she did that by joining the LAPD and becoming a detective. So, unless she's dead, left the force, or left the city, finding her shouldn't be that hard, should it? I still don't have a phone, so I can't call around or look her up online. I know she was working out of Downtown, though. The new LAPD headquarters burned down in the L.A. Firestorm, so last I saw her she was working out of the old decommissioned Parker Center that they'd had to reopen. It's not much to go on, but it's a start.

Getting out of the Ambassador proves to be easier than going in. I slide back to the living side while still on the hotel's grounds and appear on a basketball court on the other side of the school. I wish I'd known about this earlier. From there I simply walk to another gate and pop the lock.

There's something about this specific basketball court. It's important, but for the life of me I can't remember. One more mystery to toss onto the pile, I guess.

The sun has only just come up in the last half hour, painting the sky in thick oranges and reds. The last time I saw an L.A. sunrise, the fires had only been out about a month and the sky was overcast with clouds and ash. Now all the ash has cleared enough that you can only see it by how it reflects the light. Shit'll still give you lung cancer, but goddamn does it look pretty.

I steal a different car. It's more of a pain than it's worth to hang onto the same one for too long. Eventually somebody will notice, and though I'm not worried about cops, they can be a pretty big waste of time. I wonder how the owner will react when they find it's been stolen and the GPS tells them it's parked at police headquarters.

The early morning traffic is lighter than it was before the fires, but still heavier than it was right after. A lot of freeways collapsed, and a lot of people either moved away or were homeless and staying in a FEMA camp. The campsites I pass are all vacant now. Torn down and stored away for the next national disaster.

I see a lot of construction going on as I head into Downtown, and the charred stump that was Skid Row has been razed to the ground and fenced off. Weird place, Skid Row. It's like a funnel that all the homeless and destitute roll into. And once they're there, the only way out is the hole in the bottom.

Skid Row was one of the worst hit spots in the whole county. Something like ten thousand people died inside a four-square-mile area. Lots of reasons why, but mostly because they were poor. The ghosts and a swath of prime L.A. real estate are all that's left. Of the ghosts, most are Wanderers. Some Haunts, not as many Echoes. I can only hope that the souls they came from are doing better than when they were alive. Of the real estate, the property values? Some asshole billionaire's gonna make a killing. So to speak.

Enough of Downtown has changed that there are only a handful of buildings I recognize, but it's similar enough that I find the new LAPD headquarters built on the burnt-down foundation of the old one. I abandon the car in a red zone out front and slap a

sticker on my jacket where I've written VERY IM-
PORTANT POLICE PERSON WHO NEEDS TO
SEE LETITIA WASHINGTON ASAP in Sharpie.
I figure that should at least get somebody to look her
up for me.

The building is all concrete and glass with an almost Brutalist feel that carries over to the interior. I
breeze past the metal detector, the officers caught by
the magic of the sticker, letting me through with worried glances. If there's something about Letitia they
know that I don't, a chance that's probably somewhere
in the neighborhood of one hundred percent, this
might have been a remarkably bad idea.

I'm not worried about getting arrested. I've been
arrested lots of times. It gives the police a strong sense
of accomplishment, and I'm a giver. I even spent a couple years in a Las Vegas jail cell. But that was on purpose, to talk to the ghost of a dead necromancer and
pick up some tips.

What I'm worried about is that Letitia's in some
sort of situation that I'm about to make worse. Not
that that's ever happened, of course.

"Hey," I say. "You know where I can find Letitia
Washington?" They both say "third floor" so fast and
in sync that they're almost in harmony. They look
worried. This is not a good sign. I figured they'd shrug
their shoulders and direct me to an information desk.
But they know her, and they know where she is, and
she's in the rumor mill enough that they're more than
a little nervous.

The directory by the elevator tells me that the third
floor is Homicide, so at least she's in the same department. The officers and detectives in the elevator with
me are giving me nervous glances. The ones who exit
at the third floor hurry off like I've got the plague.
Maybe I should have written SANDWICH DELIV-

ERY FOR LETITIA WASHINGTON instead. Probably would have gone over better.

In through a pair of glass doors to a reception room where a Latino officer is manning the desk. "I'm looking for Letitia Washington. She in?" He looks up and his eyes pop a little too wide. He pushes a clipboard with a sign-in sheet toward me, gets on the phone.

"Captain, there's somebody to see you. I really think you need to talk to him." He looks at the sign-in sheet where I've penned my name in big letters to make sure there's no doubt who I am. "Yes. He does fit the description. His name's Eric Carter. I—Ma'am? Are you there?" The door behind the desk bursts open a couple seconds later.

Letitia's a little taller than I am and she uses her height to stare down at me, shock on her face. She has her hand on the butt of her gun and I have absolutely no doubt that she will use it on me, whether I know what she's pissed off about or not. She doesn't say anything, so it's up to me to break the silence.

"Ta-da!" I say, throwing my arms out and doing jazz hands.

She punches me in the face.

Chapter 5

Jail. Everyone should try it at least once in their life. It gives you a strong appreciation for not being in jail. The holding cell I'm in has a sink, a toilet, and a metal bench bolted to the floor. The bench isn't comfortable and it smells of urine, shit, and for some reason burning rubber, but after getting smacked around by angry police officers it could be worse. Overall the cell's pretty sparse, even by the standards of holding cells. I mean, it beats any cell in Arizona, but compared to this Vegas was fucking luxury.

So, Letitia punched me, I went down, and five more very large police officers jumped in, did a lot of punching themselves, then tossed me in here. I could have fought them. But that would just exchange one set of problems for another and piss Letitia off even more. I need to talk to her, and if the price of admission is a black eye and bruised ribs, well, I've paid more for less.

The thing is, there's nobody else down here with me, which strikes me as a bad sign. These cells are designed to be temporary, until sheriff's deputies come to cart the prisoner away to the central jail across the river. Unless things have changed since the last time I was in an LAPD holding cell. They should be packed.

It's technically possible that there would be no one in here except me, but that's a bit of a stretch. More likely is that I have this entire chunk of LAPD real estate to myself because somebody made a whole block of cells disappear for a couple of hours. Doesn't take magic to make that happen.

I hear a door at the far end of the block open and close, sharp footsteps snapping against the cement floor. A moment later Letitia is at my cell, placing a plastic chair in front of me and sitting down, her face a mask.

Letitia is dark, like teak. Hard as teak, too. She's tall, especially in anything that's got a heel, but she's not necessarily big. That doesn't stop her from filling a room with nothing but sheer force of will.

In high school she was angry, easily triggered. Mohawk, army surplus trench coat, curb-stomper boots. Kinda cliché, really.

Mage high school is designed to do basically one thing: teach young mages how not to kill themselves. It's more boot camp than Harry Potter, and it needs to be. You get a few dozen hormonal teenagers who can chuck fireballs all in a room together, you need to teach them both how to not blow themselves up and how to rationally deal with other mages.

For a very loose idea of "rational," of course. Letitia, for example, stabbed me with a knife. I was surprised. Not that she'd attacked me—if anybody was going to do it, it'd be her—but that she'd actually used a knife. She didn't sucker punch me or use magic. No, she shoved a combat knife between my ribs.

I respect someone who goes straight for the knife. They're making a bold, unmistakable statement. And that statement is, "I'm going to fucking kill you now." There's honesty in that.

Letitia opens her mouth to talk, but I raise my hands to stop her. "Before you say anything, I would just like to apologize unreservedly for whatever I did that I can't remember, but I assume it was something truly egregious and I am sincerely, sincerely sorry."

"That sounds rehearsed."

"I said it a lot to Vivian when we were dating."

"Right," she says. "Tell me why I shouldn't shoot you right now?"

"Can I get this as a multiple-choice question?" She draws her gun from its belt holster and puts it in her lap, finger just above the trigger. Okay. That's probably not good. What the hell did I do? "Whoa, there. I said I was sorry. I don't know what I'm sorry for, but I did say it was a very sincere sorry."

"Who the fuck are you?"

"I—don't know how to answer that?" I say.

"Carter was pushing forty. You look all of, I'll say thirty? If that? He looked like twenty miles of rough road. You don't have a scratch on you."

"For the record, I'd like to point out my newly acquired bruises, contusions, and the beginnings of a pretty nice shiner."

"Yeah? The tats new, too? I can see a few poking out of your collar and shirt cuffs. Carter was a little less colorful."

"Would you believe I woke up this way?"

"I don't know. Try me."

"I woke up this way," I say.

"Nope."

"Worth a try."

"Carter was as big a pain in my ass, though, so you got that down."

"Why do you keep referring to me in the past te—" My voice drops off into silence as it clicks. How did I not see it before?

That's a question I can answer. Denial. I didn't want to see it. It explains, not everything, but a lot.

"How long have I been dead?" I say.

It's the only thing that fits. It can't have been a resurrection. I don't know how to do one, but there are legends that they've been done in the past, and they're horribly complicated. Everything I've read says you need the original body for a spell like that, and then I shouldn't look any different than when I died.

"Five years."

"Jesus. Five years? What the hell happened?"

"You tell me," Letitia says. "You're claiming to be the one who died."

"Jesus fuck, Letitia. Look at me. Am I lying? About any of this?" Letitia's knack, that one thing a mage is really good at, is alethemancy. Truth magic. In her case, she sees lies the way I see the dead. She doesn't say anything, but she also doesn't shoot me.

"No," she says. "But that only means you believe it."

"Oh, for fuck sake. What makes more sense here? That a dead necromancer who deals with the dead and is married to an actual goddess of the dead was somehow magically made not dead," I say, "or that somebody, anybody, would want to be me? Would you want to be me? I don't even want to be me."

"Shit," Letitia says, holstering the gun. "It really is you. How? Fuck, why?"

"Don't look at me, I've been dead for five years, apparently. I don't even remember dying. How did it happen?" I feel vaguely insulted, like I got left off somebody's guest list in a Jane Austen novel: "How rude! Nobody told me I was dead!"

"You got beat to shit in a school basketball court, had a stroke, and bled out all over the blacktop."

"Hank. Motherfucker." I can feel the shape of the memories now. Some of them, at least.

"Who?"

"Demon who was working with Darius. It's not important. Why can't I remember any of this?"

"Like you said, you've been dead for five years," Letitia says.

"Funny. But no," I say. "Souls endure unless something goes to the trouble of destroying them. Souls keep their memories. That's what shapes who they are, keeps them all in one piece. Even ghosts left behind usually remember something of the original person and how they died. So why the hell can't I remember?"

"That's what you're worried about? I think the takeaway from all this is more 'I came back to life' than it is 'I can't remember what happened while I was dead,'" Letitia says.

"You don't get it. There is, or at least was, a claim on my soul from Santa Muerte. The second I died, she should have taken me to Mictlan. I remember up to the point where I hit the ground, but everything else is a hole. Why is there a hole? If she didn't take me to Mictlan, where was I? And if she did, why hasn't she come to take me back?"

"Maybe she got sick of your shit."

"If she did, she wouldn't have brought me back to life. She'd just lock me in a hole in Mictlan for a few hundred years. No, this is something else." I roll up a sleeve and look at the tattoos on my arm. "Why don't I have any scars? Why do I still have my tats? They're essentially the same thing. I've got one, I should have the other. I'm out of my depth here. What the hell happened to my body?"

"Cremated," she says.

"Huh. That's weird."

"That's weird?" she says.

Cremation is a good general practice with mage corpses. There can still be magic lingering around them. Tough to access, but if you know what you're doing you can use it.

"I'd assumed this was my body. If it's not, whose is it?"

"Fucked if I know," Letitia says. "I pushed the button that lit you up, and then I scattered your ashes all over the place to make sure you stayed dead."

"Should have buried me at a crossroads at midnight with my head cut off and a stake through my heart."

"Cremation was cheaper."

This isn't my body. Is this even a human body? It could be a construct that somebody shoved my soul into. I might not be able to tell, but I think I'm remembering everything but the last five years. You'd think I'd remember what it's like to feel human.

"Any idea who might want to do this?" I say. "I'm drawing a blank."

"No," she says, a little too quickly. She could at least sound a little regretful. "I mean, no offense, but nobody showed up for the funeral."

"I had a funeral?"

"No, but if you had, nobody would have shown up for it. The world's better off without you in it, and everybody knows that."

"Ouch." That stings. Not unexpected, but still. "Well, somebody wants me walking and talking, or they wouldn't have gone to all this trouble. We find ourselves a manic Indian woman and I bet she'll have some answers."

"No," Letitia says. "I am not getting involved in whatever the fuck this is. Not my pig, not my farm. I'm barely holding my own shit together as it is. I don't need your bullshit on top of everything else."

I was hoping she wouldn't say that, but really I had no reason to expect otherwise. Guy supposed to be a corpse shows up on your front door, you know nothing good's gonna come of it. Her wife almost died because she got caught in the crossfire between me and a psychopathic cartel killer. I can't say I blame her.

"Fair enough," I say. The look of relief on her face is heartbreaking, but it is what it is. Can't say I've been very good at being anybody's friend. "Can you at least give me some information? I'm stumbling around in the dark here. I've been dead five—Jesus, it's really been five years?"

"Give or take. Honestly, not a lot's changed. There's more free porn on the Internet, we have another ass-hole in the White House, there are more electric cars but just as many idiots who can't drive in the rain."

"Ten-story digital billboards showing geishas eating candy?"

"This isn't *Blade Runner*, Eric. The billboards top out at five stories."

"What is the world coming to? Speaking of which, Police Captain?" I say.

She lets slip a smile. She's proud of that fact. And she should be. "Yeah. Couple years ago."

"How's everything else?"

"Up and down. Annie's good. We're, well, I don't want to say we're past things, but we've reached a bit of a detente. She doesn't want to know about magic. Wishes she'd never found out. Really fucked her world-view."

"I can imagine. Didn't you tell me she's Catholic? Or was?"

"Yeah. She'd already had to reassess the Church when she realized she was gay, and then when she came out to her family. It was a rough time for her. Having to do it all over again because the entire world has flipped on its side? It was all too much. So I don't tell her about it, and she doesn't ask. If I'm working late, I don't say whether it's catching normal bad guys or cleaning up after magical ones."

"I'm glad you two were able to work it out."

"Thanks. You dying helped."

"That, I didn't need to know, but it's nice to see that my ugly demise contributed to your domestic bliss. A regular fucking Cupid, that's me. How about Gabriela? She still around? I went by the warehouse. It was abandoned."

"Yeah. We talk every once in a while. Gone legit, or she's got a legit front, at least. Still hanging onto her idea of protecting all the supernaturals and giving them a place where they don't have to hide who they are. She still had the property her hotel was on, and the owners and next of kin for the rest of the block had all died in the fires. She bought up the whole block at auction."

"Damn. That's some impressive real estate. Bigger hotel?" I wonder if I passed it as I was going by Skid Row.

"Community center, homeless shelters, food bank. Caters to pretty much anybody. The supernaturals get screened and don't mix with the humans. Plus she's been building low rent housing. She's using the same enforcers she always has, only now they're doing more community outreach than B&E. She does good work. The right-wingers hate her because she's helping the homeless and the progressives hate her because she doesn't let them into her club. She pisses everybody off."

"Knew I liked her for a reason."

"She still murders people if they get in her way," Letitia says.

"You're getting me all hot and bothered over here, Tish. At least she's staying true to her roots. How do you think she'll take me coming back?"

Letitia cocks her head in thought, a frown on her face. "Honestly, I don't know. She got . . . weird when you died."

"Weird?"

"Weirder," she says. "I don't know what was going on with her. There were a couple months I didn't see her, but I did see a whole lot of corpses in the morgue that I'm pretty sure she's responsible for. Can't prove it was her, and I'm not sure I'd want to anyway. These people were hardcases. They're better off dead."

"Like me," I say.

"I—Look, I'm sorry. I shouldn't have said that."

I wave it off. "We both know it's true. I doubt putting a bullet through my head's gonna solve anything. Whoever did this would probably just bring me back again. Goddammit."

"You're the only person I know who can get pissed off at being brought back to life," she says.

"I'm not pissed off about that. It's that somebody did it to me. I'm fucking tired of being a goddamn chess piece. Fuckers can't even let me stay dead." I don't like choices taken away from me. I don't like having to dance to somebody's else's tune. Been there, done that. I'm pissed off that I was brought back to life because I didn't have a say in it. Somebody's pulling my strings, and I'm not gonna hop around like a fucking puppet.

And dying in the first place? Death is the ultimate fuck-you to free will. See, unless you're pulling that trigger yourself, and sometimes even when you are, it isn't a choice. Everybody's human suit is going to take a dirt nap at some point, and almost no one's crazy about the idea. Somebody's fucking with me, and I really want to find out who.

I know I shouldn't ask, but I need to anyway. "How about Vivian?"

"Gone," she says. "She left a couple days after you died and didn't tell anybody where she was going. Haven't seen her since. I think out of anybody she really isn't one you should track down."

"Kinda figured." Five years. Jesus. I was away for fifteen once, but that was by choice. A fucked up, misguided choice that led to a lot of blood being spilled. And even then the people I'd left had an idea that I might still be alive. This is way different. These are people who saw my corpse, who lit me up and tossed my ashes like they were cleaning out a chimney. And anyone who knows I'm dead is going to wonder why I'm back, or if I'm actually me. I'm kind of wondering that myself. I don't want to play whatever game this is, but I'm going to have to until I can at least figure out the rules.

"What's your next move?" Letitia says.

"Depends. You going to let me out of this cell, or do I have to do it myself?"

"I was thinking of having you stew in there for a—"

"Excuse me." A voice from around the corner at the end of the cell block.

"This section's closed," Letitia says. "Private party." A uniformed officer steps around the corner and walks toward us. There's something not quite right with his gait. "Did you not hear what I just fucking said?"

I cast an unlocking spell that hits the cell door and handcuffs both and slide the door out of the way. My gut tells me shit's about to go down, and I get a shield up just as the cop draws his gun and fires at us.

Everything about the cop is average. Hair is an average-looking blondish-brown. Not straight, not exactly curly. Skin's an average of not quite white, not quite brown, not quite anything else.

"I don't think this is a real cop," I say. Letitia doesn't answer. When I glance over my shoulder, I see why. One of the bullets got through before I had the shield up completely and it's hit her dead center in the chest. She's lying on the floor, a little burnt hole at her heart.

I know she's not dead, because believe me I'd feel it if she were. But she's hurt. I know she's wearing a vest under her shirt, and that's the only thing saving her. My hindbrain, though, hasn't quite gotten that information.

Something inside me cracks beneath sheer rage. Some wall holding back power I thought I'd lost. A jarring awareness of two sets of memories over the last couple of days, and a wave of knowledge spanning the last five years and millennia before slams into me and I become something else.

Whether this body is mine, human or some kind of golem, is irrelevant. Whether it's meat or clay makes no difference. It is a vessel and nothing more. I am Mictlantecuhtli. I am the King of Mictlan. As a god of death I am anger and retribution. I am Eric Carter. As a human being I have my own take on anger and retribution, and right now it involves shoving that gun up this guy's ass.

I walk down the line of cells toward him, not even bothering with a shield. He fires again. Bullets tear into me, but all they do is put holes in my clothes.

I grew up around death. Feeling it, watching it, knowing the ins and outs of it in a way I didn't understand anything else. For me, death is—simple isn't the word. There's nothing simple about death. But clear. Death is a hole where a person used to be, a gap in the emotional space. And like how seeing a smile with a missing tooth throws all the other teeth around it into sharp relief, death does the same thing to life. It's harder for Eric Carter to see, but it's easy for Mictlantecuhtli, so I didn't notice this before now.

The man in front of me isn't alive or dead. He's a little bit of both. Like the driver at the motel, he's a construct, a Ken doll with a Glock. But I couldn't see then what I can clearly see now. There's a person holding this thing's reins, powering it with a little spark of their own life, a little sliver of their own soul.

As I get closer the construct is just shooting and

reloading, shooting and reloading, its hands a blur. I think the gun and the bullets are part of the same magic that powers it, because the gun never jams, and the magazines seem to appear in its hand out of nowhere. No expression on its face. A small pile of hot brass and empty magazines are forming around its feet, and my clothes look like I've jumped into a woodchipper.

I bat the gun out of its hand. The second the weapon loses contact it disintegrates into pebbles of clay. I grab the construct by the neck. It punches and kicks at me, but I don't feel any of it. I look straight into the thing's eyes, and I know that whoever is piloting this thing can see me, and I say, "I will find you."

I grab that sliver of soul and life and rip it out like a weed. The construct disintegrates into chunks of clay. Body, clothes, everything. Same for all the magazines and brass on the floor. I hold that spark in my hand, watch it wriggle like a worm. I pull the spark into myself, devour it. Its taste is an echo of the soul it came from, and it goes down like cheap scotch. I don't know who this person is now, but when I find them, I'll know.

Something goes wrong. My legs buckle under me. The veins in my hand begin to turn black. I can feel a searing in my skin, and I realize why whoever brought me back had to do it like this. They split me in pieces and brought back Eric Carter, but left Mictlantecuhtli behind.

This body, wherever it came from, can't contain all of me. Human bodies are not meant to hold gods. I'm burning through it like a lit match, and I make a split-second decision. I rebreak what I just fixed. I split myself back in two, hanging onto whatever can safely stay behind. I let Mictlantecuhtli go.

As that part of me drains away, I'm changing into good-for-nothing Eric Carter again. Plain old necro-

mancer, Lazarus cosplayer, overall pain in the ass.
But it's not a clean separation. There are pieces of
Eric Carter in Mictlantecuhtli, and Mictlantecuhtli in
Eric Carter. It's like the worst Reese's Peanut Butter
Cup commercial ever.

I feel a tearing inside my mind as the last connection between the two of us separates. Exhaustion washes
over me and I fall unconscious to the floor.

Chapter 6

I come to next to the pile of clay that was shooting at me just a few minutes ago. I feel raw, hollowed out. Everything hurts, my brain most of all. I think I'll go back to being unconscious for a while until I stop feeling like my skull's been opened up with a belt sander. I close my eyes and wait.

"You still alive?" Letitia. She sounds winded, grunting in pain as she moves. Of course she's in pain. This asshole just pumped a bullet into her chest. Kevlar might keep it from penetrating, but it still hurts like a motherfucker.

"That might be stretching things a bit," I say. "How are you doing?"

"Enh," she says, strain in her voice. "I've been shot before. I'll get shot again. The hell happened to that guy?" She leans on the wall for support and slowly makes her way toward me.

"Wasn't a guy. Some kind of construct. Never seen one like it before. Had a little bit of somebody's soul in it, though."

"Somebody's soul?"

"Yeah," I say. "I think they were, I dunno, piloting it? Anyway, I ate it." I don't want to tell her what else happened. To her I probably looked like I just choked the guy out and he disintegrated into a bunch of clay blobs. She doesn't need to know the rest. At least not until I've had some time to think about it.

"I do not even want to try to process that sentence," Letitia says. "Can you walk?"

I pull myself up from the floor, sliding up the wall. My legs are weak, but they're already feeling better. "Looks like."

"Jesus, what happened to you?" Letitia steps back, staring at me. Now there's a loaded question. Where do I even start? I'm not even sure myself.

"Lots of things, I'm sure. Are you asking about anything in particular?"

"You have a lot of new holes in you."

"Oh. No, just my clothes."

"Okay," she says, her breath coming out in short, ragged gasps, sweat beading her forehead. "I'm not hearing any alarms. Looks like when I told people to clear out and leave me alone, they cleared out and left me alone. I'll have to make sure there's no surveillance footage or anything. I had the cameras turned off, but you never know when—"

"Tish," I say. "You're babbling."

"I am, aren't I? I do that when I get shot. Give me a second." She visibly calms herself, finds her center. Her breathing eases a little, and she no longer looks like she's about to have a stroke.

"Better?"

"Yeah. Let's get you the hell out of here." She looks me up and down. "First maybe let's get you some clothes."

"And my stuff."

"And your stuff." She looks into my eyes and frowns. "And maybe some sunglasses."

Shit. "Let me guess. No whites in my eyes? All black? Kinda like shark eyes?"

"Yeah. What the hell, Eric?"

"It happens." I thought I was done with that shit. The first time this happened it took me over two years to get them back to normal, and that was only after I'd killed Santa Muerte and Mictlantecuhtli. They weren't special or anything, just black. Had to wear sunglasses all the time to hide them. Real pain in the ass going out in public at night.

"On a regular basis?"

I'm not sure how to answer that. Before I died, they were only changing when I did something that bumped up against Mictlantecuhtli's magic. After, when I took over the role completely, they were just my eyes.

"It'll go away eventually. Don't worry about me," I say. "I'll snag some new clothes when I get out of here. I've got a Sharpie and some stickers in my bag. Nobody'll see me. Speaking of which, where is it? You didn't stick it into evidence, did you?"

"I brought it down with me. If nothing else it looked like it was your shit in there, and I didn't want anybody else getting their hands on it. Come on. It's next to the door." I follow her down the row of cells, both of us moving like a geriatric couple after taco night at the old folk's home.

"How's your chest?" I say. Her breathing is shallow but not labored. The bullet hit her vest dead center. The bruise is going to be magnificent. I've been shot while wearing a vest, so I can sympathize. Main reason I came up with that shield spell. Got tired of bruised ribs.

"I've had worse. Annie's gonna be pissed off at me when she sees it."

"You gonna tell her how you got it?"

"Fuck no. I'll say it was an accident at the range, or something. These guys are shooting themselves in the foot more often than you'd think, so she won't question it."

"I don't think you give her enough credit. She

seemed to be pretty good at seeing through your bull-shit. I mean, the usual married bullshit, not all the magic bullshit you wouldn't tell her about."

"You know you're not helping, right?"

"Sorry." I stop and lean against the wall. "Need a second."

I need more than a second. I need a lifetime. I've had my soul ripped apart, stitched together, and ripped apart again. I'm weak like I just ran a marathon. My mind is spinning with questions I don't have any answers for.

"Eating souls take a lot out of you?"

"Something like that." We reach the door and I grab my bag. Pull out a HI, MY NAME IS sticker and write JUST SOME GUY on it with shaking hands in Sharpie before putting some juice into it. That'll last long enough for me to get some new clothes and find a place to hole up nobody knows about.

I don't know how those guys found me at the mo-tel, and if Demon Hank knows about the room at the Ambassador, Darius probably does, too. I really wish I hadn't gone there and run into him. And since I'm wishing, I think I'll wish for a handjob, a bucket of cocaine, and a redheaded pony girl.

"Hey, thanks for the information," I say, checking that everything is in the bag. I think about transfer-ring the watch and razor to a pocket, but my clothes are so badly torn up they'd just fall through. I leave them in the bag, slide the Browning into its holster in the small of my back. "Once I'm gone you shouldn't have any more problems like that again. I'll get out of your hair. Say hi to Annie for me." I think about that for a second. "Actually, no, that probably wouldn't be a good idea. But keep your head down. Things are gonna get messy." Messy how, I can't answer, but things get messy as soon as I walk into a room.

Letitia closes her eyes, pinches the bridge of her nose. "I can't believe I'm saying this. I'm in."

"Sorry?"

"I'm in. I'll help you."

"I thought you didn't want any part of this."

"That fucking thing shot me. I want to find who sent it and kick their teeth so far down their throat they're shitting molars for a week."

I can respect that. It's a very Letitia thing to do, so I'm not too surprised, but still. I think about it for a second and much as I'd like the help, much as I need it, I can't. "No," I say. "This is too big. Maybe too big for either one of us. If anything's going to happen, I won't have you taking any more hits."

"Eric, don't get in my way," she says.

I know that tone. If I don't bring her in, she'll come in on her own, and fuck only knows where that'll take us. "Are you sure? Whatever the hell is going on here, it's nothing small. I have to figure out a couple of things still, but I think I know what happened, and if I'm right it would have taken a serious fuck-ton of power to pull off."

"Sonofabitch. I just put this together," she says.

"What?"

"It did take a lot of power. Last night. Somebody set something off down near San Pedro. Everybody felt it."

San Pedro? What the hell is in San Pedro? That's the Harbor. Boats, trucks, shipping. Something else. I was in a cement bunker. What the hell is it? It comes to me. "Fort MacArthur," I say.

"Isn't that a museum?"

"It's an old World War II gun emplacement," I say. "Museum, memorial, something like that. Most of it's closed off, but part of it is an old concrete bunker. I woke up in a room like that. That had to be where it happened."

"Got any other leads?" she says.

"No," I say. "But I think if I poke around I'm probably going to find a few things."

"I know a place down that way," Letitia says. "The Down And Out. It's a bar on Gaffey. I can meet you there in"—she looks at her watch—"about four hours. I have to clear things here, make sure nobody heard all the gunfire. And you should get yourself new clothes. You go through a lot of those, don't you?"

"You would too if you got covered in blood as much as I do. What's your number? I'll grab a phone on my way there. And do you have Gabriela's?" She rattles off a string of numbers and I jot them down on one of the stickers.

"Four hours?" I say.

"With traffic, yeah. Oh, and stay off the 110. It's still collapsed from right before the old USC campus all the way down to Firestone."

"Still?"

"It's a toxic wasteland down there. When Vernon went up, all the chemicals settled there. It won't be clean for decades, if ever."

———

Vernon. I'd almost forgotten about Vernon. It is—sorry, it was—a city just east of South L.A. By the time I actually met him in person, Quetzalcoatl was so whittled down that he had to create a form out of pulled-together trash. Fine motor skills weren't exactly his forte. What's a god who needs hands to do? Why, enlist a Mexican sicaria who likes to set shit on fire, of course.

La Niña Quemada, the Burning Girl. Cartel killer named Jacqueline Sastre who'd had quite the reputation. She'd been gunning for me when I was in Mexico blowing up heroin distribution centers for shits and giggles, and we just missed each other. Pity. Might have saved a whole lot of people.

Vernon was built for light and heavy industry. Warehouses, manufacturing, trucking. The place only had like a hundred people actually living there. During the day it's wall-to-wall drone workers. At night, you get truckers passing through, not much else. Gabriela and I knew Sastre was holed up in one of Vernon's abandoned factories, which is like saying there's a needle in one of these haystacks, good luck and have fun.

We found her in one tying little bundles of fatwood together. Wouldn't find out until later that they were firestarters. Magical firestarters. I think you can see where this is going. Things went poorly for us. Gabriela was gutted and almost died and to save her I had to let the Burning Girl get away.

Then Sastre blows up Vernon. Not a building in Vernon. Not part of Vernon. The whole. Fucking. Thing. Three-hundred-foot-tall wall of flame inside a five-square-mile crater. The blast took out eight hundred people from surrounding neighborhoods in the first few seconds.

But the real problems were right on its heels. Remember all that manufacturing I was talking about? Some of it used some pretty toxic stuff that all got hurled into the air and blown out over South L.A.

Nearly eight hundred thousand people lived in that area. Biggest evacuation in—well, shit, maybe ever. It was certainly one of the worst humanitarian crises the country's ever seen.

Until the real fires started, of course. Vernon was just the practice run.

———

Letitia's not kidding when she says South L.A. is a wasteland. It looks like the fucking moon. Most of the buildings haven't even been torn down yet. I see it to the south as I take the 10 Freeway out toward the 405. Two freeways I watched collapse as Letitia and I chased Sastre down and all the while she was tossing those fucking firestarters out her window.

The rest of the drive down to San Pedro is a crawl just like normal. Except for all the new buildings, vacant lots, for-sale signs. Five years might be a long time to be dead, but it's not nearly long enough to recover from the fires. Although the Port of Los Angeles doesn't seem too different, or at least I don't remember enough of it to notice. When I get off the freeway onto Gaffey in San Pedro, though, I can see it.

Like everywhere else there's new construction, but mostly there are just vacant lots. San Pedro looks to be on its last legs. But people have said that about it before and it's always hung on, like that one racist uncle who shows up every year at Thanksgiving and won't do everybody a favor and just fucking die.

The Down And Out is easy to find. It's the only open business in a strip mall surrounded by vacant lots littered with desperate looking for-sale signs, like profile pics of bros on Tinder who think having a tiger in the frame is somehow going to get them laid. On the trip down I've been thinking. But I need some visual aids to see if I've got things right and I think a few glasses and a bottle of scotch might be just what I'm looking for. I could also really use a drink.

I park and text Letitia that I'm down here. I start to dial Gabriela's number a few times but stop just shy of hitting the call button. What the fuck would I say? "Hey, Gabby! How you doin'? Yeah, this is Eric. You know the dead Aztec god stand-in? I was just in town from the Underworld and thought I'd give you a ring." If my meeting with Letitia is any indication, I don't think that'll go over very well. Maybe after Letitia and I check out Fort MacArthur.

The Down And Out is not classy. It isn't hip. You want a twenty-dollar Manhattan, this isn't the bar for you. It looks and smells like what it is, a locals sort of hangout that can barely keep the floors clean of beer, the bathrooms clear of the stink of urine, or anything more complicated than football trivia on the TVs.

The lights are dim and the bar's almost empty. Not exactly a happenin' place. The smokers have found it, though. A thick haze of cigarettes and cigars hovers over everything like smog over the Valley. Guess when you're living in an economic Chernobyl nobody really cares about pissy little no-smoking laws.

I settle into a booth in the back. A nervous-looking waitress, presumably nervous because of the weird guy in sunglasses in a dark corner of the local shit-kicker bar, comes by and takes my order.

"Gimme"—I do a mental count and realize I have no idea how many I'll need—"half a dozen empty shot glasses, half a dozen tumblers, and a bottle of scotch."

"You expecting company?" she says. I look around the room and see all the Echoes and Haunts this place has accumulated over the years, plus a few Wanderers, too. It's pretty crowded.

"Just one more. The rest are already here," I say.

"Oookay. Six shot glasses, six tumblers, one bottle of scotch. Any preference?"

"Anything that hasn't been pissed in."

"Might be a challenge."

"A little bit of piss is okay."

"You got it. Lightly pissed-in scotch. Anything else?" It occurs to me that I haven't eaten anything all day, hell, in the last five years.

"Got anything to eat?"

"Chicken wings."

"Chicken wings it is, then."

She backs away a bit before turning and walking to

the bar. My glasses, bottle, and chicken wings show up. The wings are disgusting but hell, they're calories.

If I'm right, I know what happened to me, but not how. The concept's simple, but I keep playing it over and over in my head, less to be sure that I'm right and more to figure out how they might have done it. When Letitia comes in and sees me in the corner pouring scotch into shot glasses and tumblers and back into the bottle, making notes on cocktail napkins, she slides into the seat opposite me and says nothing until I look up.

"Do I want to know?"

"I've gone through it about forty times, and just now I thought it might be an old Persian spell I heard about inscribed on a clay tablet a few thousand years old. It's sitting in the London Museum last I heard, but I don't think it's the one. The subject catches fire and turns to ash in seconds. Might be a variant, but I'm fucked if I can figure out how."

"What the hell are you talking about?" she says.

"Short version or long version?"

"Let's start with short," she says.

"I wasn't brought back to life," I say.

Chapter 7

"Okay, back up. You're not a zombie, are you? Or like that hologram of Tupac they rolled out at Coachella?"

"Neither. Nobody brought me back to life. In fact, you could make an argument that I'm still dead. Sort of. Part of me."

"I don't follow."

"I'm not exactly Eric Carter."

"But—" Letitia starts. "How did— I don't get this."

"I'm part of Eric Carter. More accurately, I'm the Eric Carter part of Mictlantecuhtli. Here, I brought visual aids." I pour some scotch into a couple shot glasses.

"Drink this," I say. "You're gonna need it." We both throw back our shots. Letitia gags, but I've already sampled it and got my gagging out of the way before she arrived. Still tastes better than that black tar crap I was puking up earlier.

I pour more scotch into another shot glass. "This is me."

"The shot glass?"

"The whisky."

"The shitty whisky," she says.

"The shitty whisky indeed."

"Pretty on brand."

"I try. Now—"

"So what's the shot glass?" she says.

"My body. If you keep interrupting me this metaphor's gonna fall apart."

"So, your soul is shitty whisky."

"Yes. My soul is shitty whisky, my body is a shot glass. Do you mind? Now I die, right? Flatline, push up the daisies, take the dirt nap. Following so far?"

"With you so far." I pour the shot into one of the tumblers. "Your soul went into a whisky glass?"

"Do you want to hear this or not? I had an agreement with Santa Muerte that I'd take the role of Mictlantecuhtli and help her spiff their place up. Was supposed to be three months out of the year but kicking the bucket kind of changed the game plan. I died and my soul went to Mictlan."

"Because of your deal with Santa Muerte."

"Not sure. Possibly it was the only afterlife that would take me. So, I go to Mictlan, and I take over as the King of the Dead."

"And the glass is the King of the Dead."

"Close. The glass is the empty cosmic space that the god Mictlantecuhtli had previously occupied before I killed him. You can see that, though I have taken his place, I don't fill the glass."

"Big shoes," she says.

"And then some. But now that there is a Mictlantecuhtli, even if it's one with Eric Carter at his core, he grows." I pour scotch from the bottle into the tumbler. "And grows, and grows, and grows, until . . ." I fill the rest of the glass with more scotch until it's almost to the top.

"Until he's nothing but Mictlantecuhtli."

"Right. He grows to fill up that cosmic space. So, now Mictlantecuhtli is aaaaall growed up, hanging out in Mictlan."

"Okay," she says. "Following you so far. What happens next."

"Eric Carter does not get brought back to life."

"Lost me again."

"Eric Carter and Mictlantecuhtli are the same person. They're so mixed up together that you can't tell one from the other. Mictlantecuhtli isn't like one of those Russian nesting dolls with Carter at the core. He's like this glass. One shot glass of whisky is blended with all the rest of the whisky. So, how do you get that exact same shot glass out of the tumbler? How do you get Eric Carter out of Mictlantecuhtli?"

"You can't. They're the same thing."

"Right. It'd be like unmixing paint. But what you can do," I say, picking up the filled tumbler, "is summon the whole god, and when it shows up, stick it into a vessel." I pick up a different shot glass.

"That still you?"

"Actually, I think it's some random hobo. Just roll with it. Now, what's wrong with this picture?"

"Why's it a hobo?"

"I merely assume it's a hobo. It's a body. Not sure whose, and I don't see how it makes much of a difference."

"I think it makes a difference to the hobo," Letitia says.

"What did I tell you about this metaphor falling apart?" She makes a zipping motion across her lips. "Thank you. Where was I?"

"Shot-glass hobo."

"Right. What's wrong with this picture?"

"There's not enough room in the shot-glass hobo," she says.

"Exactly. Mictlantecuhtli is too big to fit into the shot-glass hobo because the shot-glass hobo is very, very small compared to Mictlantecuhtli, who is very, very large."

"Somebody tried to summon Mictlantecuhtli and shove him into a human body," Letitia says. "And since not all of Mictlantecuhtli could fit, only some of him went in?"

"And trapped him." I place my hand over the mouth of the shot glass.

"Are you saying that you're Mictlantecuhtli in Eric Carter's body?"

"Close," I say, and throw the shot back. "I am an Eric-Carter-sized piece of Mictlantecuhtli because that's all that will fit into an Eric-Carter-sized body. When I woke up and couldn't remember anything, I didn't realize anything had happened. I thought I was just me. Eric. Not. You know what I mean. I don't know why I couldn't remember, whether that was on purpose or an accident, but I've got all my memories back now. His memories. Something."

"Then what happened? Why do you know this now?"

"You got shot. I don't like my friends getting shot. I got angry. The rest of me came pouring back in."

"The black eyes are, what, residual death god?"

"Pretty much. That and my memories. But even though I remember everything, the problem still applies. This body can't hold all of Mictlantecuhtli. I was starting to burst at the seams. So I let the rest of myself go back to Mictlan."

"Let go" makes it sound so innocuous. Simple. Easy. Comfortable. The process was anything but. I was burning from the inside out. The body was going to disintegrate at the very least—not that I cared much about a husk of meat. But I don't know what the proximity would have done to Letitia. Or what would happen with Mictlantecuhtli. And I couldn't figure out how to take the rest of Eric Carter with him.

When I released the part of me that's Mictlantecuhtli, it was not a clean separation. It was like ripping through a dozen folded newspapers. My soul shredded along the tear. And I did it on purpose. Imagine having to chop off your own leg with a dull hatchet.

It makes me wonder what would have happened if the original Santa Muerte and Mictlantecuhtli had succeeded in shoving my and Tabitha's souls out of our bodies and replaced them with their own. Would they have just blown up? That would have been embarrassing for everybody.

"So what does that make you?" Letitia says. "Exactly."

"Unless I can think of something better, I'm Eric Carter. I have Eric Carter's memories. But I also have Mictlantecuhtli's up to the point where we split off."

"I see a flaw here," Letitia says. "What about the hobo?"

"What about the hobo?"

"Why don't you look like the hobo?"

"That is a very good question that I'm still trying to figure out," I say. "It's possible that the spell, or Mictlantecuhtli's will, or mine, or whatever, was able to reshape the body. I think it's related to how people view their bodies and identities.

"When I picture myself, there are no bullet holes or broken bones, but I do see my tattoos. They're more a part of my identity than any of my scars are. There's an ideal in our minds of who we are. There's also the self-image of us as ugly, horrid blobs of flesh that aren't worthy of love, of course."

"But you've got enough of an ego that's not a problem. You picture yourself like ten or fifteen years younger?" Letitia says. "There's some Freudian childhood shit in there somewhere. What about all the color in the tattoos? You got some secret sparkly My Little Pony fetish going on?"

"Pony something fetish, at least. I think I know.

And it supports the rest. Mictlantecuhtli is usually depicted as a gaunt scarecrow of a guy, wearing a necklace made of eyeballs and a headdress, who's so skinny you can see organs hanging out of his rib cage."

"Charming."

"Yeah, I'm not crazy about it either. But I look however I need to in Mictlan. Or he does. Or I do as him. I'm going to have to figure out my pronouns. Anyway, he takes other forms. Now, the Aztecs had a thing for feathers. They put feathers on fucking everything. Feathered headdresses, feathered capes."

"You wore a feathered cape."

"Occasionally, yes. Go ahead and laugh. I looked just as stupid as it sounds. They're all feathers from tropical birds."

"Bright colors," she says. "So, instead of a bright feathered cape, you get bright colored tats? Does that mean you've got some of Mictlantecuhtli in you and vice versa?"

"Technically—"

"No, I'm not doing that. You're you. You're Eric Carter. I try to think of you as a piece of some Aztec death god and my brain's gonna pop."

"I don't know how precise the ritual was," I say. "But I think so, yeah."

"And you have no idea why?"

"I have some guesses, but I don't know if they're right, and I don't want to go down those paths until I have a better idea of what's happening. I need to see the bunker where the ritual was performed. Might tell me something."

"Then let's go."

"Hang on," I say and dig into a pocket, pulling out a wad of the bills I stole from a couple ATMs on my way down. I put the bills on the table and an empty shot glass on top. There's probably four or five thousand dollars there for the waitress.

"Big tip," Letitia says.

"For dealing with my shit? I think it's a little light."

"You won't get an argument from me."

———

The Fort MacArthur museum is at the top of a hill in San Pedro that faces the ocean. It was a gun battery set up to defend the L.A. Harbor since around World War I. It was shut down in the seventies and turned into a museum in the eighties. The guns are all gone, but the concrete structures are still in place.

Getting in is easy. Letitia casts a don't-look-at-me spell on the car and I snap the lock holding the gate in place. If there are any guards patrolling the grounds, we're not seeing them. Still, I make us both HI, MY NAME IS stickers declaring that we're not here, just to be on the safe side.

She pulls up in the lot just outside the museum and we walk down into the main grounds. I can tell we're in the right place because I get more and more uneasy as we walk the grounds. Eventually we come to a set of double metal doors set in the concrete wall of the battery with the sign MUSEUM next to it. My gut tells me that what I'm looking for is somewhere behind that door.

"You doing all right?" Letitia says. "I don't know about you, but I can feel the leftover magic in this place."

"Yeah," I say, not sure if I'm saying that I'm all right, or agreeing about the leftover magic. She's right. Whatever was done here, it was fucking huge. I snap the padlock and send some electricity through the doors, frying the alarm.

The doors need maintenance. The hinges scream in the quiet emptiness loud enough to make us both jump. They sound a lot like the door that was open when "Joseph," whoever the fuck he is, left to get into a gunfight. We leave the doors open, not wanting to make more noise than we have to, and head into the warren of halls and tunnels underneath the battery. I cast a light spell, creating a small, hovering globe that illuminates the darkened hallway.

"Is this place haunted?" Letitia whispers.

"Every place is haunted." I can see a few Wanderers and a couple of Haunts walking the grounds. Some look like they were soldiers, World War II uniforms, but there are a couple that are clearly modern tourists, oohing and aahing at everything they pass by. I don't have the heart to tell them that they're dead.

"You know what I mean, smartass."

"Would it help if I told you it wasn't?"

"Maybe. This place is creepy as fuck. And that light isn't helping anything. All it does is throw shadows around."

"I can get rid of it," I say. Letitia casts her own light in case I'm serious.

"Screw you. Let's just find this place and get out of here. You might be just fine with ghosts and dead people, but it freaks me the hell out."

"They're harmless," I say.

"Yeah, that's what you said about all those ghosts stuck in paper traps. How many did they kill?"

"Totally different thing," I say. "Those were already over on this side. None of these are. So relax." I wish I could take my own advice. It's not the ghosts that are getting to me, it's the growing sense that everything here is wrong. If we take a turn and the feeling fades, I turn us around and head the other direction. It's like playing that hot/cold game. The warmer I get, the sicker I feel.

"If ghosts eat me, you're gonna be hearing from my wife," she says.

"Look, I promise you the ghosts will not eat you."

I stop in front of a single metal door, recently broken rust on its hinges. "This is it."

"You sure?"

I want to run, scream, claw my eyes out. "Yeah, I'm sure."

We both draw our guns and I ready a shield spell in case there's something on the other side we don't want to tangle with. We pull the doors open and I almost throw up from the stink. Thick and acidic and rotting. It smells like a morgue that lost power a week ago.

Yeah, this is it. The summoning circle is still in the middle of the room, candles sit in tall candelabras waiting to be lit. I can tell it was abandoned in a hurry. There are still reagents and ritual items that wouldn't have been discarded otherwise.

"You like tequila?" Letitia says. She picks up a bottle at one of the cardinal points of the summoning circle.

I find a large notebook, pages filled with arcane symbols, chants, visualizations that help in casting spells. A handful of pages seem to be working out the problem of how to summon a god and stick him inside a meat suit. I slide it into my messenger bag to read later.

"Yeah," I say, though the idea of tequila makes my stomach churn. "Sort of. Mictlantecuhtli's more a pulque fan, but tequila will do in a pinch. What else do you see?"

"A human skull, a finger bone with a really sick aura around it, a rat nailed to a board, and a dead coyote wrapped in barbed wire."

"These guys weren't fucking around," I say, and pick up the finger bone. She's right. I don't know that I'd say it had a sick aura around it, but then, I wouldn't. "You sure you cremated all of me?"

"Thought so, yeah. Why?"

"Pretty sure it's my finger." I slide that into the messenger bag along with the notebook. "I recognize all of those symbols. Each one means something different either to me or Mictlantecuhtli, even if some of them have a modern twist, like the barbed wire."

"So, they really were summoning an actual god," Letitia says. "I'm not up on my Cosmic Entities, but that seems like a bad idea. How did they do it?"

I walk around the circle. It's formed of multi-colored powders; some of them have been burnt, and orange flower petals and thorns are scattered across throughout. In all the mix of scents I can pick out familiar smells. Something from Mictlantecuhtli's past. I bend down and close my eyes, searching through inherited memories that were never mine.

"Burned ahuehuete and pōchōtl," I say. "Sacred trees tied to kings and symbols of their power. Cempasúchil, Mexican marigolds. They draw out the souls of the dead. You see them a lot during Día de Los Muertos. I can see how they brought him here, but I don't know what they trapped him with."

"You woke up inside the circle?" Letitia says.

"Yeah. It was unpleasant."

"Maybe it was the body that did it. Like a bucket catching rainwater. The ritual circle didn't trap him so much as it filled up, and there was only one place for the spillover to go."

"That actually makes—" I stop when I hear the distinctive sound of the spoon of a grenade ping and the primer snap. I slam into Letitia, trying to get us both behind a couple of concrete slabs.

The grenade lands about ten feet away from us and turns out to be a flash-bang. It won't kill us, but the deafening noise and blinding flare are more than enough to take me down. I can't hear anything but a high-pitched whining in my head and I'm half blind.

I try to stand up, but gravity and I are no longer on speaking terms.

Something grabs me from behind and slams my head into the floor. That and the assault on my senses from the flash-bang and it's game over.

Chapter 8

I have a bag over my head. I hate having a bag over my head. It's always the same goddamn thing with kidnappers. "Let's put a bag over his head. That way he won't know what's happening!"

I know what's happening. I'm being kidnapped. Don't have to be Sherlock fucking Holmes to figure that one out. Oh, and protect the location of your secret hideout? Really? Do you have any idea how easy it is to track a cell phone? I can feel mine inside my pocket.

But wait! What about frightening and disorienting your victim? Blow me. I'm already disoriented. Fucking flash-bang did that for me. And frightened? Seriously? Do you have any idea how many times I've been kidnapped, stuck in a trunk, handcuffed, or left for dead in the desert? Try something new. Shoot me into space or something.

The bag is pulled off my head and I'm not surprised to find myself sitting in a leather club chair in a smoky jazz bar, all oak paneling and dimly lit tables. A woman in a red cocktail dress is on stage singing "My Funny Valentine," a four-piece band backing her up. The small table in front of me holds two glasses of no doubt excellent whisky—one for me, and one for a man with skin the color of ebony, biceps like tree trunks, and a broad smile full of teeth promising that he'll be very polite about it when he eats you.

"Darius," I say, popping the handcuffs off my wrists with a thought.

"That'll be all, Hank." I can feel the demon hovering behind me.

"Oh, hey," I say. "Got tired of German Expressionism?"

Hank shrugs. "If he'd just gone Cubist like I asked I'd have stuck around."

"Fair enough." I'm not particularly comfortable with him this close, but at least he isn't trying to kill me again.

"I'll call for you soon, Hank," Darius says, voice smooth as lubed-up satin.

"Yes, sir," Hank says. The looming presence behind me fades.

"It's good to see you, Eric. Wasn't sure I ever would again."

"Kind of surprised myself." I put the handcuffs on the table in front of me. "Was that really necessary?"

"Can I trust you?"

"Oh, hell no."

His booming laugh drowns out the singer, the band, the entire room. And when he stops everything is silent. The bar is empty. Darius waves his hand, dismissive, and the cuffs disappear.

"They were just for show," Darius says. "One must respect decorum, after all."

"Oh, of course. I wouldn't want to get in the way of decorum," I say. I look around the bar. "Is this your thing now? Like permanently? I went to a lot of trouble to help you get the CBGB look. Didn't hang onto that very long, did you?"

"I'm old," Darius says. "Set in my ways. I'll keep this, oh, I dunno, another hundred years or so? Punk was nice and all, but the urinals kept filling up with vomit and there was just too much fucking in the stalls for my taste."

"I can appreciate that," I say. Bathroom stalls are terrible places for fucking. "So, to what do I owe the pleasure of your company? Clearly I'm not here for you to kill me. You would have done that already. Oh. Wait. You did."

"That was the passion of our mutual demonic friend. I just wanted him to bring you here to have a talk."

"And get the bottle."

"Yes," Darius says. "And that. You know, despite your protestations, I never thought you didn't have it."

"Pfft. I know that. Everybody knew that. Even if it turned out I didn't have it, everybody would have thought I did. I wasn't lying so much as giving a wink and a nudge. I'm assuming that's why you brought me back. To open your bottle."

"Guilty," Darius says. "Guilty of many things. So many sins writ upon my skin. I will admit to each and every one of my crimes. And so it is with the deepest regret that I cannot claim this one."

"What?"

"You just need who, where, when, why, and how and you'll have a full set. I'm telling you that I did not bring you back. This time, my friend, you are not a piece on my board. Don't get me wrong. I'm grateful to whoever pulled you from a no-doubt-comfortable afterlife banging the Queen of the Dead beneath Mictlan's skies. Gives me hope that you might see fit to assist me with my current residential issues."

Okay, well, that's that theory shot. But then, Darius enjoys lying. He's very good at it. Especially when he uses the truth to do it. So of course he could be lying. He's Darius. But he never does anything without a reason. So why would he lie to me about this?

Fine, I'll play his game. "If not you, then who?"

"I have no idea," he says. "Which surprises me. Seems there's a new player at the table. Or an old one who is very well hidden. And I must say, they've chosen themselves an excellent piece to play with."

Anger courses through me and I consider trying to kill him, but I know it won't work. He'll just shrug it off and laugh at me. This is his world inside the bottle. Not mine. "I am not a pawn," I say.

"Oh, no," Darius says. He picks up his whisky and sniffs it before taking a sip. A blissful smile, a tip of the glass. A toast? Salute? Challenge? I can never tell with him. "You really ought to try this. I purchased it from a gentleman in Hong Kong who paid almost eight million dollars for it. A Macallan 60. Excellent nose on it. But as I was saying, no, you are no one's pawn."

"Glad we cleared that up."

"Maybe a rook," Darius says. "No. Bishop? Fast, striking at an oblique angle? Ah. A knight. Attacking from the enemy's blind spot. Coming out of the shadows. And you are such an easy piece to move."

"Okay, now I really want to kill you."

"And you didn't before? I didn't know there was an even higher setting for your rage." He holds his whisky glass in his hand palm up. An ornate bottle appears in its place. It's a perfect reproduction of the one he's trapped inside.

"Hey, I can see your house from here," I say. He ignores me.

"Have you ever heard of a Devil's Flask?"

"Can't say I've run into that one. I have heard of a Devil's Jockstrap, though. It's like an Eiffel Tower except that—"

"It's stage magic," he says, cutting me off. "Little ironic you've never heard of it before. You should look into what the normals can do some time. The magic of perception is a fascinating subject. A Devil's Flask is a bottle that's been heated and the outside rapidly cooled. The inside, however, cools slowly. The difference between the two makes the outside very strong, but the inside—"

He waves his hand over the bottle and the cork disappears, to be replaced by a nail hovering an inch over the opening. It floats for a moment and then drops into the bottle. The bottle explodes, showering us in glass. I jump a little, not expecting that.

"The inside is incredibly fragile. The slightest scratch in the right place and boom. That's you. You've been through a lot, my friend. You are covered with armor thicker than the Wall of China. But get behind it, hit you in just the right place. And you shatter." The bottle and shards of glass disappear.

"I'll get that looked at. Hell of a metaphor you got there."

"I thought so," he says. "Did you understand it?"

"Which part? The insult about being fragile on the inside or the insult of shattering if you hit me in the right spot?"

"Before you came in, I had no hopes of ever getting out of here. All my work to groom you into the perfect key wasted."

"Groomed."

"Just so. Who nudged you toward Santa Muerte, even if only by pulling my support? Who helped you in Mictlan? Who made you King of the Dead?"

"You're saying this was all planned? Horseshit. You're good, Darius. You're not that good."

"Oh, I'll admit I took advantage of other circumstances a time or two, but once you came back to Los Angeles after your sister died, I saw an opportunity. Only Mictlantecuhtli can let me out of here, so I needed to make a new Mictlantecuhtli."

Motherfucker. I can see it now. He didn't have to arrange much. Just steer me in a couple of different directions and eventually I'd end up where he wanted me.

"How'd that work out for you?"

"Things have taken a promising turn, actually. I'm very patient, Eric. I have to be. I'm over eight thousand years old. I waited five hundred years to get this close to freedom. I'm not about to squander that opportunity. But if things don't work out, I'll wait another five hundred years. It's not like I'm going anywhere."

"And there will always be another sap out there to con into helping you."

"There always is. Really, Eric, don't waste that whisky. Unlike much of what's in here, that's real. Never waste good whisky, son. It's a crime against nature."

I throw the whole glass back, barely tasting it. I swallow it, let it burn down my throat. "All right," I say. "What's your pitch?"

"My pitch?"

"Yeah. I'm not about to just open your fucking bottle for you. So what do I get out of it?"

"I'm a djinn, Eric. I can give you whatever you want. Riches, fame, power."

I can't help but laugh. "The fuck would I do with any of those things? I've already got more power dribbling out my ass than I know what to do with. Fame? Shit, I had all of L.A. hunting my ass down trying to kill me. Mothers use my name to scare their kids to go to bed. And riches? Did you seriously think I would jump at cash? I'm kind of insulted."

"What if I brought your sister back to life?"

It takes me a second to realize I've stopped breathing.

"Do not fucking jerk me around Darius," I say. "Not about that."

"I'm not. I could do it. Bring her back from the

grave. Wipe her memories of what happened to her. You could tell her she was in a coma. Why don't you think I can bring her back? A moment ago you were accusing me of doing that very thing to you."

I'm irritated that he actually had me considering it. But trying to use me as the poster boy for resurrection tells me he's just stringing me along. He doesn't know a goddamn thing. If he did, he'd know nobody brought me back to life. But it always helps to play along.

"How? I don't even know how I was brought back. I don't think you do either."

"Please, Eric. Now I'm insulted. I'm not like you. I'm a djinn. I don't need silly rituals, or complicated negotiations with the world around me. I tell the universe what I want and it simply accommodates me. If you want your sister back, I'll bring your sister back. Hell, I could bring your whole family back if you wanted."

"Don't overplay your hand, D," I say.

"Forgive me. Is it wrong to be grateful to the one who could free me from this prison?"

"I haven't said yes yet."

"True. But I'm confident you'll come around. In time."

"So, can I leave, or are you going to keep me trapped in here with you? Bear in mind I can't exactly pop the cork from inside."

"You are by no means a prisoner."

"That's funny. The flash-bang and the bag over my head kind of gave me a different idea."

"I'll speak to Hank about his overenthusiastic methods."

"You might also want to tell him that since he killed me in the first place, the next time I run into him I'll be returning the favor."

"I'll make a point of it." He nods and a door appears next to me. It's not in any wall, it's just sitting there in its frame in the middle of the room. "Your door."

"I'll keep in touch. Let you know what I decide."

"Oh, please do," he says.

"I'm probably going to say no."

"Possibly. Possibly. We'll just have to see, won't we?"

"See you around, D," I say. I stand up and push open the door. The other side is the park next to the grounds of Fort MacArthur. I can see it within walking distance. I walk through and close it behind me, the door disappearing as soon as it shuts.

"Really, D?" I say. He's put me next to the Korean Friendship Bell, an enormous bronze bell hanging in a pagoda that was given to the U.S. by South Korea in the seventies. I know Darius is more subtle than to shove a "Hey, we're buddies, right?" message in my face and expect me to buy it. So why—

A groan interrupts my thoughts and I realize why I've been dropped here instead of where I was taken from. Hank must have brought Letitia here and stuck her somewhere she'd be out of the way. I run around the pagoda and see her propped up against a column on the other side.

I crouch down in front of her. Her eyes slowly refocus until she notices that it's me. "The fuck happened?"

"Flash-bang. You got dumped here, I got tossed into the dimensional prison of a djinn who thinks I'm going to let him out of his bottle."

"Darius? What the hell? Oh, fuck this hurts. How are you okay?"

That's a good question. "Darius's doing, I think."

"Least you could have done is share."

"Sorry. I'll remember that next time. Can you stand?"

"With or without throwing up?"

"Preferably without."

"No promises." I help her up and we stagger toward the parking lot. There are a couple L.A. Public Works trucks parked there. I pop the locks and get Letitia into the passenger seat. I start the car with a snap of my fingers and head down the hill. It's a truck with a truck suspension and every little bump and pothole feels like falling into a crater.

Letitia's starting to look a little green. She lowers the window and sticks her head out, either to get some air or because she doesn't want to throw up inside the truck.

"Hey, you know how I said I was in?" she says.

"You reconsidering?"

"Kinda."

"If there's one thing I have learned over the last several years, it's that I can't guarantee anybody's safety. You need to walk, I totally get it. Hell, I might kick your ass to the curb myself." It would be kind of a relief. I'm a shit magnet, and anybody in my orbit gets coated with the stuff.

"I'll let you know. Hey, you think you can drop me off at home? I'll have Annie take me into the station tomorrow."

"How about we take you to a hospital?"

"And let normals work on me? Not gonna happen. I'll call a guy I know in the morning." We all have a guy. Mage doctors are always in high demand. No sane mage wants a normal cutting them open, resetting a bone. Having normals do medicine on us is like being a kid facing an epileptic mohel at his bris.

"You've probably got a concussion. How about you call him now?" I'm a little touchy about concussions. Technically, that's what killed me. I'd been knocked around so much, turns out I had multiple traumatic brain injuries. If Hank hadn't shown up and pushed things along, I probably would have kicked soon enough all on my own.

Letitia fishes her phone out of her pocket, focus

going in and out. She looks at first like she's considering it but then shakes her head, turning a little greener with the movement.

"No," she says. "It's too late. I don't want to bug 'em."

"Give me your phone."

"No, fuck you. I'm fine."

"Give me your goddamn phone." I snag it out of her hand. She's already unlocked it and I thumb open the phone app and check the speed dial. I hit the entry that says DOCTOR. It starts to ring.

"I wish you hadn't done that," she says. "You're gonna wish you hadn't done it too."

"I don't see—"

"This is Vivian," comes in clear through the phone. I seize up. I don't know what to say, which is just as well because my throat has closed. I hand the phone over to Letitia so she can talk. She looks at me through her concussion haze trying to see if I'm okay. Jesus fuck, Tish. You're the one with the concussion.

Letitia tells Vivian that she got caught by a flashbang and thinks she might have a concussion. They talk a little for the next minute or two and then she hangs up.

"So where am I taking you?" I say.

"Harbor-UCLA," she says, pocketing her phone. "She's going to meet me at the ER."

"You want me to drop you off there, or around the corner so she doesn't have to see her dead ex?"

"Fuck, Eric. Don't blame me for you calling her."

"I don't. I blame you for telling me she skipped town." I tell myself that the only reason I'm so pissed off is that I don't want Viv to know I'm alive, but in all honesty, it's because Tish lied to me.

But she's right. I can't blame her for Vivian finding out. She was doing what she thought was the right thing. Don't tell me Viv's still in town, and don't tell Viv that I've come back from the dead.

"What was I supposed to do, Eric? Make things even more awkward? And that was before I knew about you being snipped off your god self like a fucking skin tag. I really wish you hadn't called her."

"You need help, Tish. Viv's the best person to give it to you."

"Are you doing the martyr thing? You're doing the fucking martyr thing, aren't you? Goddammit."

"No, Tish. You're right. I would have preferred you told me the truth and then said, 'And stay the fuck away from her.' But I get why you didn't. Just do me a favor and don't mention me to her."

"Do you a favor? Shit, man, that's just self-preservation. I don't need to piss her off while she's poking around in my head."

"I'll drop you off right next to the ER entrance," I say. "Unless it's changed, there's a spot to the side where you can get to the door quickly and she shouldn't see me."

"Thanks." We drive in silence for a couple of blocks, windows down, cold air blowing into the car. "For what it's worth, I'm sorry."

"Nothing to apologize for," I say. "You didn't do anything wrong."

I did.

———

I keep Letitia awake for the whole drive. Talking really loudly whenever she seems about to fall asleep. Sleep and concussions aren't a great mix. Once she's in Viv's care she's not my problem, but I don't want her dying in the truck before I get to the hospital.

I get her to the ER and offer to help her walk in. She waves me off and staggers toward the entrance. I don't follow, but I'm watching her closely. She stops to talk to someone who's blocked by the side of the building, Vivian presumably, and then steps out of sight.

I slump in the seat, take a deep breath. Hopefully, Tish keeps her mouth shut. There are already too many people who know I'm back. Besides Tish, there's at least the crazy Indian chick, the guy with the gravelly thug voice, whoever hired them, the guy with the mannequins trying to kill me, and Darius, who might or might not be one or more of those.

Oh, and me. Or at least the rest of me, who I reconnected with and had to let go back to Mictlan. If he didn't tell his wife—our wife—fuck. Am I even me, anymore?

Goddammit, Tish. Why didn't you tell me? I did everything I could to distance myself from Vivian before I died. I avoided her. I avoided her side of town. The places I knew she worked or hung out. I didn't ask about her. I didn't want to know what she was doing or have her know what I was doing.

Fifteen years on the road and then BAM, I'm back causing nightmares and chaos like a monkey with a blowtorch. And when the smoke clears, Alex, her fiancé, my high school best friend, is dead. Not just dead. Gone. Soul devoured, body taken over by the ghost of the man who killed my parents.

So I killed him. He was already dead when I pulled the trigger, but I killed him just the same. If not for me, he'd be alive, Vivian and he would have a life together. Fuck, maybe they'd have kids.

I was a shit magnet that had to, wanted to, stay away. So, of course, I come crashing back into her life. Every time I saw her, everything she hated—me, what I'd done to her life, where she would be now if I hadn't fucked everything up for her by doing nothing more extravagant than simply being there—would all come screaming to the surface through a ripped open wound.

It must have been a relief when I died.

But now, Jesus. I really need to make sure she doesn't find out I'm back. Or at least delay it, muddy the waters. People are going to talk, if they haven't already, and word's going to get around. I give it a day at most before it gets to her. Probably sooner.

I'll have to cover my tracks. Make sure any rumors stay rumors. I don't have the best track record for that sort of thing. I'm better at loud and violent. But I can at least try.

Or I could figure out how to fix this whole thing.

Might need some help on that.

"You there?" I say to the empty car.

"Hello, Eric." Santa Muerte sits in the passenger seat in her Tabitha form: a short Asian woman with shimmery black hair falling over her shoulders. She's wearing a faded red t-shirt with a silk-screened sugar skull on the front and a pair of jeans. The sight of her has me running through five years of memories. None of them are what I would have expected when I agreed to be Mictlantecuhtli.

"Well, isn't this a pickle?" I say.

"If you mean vaguely dildo-shaped and shoved repeatedly up your ass," she says, "sure."

Chapter 9

"Mmm. Dill pegging," I say. "My favorite. So, what do you make of this shitstorm?"

"It's . . . not good."

"Not good as in, 'This is a pain in the ass,' or not good as in, 'You're fucked all to Jesus'?"

"Bit of both. Do you know what happened?"

"Not the details of how but I figured out what's been done. I assume you or my larger half did, too. Any idea how to reverse it?"

I'm stuck in one of those games where the only way to win is not to play. I shouldn't be here, no matter what whoever resurrected me thinks, and I'm tired of being somebody's piece on the fucking Monopoly board. I want out.

"Yes. We figured it out, too."

"And?" She looks like she's just bitten a lemon. "Fuck. That bad?"

"We can't reverse it. Not exactly. And there would be consequences."

"There always are. Hit me. What's the plan?"

"It's not a plan. It's a bad idea and dangerous and neither of us want to do it."

"Excellent. I am all about bad ideas. Where do I sign up?"

"This isn't a joke, Eric," she says, heat in her voice I haven't heard in a very long time. "You, the piece of you I'm talking to right now, will disintegrate. You won't just be dead. You'll be gone."

"I admit that sounds bad," I say. "So, explain it to me. I know what happened. Why can't we fix it?"

"The spell didn't just split you off from Mictlante-cuhtli. It took everything that was Eric Carter, that was still human, and put its claws into it and hung on. There was nothing left of you until you reconnected. When you let the rest of yourself go back, a little bit of Mictlantecuhtli was left inside you, and some of you in Mictlantecuhtli."

"Figured that. So, what's—"

"His . . . system, his godhood, whatever, treated that piece of humanity like a virus and killed it."

"I would like to refer to my previous statement that it sounds bad, but I'm a lot more than a little bit of me. And I'm where he came from. I should be able to just slot back into place."

"He's already grown over the gap."

I chew on that for a minute. My voice is surprisingly calm when I say, "To stretch a metaphor, you're saying that after someone evicted me from my own place, my roommate bulldozed my old room and stuck up a new wall where it used to be."

"Worse. Your roommate built a brand-new room where the old one was standing, moved all his shit in, and changed the locks. There's no place for you. There's no you-shaped slot to fit back into. There's nothing but Mictlantecuhtli left over. You're still his . . . template? I guess? But you can't come back."

"So, I have all the human parts," I say. "And he's lost them all. What's happening to him?"

"He's . . . different. Not a lot different. Not yet. He remembers what it's like, being human. He has echoes of you, but I think they're going to fade. It will probably take a few hundred years, but he's already more focused on the tasks of making Mictlan whole."

"The subtext here being that without me, he's doing a better job." Who knew coming back to life could be so fucking complicated?

She pinches the bridge of her nose. A particularly human expression of frustration that she hasn't given up. Maybe she can't give it up. She's equal parts Santa Muerte and Tabitha Cheung. She says she isn't at war inside her own head, that she's neither of them, but her own being. I'm not always sure I believe her.

"So what do we do?"

"Nothing," she says. There's regret and anger, hopelessness and futility, all rolled up into that one word. "There's nothing to do. You're Eric Carter. Completely human. Mostly human. You still have some bits and pieces of his power, but I don't know how much." She looks at my face. "Except for the black eyes, maybe. Have you tried willing them away?"

"It's been a busy night," I say. "So, there's no going back. I'm on my own."

"Not entirely. I can still hear you. If I can help you, I will. It's difficult, though. You're not tied to me anymore. At all. Picking out your voice from the billions of others on the planet is difficult. If I'm not searching for it, I won't hear it."

"And him? Can he hear me? He have the same problem?"

"He can hear you better than I can. You still have a connection since you have some of him in you. But I don't know what he would do if you asked for help. He can't leave Mictlan on his own, and without something physical to go into, he'd just slide right back."

"Like I said. There's no going back, and I'm on my own."

"Eric—"

"Yes or no?"

"Yes. All right? Yes, that's what it means. You're human. You've got your life back and I—Goddammit." Her body shimmers a bit and I can see Santa Muerte just under the skin, all angry bones and threadbare clothes. I used to tease her about saying 'goddammit' since she's actually a goddess, but I figure now isn't the right time.

"Okay," I say. "I'm human. And I can't go back. Except I really am already back. We're still the same person. We can fig—"

"No," she says. "You don't understand. You are different people now. There's him, and there's you. You're separate. You'll always be separate. He's Mictlantecuhtli. Completely. He's my husband. I have a claim and connection to him, not you."

It took me a while to get used to the idea that she isn't the same Santa Muerte who caused so much grief and damage for me and so many others. Got used to the idea that Tabitha was as much a part of her as the original Santa Muerte was. She had her own identity, made her own choices, and they were based on compassion as much as they were on purpose. The rage had, not exactly left her, but become more channeled.

Santa Muerte has traditionally been about more than death. Tabitha's influence brought those pieces to the fore: protector and lover, a deity for broken hearts, one you can grieve with, who will understand your struggles more than some distant god behind tall spires and stone walls. Someone to turn to when there is nothing left. She wasn't the same. She had truly become the Saint of Last Resort.

And I wasn't the same, either. Dying, becoming Mictlantecuhtli, seeing what it truly means to be a guide to the dead has . . . I'm not sure changed is the right word. Let me be something I had always tried to be, maybe.

My understanding of death has changed. While I

was dying, she had to point out that with everything I knew, everything I'd experienced, I was still seeing death as a binary. Death is so much more than a transition from alive to dead.

So yeah, it took a while to get used to it all. But I did. I saw that it was right. That it was who I needed to be. What I needed to be. I had a purpose, a reason to simply exist. And now all the worst parts of me have been thrown back into a meat suit. Jesus. I feel like I'm in prison and we're talking on phones with glass between us.

"What now?" I say, and I'm not entirely sure what I'm asking about.

"Try not to die," she says. "I don't know what would happen to you. You might come to Mictlan as one of the dead. Or you might go somewhere else entirely. I just don't know. You're not exactly popular with the god crowd, you know. They tend to frown on deicide."

"Thanks for the pep talk, Coach. Maybe I should try to get in good with Odin. There's gotta be a position for an ex-god in Valhalla. Maybe I can shine up the war hammers. I was hoping you might have something a little more concrete."

"Find who did this to you," she says. Her eyes shift to a glowing red. "Who did this to us. Make them pay."

"Oh, believe me, I'm planning on it."

There's really nothing left to say after that. We say we'll see each other around, but I know it's not going to be that simple, not now that I'm flesh and bone and she isn't unless she wants to be. She has what she needs. She has a Mictlantecuhtli, and he isn't me.

She pops out of existence a moment later and I'm left alone in the car. I can feel the weight of the wedding ring I don't wear anymore, like a phantom limb, reminding me that I'm not who I thought I was. Who I'd hoped I was.

It's suddenly too hot, too stuffy, too everything. I throw the door open and walk in fast circles around the car, my hands clenching and unclenching, clenching and unclenching. I want to punch someone. Want to rip into them and tear them apart. Want to feed them to ghosts. Want to devour their soul, head to tail.

I'm back. I don't want to be back. I was done. I was over this bullshit. And then some fucker yanks me here and throws me into this chunk of dead hobo flesh. That explains all the puking. Probably embalming fluid, probably with a few chunks of old meat in a frothy rotten zombie milkshake.

What the hell am I going to do now? When this shell finally kicks the bucket, what then? I'm gonna go somewhere. Back to Mictlan? Somewhere else? Who's going to try to claim my soul this time? I am going to find whoever it is who did this and kick their asses into next week.

Nobody brings me back from the dead and gets away with it.

I'm driving around L.A. in the middle of the night, passing new buildings and vacant lots and places where the bones of burnt houses jut up from the ground like hands reaching out of open graves. Five years and the places I expect to be rebuilt, freeways, big money buildings, rich communities that didn't completely clear out when the fires hit, are doing pretty well. The rest? It's a repeat of the aftermath of the '92 riots, where the hardest-hit places got fuck all. Only this time with the added nightmare of an uninhabitable wasteland where chunks of South L.A. used to be.

I'll have to ask Tish what the deal is with that toxic zone. Is it heavy metal poisoning? Radiation? Toxic chemicals? All of the above and then some? Places like that, you don't just have to worry about the chemicals, you have to worry about what comes out of the sludge to eat your face. I wouldn't be surprised if there was some toxicity in the magic there, as well. I've seen how a place's magic can be twisted up.

Good for death and destruction magic. Not the kind of death magic I practice. Well, okay, technically it is, but that shit never comes out right. Call the dead in a place like that and you're more likely to get animated corpses than ghosts. Or ghosts in animated corpses. Or just a bunch of corpses. Like out of nowhere. I tried to do a mass call for ghosts in a dump in New Jersey one time and instead it rained dismembered body parts for almost an hour. I bet the Cleanup Crew has their hands full hiding all the magic crap that wanders out of the zone.

I should hit the 15 and not look back. I did that before. I can do it again. Get into Vegas, look some people up. No, wait. The people I'd meet in Vegas are not ones I want to see again. Mexico's right out, and San Diego, pretty much everywhere in the South. Florida and Georgia would be a bad idea. North and South Dakota would be a horrible idea. Have I pissed off any Canadians? I can't remember. It doesn't matter. Sure, I should go, but I know I won't.

My drooping eyelids remind me about another fucked-up thing about being alive. Warren Zevon to the contrary, you don't sleep when you're dead.

The 110 Freeway stops at the 405 Interchange. Cones, water barrels, concrete embankments, and a big sign flashing DETOUR over and over again make it clear that people should stay the hell out. The actual toxic zone is a couple miles further north, but they're not fucking around.

I get off at Western and start looking for a place to crash. This whole area is a ghost town. Almost literally. The place is crawling with Echoes, Haunts, and a fair number of Wanderers. Vacant lots, empty buildings. I pass a couple of shuttered motels, but from the weeds in the parking lots they haven't been open in a long time.

I pull into the parking lot of a half-burned church with tents, cars and RVs scattered through the lot. A couple FEMA trailers with showers and toilets are shoved against the church wall, and a makeshift kitchen has been set up beneath a large awning nearby.

I find a spot not too far from the lot entrance. If I need to bug out fast I won't run anybody's tent over. I get some curious glances. A couple people start to head my way then think better of it.

Situations like this, there's safety in numbers. After a while the tribe starts to figure out who's dangerous and who's not. They don't kick me out, but they aren't welcoming me in either. Maybe it's the late-night sunglasses, maybe it's just my vibe. Either way, good instincts.

I set some half-assed wards, trying to be as unobtrusive as I can, acting like I'm checking the car over for damage. A couple kids watch for a bit, then get bored and wander off. That done, I push the driver's seat as far back and down as it will go and drift off to a troubled sleep.

———

Morning breaks like shattering glass. I bolt awake, sunlight burning my eyes. It takes me a second to remember where I am and what's happened. I check the rearview mirror and thankfully my eyes have gone back to normal.

People are breaking camp. Cars heading out, most of the RVs staying. People are cooking breakfast over at the kitchen. They've got themselves a nice little community thing going on here. After the fires a lot of people either left L.A. or stayed in FEMA refugee camps.

The ones who could rebuild their homes did. Problem was that over sixty percent of Angelenos rented. They had nowhere to go, so they either left or formed these parking lot communes.

An Asian woman with a ten-year-old wearing a Pokémon t-shirt trailing behind comes up to me with a plate of food. It smells good, and fuck knows I'm hungry, but this is just a pit stop for me. Guy like me doesn't belong here. Guy like me just poisons the well.

"You sure?" she says when I turn it down.

"Somebody here's gotta eat more than I do," I say. "I do appreciate nobody kicking me out last night when I rolled in."

"Don't worry about it. It's a church parking lot," she says. "Pastor won't turn anybody away. Not if she can help it. Cops try to run us off about some kind of permit or other every once in a while. It's a shakedown. Only time they ever come out here. I'm Lani, by the way."

"Eric." I lean down and smile at the kid in what I hope isn't some horrifying rictus. He's hiding behind his mom. Not surprised. I can't imagine the last few years have been kind. "What's your name?"

He looks at his mom, who's trying to encourage him, but the kid's having none of it. I'm not gonna push it.

"Sorry about that," Lani says. "That's Matthew. He's—had some trouble adjusting."

"Yeah. We all have, huh?"

"Some better than others. Having this helps. We take care of each other. Lord knows nobody else will." She catches my glance at the church and laughs. "Pastor's Unitarian Universalist. She doesn't care if you believe, don't believe, believe something else. Gay, straight, trans. And if someone does care, then this isn't the place for them. She doesn't even hold services anymore. Took out all the pews, put in bunk beds."

"How about you?" I say.

"I'm . . . undecided. Being here, seeing all this. I don't know what you'd call it. Humanitarian? I used to believe in God, but now—" She looks back at the boy who's crouched down to watch a line of ants crossing the pavement. "I believe in this boy right here. I believe in people."

At one point I would have called her naive. But now, I wonder if maybe she's got the right of it. I just wish I could share her optimism. I pull out a HI, MY NAME IS sticker, fold it in half and write down my number.

"You don't know me," I say. "But if you need help, somebody brings down the hammer, somebody gives you shit? Call me. Day or night. Especially if it's anything . . . weird."

She takes the sticker, one eyebrow cocked, a half-smile on her lips. "Weird?"

"Yeah. You'll know it if you see it."

"Like what, zombies? Werewolves? Ghosts? Wizards?"

"Yes," I say. "Especially ghosts and wizards." Her face falls into skepticism that I can totally understand. I'm a crackpot. I'm some random nutso off the street looking stink-eyed at the herd.

"Like . . . weird blobs crawling down the street?" she says. That gets my attention.

"Coming from around the toxic zone?"

"Yeah," she says. "I mean, we're not close, but there's not a whole lot between us and the quarantine zone. Looked like a rolling, slithering boulder? I've seen it once. At first I thought I was imagining it, but then half a dozen others here have seen it, too. Or something like it. Really late at night. Not very often."

"Has it hurt anybody?"

"No. It just rolls on by. It gets bigger and smaller. Seen it break into multiple pieces and then roll back together like it's made out of Play-Doh. But that's it. Nobody's gotten close to it."

Shit. This is exactly the kind of crap I was afraid was going to happen. Bad places spawn bad magic. I've never heard of whatever the hell this is, but it's something to check out. Or have Letitia check it out. Cleanup Crew's not my gig.

Still. "You see it again, call me. If you can snap a pic and text me, that'd be even better. I know some people who can help. I'll pass it onto them, but in the meantime, call me if shit gets weird." I look at the kid peeking behind his mother's legs. "Uh—"

"Oh, please," Lani says. "He hears far worse from me. All right, anything weird, especially ghost wizards, I'll call you."

"If you see ghost wizards," I say, "run first."

———

When I died, Jack MacFee was maybe thirty years older than me. Old enough to have had three ex-wives, kids, and grandkids. Big boned, surrounded by big meat. Four hundred pounds and change last I'd heard. The kind of big that's more muscle than fat, even if he always looked like he was one staircase away from a heart attack.

He'd peddle his wares down in Torrance in a stall at an outdoor swap meet where the old Roadium Drive-In movie theater used to be. Everything's still there except for the car speakers on posts. They took those down so they had one big, open space. I could always get reliable pieces for rituals and other such magical bric-a-brac from him, along with pretty much anything else.

Good man, MacFee. Had that stall long as I've known him, but I heard that he used to operate out of the back of a car in the seventies, moved from place to place like a taco truck. He was dealing slightly less esoteric items back then. Bullets, guns, medical equipment, hospital-grade pharmaceuticals. If you wanted it, Jack MacFee either had it, or he could get it.

He probably had it even if you didn't want it, like the two-headed weasel in formaldehyde he kept trying to push on me. After five years who knows where he could be. A lot of the Roadium didn't survive the fires. Guy like him isn't one to let something like that keep him down. He's probably moved on to some other venue.

I end up having to call 411 because I can't figure out how to look shit up on this phone and get connected to an old number of his. No idea if it's still valid, but it rings through and eventually hits voicemail. Sure enough there's MacFee's voice on the other end. He says he's working out of the Roman place if anybody wants to see him.

The Roman place? The fuck is that? The Coliseum? No, couldn't be that. It's just inside the toxic zone over by the abandoned USC campus. Some place with regularly scheduled orgies? I mean, this is L.A. so I'm sure somebody's doing that, but I have no idea who these days.

Takes me a few minutes to figure it out. The Forum. It's a circular indoor stadium in Inglewood that's been around for decades. Concerts, hockey games, basketball. At one point a church owned it. It doesn't take me long to get there.

The building is in surprisingly good condition, though the parking lot sure as hell isn't. Firepocalypse did a real number on it. Most of the guidelines are gone, paint boiled away by the intense heat, asphalt cracked in some places, melted into smooth, black patches that shine in the sun. What's left of any paint on the ground is bubbled and cracked and barely visible.

The outer areas of the lot are overflowing with parked cars, people looking for anywhere to wedge themselves in. I leave the car at the outer edge and walk in. I'll just steal another one when I leave.

Closer in toward the building where the cars thin out I can see that late stage capitalism is chugging along nicely. People have set up tarps, collapsible gazebos, three and four room tents. Some of them are selling junk, some are selling merchandise that fell off the back of a truck, or, if the burn marks are any indication, out the back of somebody's home.

Before I died—which still sounds bizarre to me—squatters had taken over burnt-out neighborhoods. In five years I can't imagine the situation's changed much. Too many people displaced, too many with nowhere else to go. People are surviving as best they can.

And loudly. Haggling is at a fever pitch. Yelling, arms waving around. It seems every three feet two people are having a shouting match over the cost of some inconsequential item that's turned into a post-apocalyptic necessity.

It takes me a good half hour of wandering through a maze of impromptu shops and food stalls, the smell of food from a dozen different cultures and the sound of twice that many languages, before I find him.

I walk past his stall three times before I realize it's him. He's sitting in a lawn chair under a cheap patio umbrella next to a puke-green Buick Invicta, a young woman by his side.

He's lost so much weight that he's almost unrecognizable. Mirrored sunglasses cover half his face, green cargo shorts show off almost stick-thin legs, and his bony feet are slipped into a pair of rubber flip-flops. A faded blue Hawaiian shirt hangs on him like a tent on a scarecrow.

The woman: mohawk, mirrored shades. Whip-thin and all hard angles and lean muscle. Her mohawk's not gelled up, so it hangs over one side of her shaved head. The resemblance between them is noticeable if not pronounced. The woman hovers over him, an angry bodyguard who won't let anything harm her charge. Her eyes lock on me as I step up to the stall.

MacFee's drinking a Bud, he's always drinking a Bud, selling the same bullshit occult trinkets he's always sold. Little crystal tchotchkes for weekend Wiccans, Buddha statues with big fat bellies, rabbits' feet for good luck, which never made a goddamn bit of sense to me. I mean, the rabbit had four of them and look what happened to him.

The real stuff, the reagents, potions, charms, he always kept in the back of the stall. It's all probably in the trunk of the Invicta now. He's the go-to guy for the esoteric and the mundane. If he can't find it, it can't be found. He sold to street rat witches and Bel Air mages alike. It's one of his selling points, in fact. One time he told me, "I won't cheat you because I know you can kill me. And I know you won't cheat me because you know everybody else comes to me too, and they'll kill you." It's a policy that seems to have held up.

"Can I help you?" the woman says, shoulders tightening.

"Lighten up, Casey," MacFee says, his voice almost a whisper, rather than the booming sound I'm used to. He lowers his sunglasses, gives me a long, uncompromising stare. "Heard you were dead."

"I was. Now I'm not."

"Complicated?"

"And then some," I say.

"Casey, this here is Eric Carter. I told you about him. He's fine." Casey eases her shoulders a little, but her eyes never stray from me.

"You told me he died," she says.

"Like I said, I got better."

"Don't trust you," she says.

"That is the smartest thing you could possibly do. I am a professional shit magnet. Or did your grandfather there not tell you that part?" It's a guess, because she looks too young to be a daughter, and too old for anything else.

"That's why I don't trust you."

"Goddammit, Casey," MacFee says. "Stand down. Hey, dead man, you want a beer?"

"Got any bourbon?"

"Fresh out. Sorry, Chief. But I do have a fine selection of wares otherworldly and otherwise. Come on in, let's see if I can set you up." He stands from the lawn chair like he's eighty, bony legs shaking. Casey is at his side in a flash, helping him stand and walking him into the closed-off tent in the back.

MacFee's in a bad way, but I ignore it, hoping it's all in my head. Maybe he did Weight Watchers. Fuck do I know? Only I do know. I've seen the dying and the dead enough to know when one's about to turn into the other.

MacFee's always been good at keeping wards up and running. He's not a mage, but he does just fine with his trinkets and bric-a-brac. I can feel the magic as I pass through it. Outside, nobody's going to see or hear us. Inside, my voice echoes in a space far larger than it should be.

"You've upgraded." We're clearly not in the tent anymore. Metal shelves, cement floor, air conditioning humming in the background. Creating portable universes is a pain in the ass and MacFee's not a pain in the ass kind of guy.

"Got sick of hauling all this shit around. We're in a warehouse out in Lancaster right now."

His shelves hold a fucking Wonderland for the inordinately well-armed. Saturday Night Specials to full-auto HKs, surplus Soviet SKSs and cheaper Chinese knockoffs. Flare guns, a harpoon gun, a couple mouse traps, two machetes, three tomahawks, a Louisville Slugger covered in nails, and more that I can't even identify.

One shelf is covered in all manner of magical goodies. Small bins filled with tied-up bundles of herbs, bags of bone dust, chicken's feet, athames, enchanted lanterns, pixie dust made the way they make olive oil and Girl Scout cookies, unicorn horn, which is funny because the only unicorns out there were created back in the twenties for some rich asshole's amusement. Some idiot let them loose in Death Valley and the place is swarming with the fucking things. Half the park rangers are mages who keep trying to hide them and eradicate them at the same time. Worse than cockroaches.

The thing that surprises me is how much survival equipment he carries. He'd always had a couple of pieces here and there, but now it's like half his inventory. Emergency food bars, canned water, space blankets, backpacks, medical gear, batteries, solar chargers.

"Jesus, Jack. Looks like your market demographic's changed."

"Hard times out there. Worse than they look, that's for goddamn sure."

"Yeah, I been noticing that. Looks like some spots are really kicking off, and others . . ."

"Whole city's a shitshow," MacFee says. "Rich fuckers buying up cheap land, kicking people out of their homes. Tell 'em they're gonna make brand-new homes and they'll all get their pick, like it's Chavez Ravine all over again. Bullshit then, bullshit now."

Chavez Ravine is where Dodger Stadium is now. Thriving Latino community up until nineteen-fifty-nine, when everybody got evicted to build low cost housing that never got built. It's not a thing a lot of folks out here know about. MacFee tends to know more than people give him credit for.

I can't disagree with him. Everything I've seen tells me the same thing. "Fair point. So, can you hook me up?"

"If I can't, nobody can."

I need ammo. It occurs to me that I should probably get some things to keep me alive when I inevitably get into more trouble than I can handle. First aid and field surgery kits, some Kelly clamps, QuikClot, a couple of burner phones. I haven't had to stitch anything up yet, but let's be honest, that's just a matter of time. He slides everything into a plastic Walmart shopping bag.

"How much?" I say.

"Not money, Chief," he says. "Need to know a couple things, though."

"Granddad," Casey says, warning in her voice.

"Hey, it's my life," he says. "I'll do what I want."

Resignation flashes across her face. They've had whatever this argument is before. Then she looks at me and I swear I can feel fire shooting out of those eyes.

"Need or want?" I say.

"Bit of both."

"I'm not sure what I can tell you. I've been . . . out of town for a while."

"Dead," he says.

"Yeah. Dead. Dead-ish."

"No worries, Chief. It's right in your wheelhouse."

Shit. I ignore that voice screaming in my head wishing I could stick my fingers in my ears and go "La-la-la" until it goes away. I glance over at Casey watching me with a wary eye. Whatever look is on my own face, she seems to get that I know what's coming and I'm not happy about it, either.

"Sure," I say. "If I can tell you, I will. But it might

be worth a hell of a lot more than a box of nines and some Band-Aids, so I might need some more gear."

"Fair enough. What's it like to die?"

"Goddammit, Granddad." Casey turns around and stalks back through the portal to the tent in the Forum parking lot.

"You don't ask the small questions, do you, Jack? Which part? The dying or the being dead bit? Dying kinda sucks, depending on how you die. After that your soul goes someplace else, wherever you think you belong. Near as I can tell, at least. You religious?"

Most mages aren't. It's hard to reconcile the knowledge of multiple gods by picking just one unless you're trying to curry favor with them, and not just some random Invisible Friend In The Sky.

"Unitarian Universalist."

"Huh. I don't know what they believe," I say. Maybe I can follow up with Lani back at the church, get a word in with the Pastor. It'd be good to know.

"Me either. I joined online so I could perform a wedding."

"Okay. Well, I guess your soul might go to wherever Unitarians go, but I think it's more likely going to go wherever you think it's gonna go. You're the only one who can answer that." He nods at this, like I'm just confirming something he already knew. There's a long, drawn-out silence that's growing more awkward by the second. I don't get to ignore it.

"How long have you known?" He's not surprised at the question.

"Couple months," he says. There's another cooler near where we're standing, there always seems to be one close at hand, and he pulls out another beer. "Started shedding pounds about a year ago. At first I thought it might be healthy eating, but we both know that's bullshit."

"How's it looking?" I say. More of a formality because I know what the dying look like.

"Bad," he says. "I was getting treatment down at Harbor, and there's a couple mage docs who owe me favors. They've slowed it down, but even with that, I'm in the endgame, ya know?"

He's right. It is the endgame. I can see it shot through his entire body. Weeks, probably days. I blink and will the vision away.

"Fucking cancer."

He raises his beer, pops the top and gives a mocking toast to the air. "Fucking cancer."

Chapter 10

You can't shoot cancer. You can't go over to cancer's house and break its kneecaps, stick its hand down a garbage disposal until it promises to leave you and your friends the fuck alone. Everybody dies, sure. But cancer's a shit way to go.

Mages can usually do something a little more proactive about their own lives. Lots of ways to keep death at bay, keep from dying for a good, long time. They usually involve deals at midnight at a crossroads, and they rarely go well.

But normals, even ones as well connected as MacFee, only have so many options, and all of them suck. Even with magic, you're still looking at chemo. I couldn't tell you why shrinking a tumor is any harder than, say, throwing a fireball. Vivian tried to explain it to me years ago. Something about the precision required.

"A cold is easier to cure than cancer," she'd said. "You just do a blanket 'kill all the rhinovirus in the system' sort of spell. But cancer is a normal cellular process that's gone nuts. Picking out which bits are cancer and which bits are healthy cells is a major pain in the ass. At most, you'll slow it down. Do it wrong and you can make it a hell of a lot worse."

"Never thought I'd go out this way," he says. I can

see the pain in his face now. He hides it well, probably on half a dozen pills just to keep upright without screaming in agony. "Did you think you'd die the way you did?"

"I figured there'd be more bullets involved," I say. He laughs and winces.

"Hell, everybody figured that. When you kicked the way you did, goddamn did a lot of people lose money. Nobody saw that coming."

"Kind of surprised Vivian didn't bet on my having a stroke," I say. "She's the one who warned me about it."

"She bet on a knife in the back. That was a few years before you died. She never changed it."

"How do you know so much about this?"

"I was the bookie," MacFee says. I can't help but laugh.

"Of course you were. You get everything ready for your big send off?"

"What, like a will and stuff? Damn right. Casey gets everything. She's goddamn smart, and a better haggler than I'll ever be. You watch out for her. She'll take the clothes off your back and make you think you got the best end of the deal."

"Even the Buick?"

"Oh, hell yeah. You should see her eyes light up when she gets behind the wheel or sticks her head into the engine to swap out some worn out part or another. She's good people. I expect the two of you to play nice."

Casey. A granddaughter. I still have trouble picturing MacFee married with a family. Shit, he's done it like three times or something and it just doesn't fit in my head. But right now I'm really glad he's got one. Or at least part of one.

"If I live long enough, maybe," I say. "Seems some people don't like my coming back from the dead."

"Imagine that. It's like they don't like you or something."

"Right?"

"I'm okay with being dead," he says. "I'd just like to skip the whole dying part. You know the worst part of it?"

"Dying isn't bad enough? From personal experience I can say I'm not a fan."

He waves a hand like he can shoo my bad jokes away like flies. "It hurts. Hurts all the goddamn time. Even with charms and pills and potions. It all hurts. Doc tells me it'll hurt worse in a little while. The spells they been using to keep the cancer from going crazy are wearing off, including the pain charms. It's too late to do anything now. That's really what scares me. Dying in pain. Dying alone."

"Casey will be there. I'll be there if you want me to. But you might have angry gods and pissed off djinn swinging by the wake. Be a hell of a party."

"You really do know how to make friends."

"Not really," I say. "I got a few." Soon I'll have one less.

"You know, I could keel over any time. Could kick right here and you'd be the only one to see me go. With a Bud in my hand, of course."

"Can't imagine you going out without one," I say.

MacFee sways and I go to catch him but he rights himself with a shaking hand against one of the shelves. He sits down into a lawn chair behind him that I swear wasn't there a second ago.

"You need anything?"

"Just need to sit and rest a spell. That's all."

"Sure," I say. "I got nowhere to be." I look for another chair and as my eyes pass back over a patch of what was empty floor a second ago, there's another lawn chair. This is some handy magic. I mean, it's a shitty lawn chair, but still, it's always ready for your ass to fall into it.

I pull the cooler closer, pull out a can and take a

drink of his nasty swill beer. Because sometimes you just need to have a drink with a friend.

"I got one more question if that's all right." A spark of hope in his eyes and I already know what he's going to ask.

"I have no idea who or what brought me back, Jack. And whoever did it, didn't really. It's complicated. But don't go there because it's just gonna make everything worse."

"I was about to say, 'Yeah, but you ain't the one dyin',' but you've been there, done that, already."

"I know you're scared. It's scary for everybody. But that's just because we don't know what will happen next."

"Oh, and I suppose you do?" he says, skepticism in his voice.

"Little bit. Like I told you, far as I know your soul's gonna go wherever it's supposed to. Could all be horseshit. My death was kind of a special case. What I can tell you is that something will happen next. And there might even be a next after, or one after that. I don't know. I don't know if it'll be good or bad. Somebody had to point out to me that even with knowing everything I do about death I still kept thinking about it as one of two things, dead or alive. But it's not that simple. It's not simple at all. I'm sorry. I know that doesn't help."

"It does, actually," he says. "A little bit. You think it'll hurt?"

It's fucking cancer, Jack, of course it'll hurt, I don't say. Because it will. Especially the kind he's got. I saw it in his bones, hollowing out craters in his legs, his ribs, his back.

"I think," I say, instead, "dying is gonna hurt a hell of a lot less than the trip getting there." That's as close to the truth as I'm willing to go. It's not like he doesn't already know. "How do you want to go out?"

He doesn't even have to think about it. "Peaceful, I think. Quiet. Without any pain." I feel someone behind me before I hear her.

"Gramps?" Casey's voice behind us. I don't know how long she's been there, but presumably long enough to hear what we've been talking about. There's an uncertainty in her voice. Am I helping out her grandfather? Or making it all worse? Either way, I try not to make any sudden moves.

"All good, honey," he says. "Having a beer with a friend."

"I keep telling you that shit isn't beer," she says. I can hear the smile in her tone, even if I can't see it on her face.

"Then grab a can of shit that ain't beer and join us."

"Sure," she says dropping into yet another lawn chair. I wonder if they already exist and they're being pulled into the precise location, or are they spontaneously created when somebody tries to sit down? I reach into the cooler and toss her a beer.

She looks over at me as she pops the beer open. "Can you—"

"No," I say before she can finish. "I wish I could. I wouldn't even know where to start. I can do some things, but they won't heal him." I put emphasis on the word 'heal,' wondering if she'll catch on.

She seems to. "I want him to go without pain," she says.

"You and me both, hon," MacFee says. "But ain't nothin' he can do. You know what the docs said."

"Jack was telling me you're pretty deft with a wrench," I say.

"I'm handy. Got that wreck outside running again."

"Used to have a Cadillac Eldorado, myself," I say. "That thing took me through hell and back before it finally went. Would have liked to have given it a more graceful exit, but I didn't get the chance."

"That's too bad," she says. "When this old Invicta goes, I want to make sure it goes out good. Know what I mean?"

"I think I do," I say.

I look at MacFee more closely. I revived somebody once by grabbing his soul as he was dying and slamming it back in. Turned out I'd made a huge mistake letting him live, but shit happens.

I can't stop MacFee's death, reverse his cancer, or anything like that. But I think there is something I can do to make the transition a little easier. The two of them are talking about something. Bickering lightheartedly. I'm only half-listening.

"You sure about that Invicta?" I say, breaking into their conversation. "Some people think a car needs to go on until it's all over and done with."

"That's cruel," she says. "Nobody—no car like that should go out bad. If you can let them down easy, you do that."

"Even if it means making a choice to let it go, knowing that you made that choice? Easy thing to regret."

"Letting him go on in pai—" She catches herself, takes a deep breath. "Letting it go on with oil leaking out and a grinding transmission is no way to spend its last days."

"Fair enough. I think I could give you a hand with it while I'm here." I tip my head toward MacFee, who's still paying attention, even though his eyes are closed.

"That car's been with me since the sixties," he says. "You don't do a goddamn thing to that car."

"It's okay, Granddad," Casey says. "We're just talking about him helping us out. That's all." She looks MacFee over and I can see she's weighing her choices. What's best for him. What she wants. What he can bear.

"Yeah," she says, her face falling a bit. It's a betrayal, I know, a hard decision that's got no right choice. "I think we could use your help."

"You absolutely sure?" I say. "Having a stranger poking around inside your car is a big decision." She nods her head. She can't talk. She's trying really hard to hold back tears.

When I focus on it, I can see MacFee's soul. It's almost like he's a ghost already. I slide the thinnest force of my will under where the soul and the body meet up. Ever so slowly I peel it back, like removing a Band-Aid from a toddler prone to tantrums. If I fuck this up, I'll have made things so much worse.

"I think when I get home I'm gonna take a nap," MacFee says. I catch Casey looking at me with a question on her face. I nod. She goes to him, kneels down and takes his hand.

"You can take a nap here, Gramps. I got everything covered. Go ahead. You're safe."

"I suppose," he says, his voice quieter, slower. "Hey, Carter, watch out for her, would ya?"

"You got it, man," I say, though let's be honest, I can't think of a worse thing to wish on somebody. I can hear his heartbeat, feel it pulsing in my bones. It's weak, but he's a survivor. I peel off a little bit more of his soul.

Casey leans in close, kisses MacFee's cheek, lays her head on his shoulder, tears soaking into his shirt. "I love you, Granddad. Get some rest."

"Love you too, hon." His voice is barely above a whisper, or maybe I just can't hear it because his heartbeat is growing louder and louder in my head until it's the only sound I can make out. It's a clock running down, the pendulum slowing a touch with each beat. Slower . . . slower . . . slower.

Stop.

MacFee's head slumps onto his chest. He lets out one last breath. His soul hovers in front of me, burning like a jewel in the sun. I lift my hand, feel its weight. It's so light I can barely feel it. This is familiar. Holding a soul in my hands is something I occasionally had to do in Mictlan. Some people die with so much suffering that it's cruel to let their soul continue on. They couldn't let it go in life, and they don't know how to let it go in death.

They'd ask me to help them. And the only help I could offer was for them to never feel anything ever again. This is different. I'm not obliterating MacFee's soul. I want to take care of it. Make sure it gets to where it needs to be.

I don't know what to do, exactly, but it feels like it wants to leave, has to, and I'm holding it back. So I let it go. It spreads, drifting and fading like glowing smoke.

And then it's gone.

Casey holds onto MacFee's body, crying. Grief and pain and relief and so many conflicted emotions. Grief will break you if you let it. Hang onto it and it'll eat you from the inside. I hope, in time, Casey will be okay. And I hope she won't blame herself if she comes to regret what's happened here today.

I put together a spell to slow down the inevitable indignities of death. It's nothing big. It'll keep decomposition at bay long enough to get everything squared away. I have a feeling that there's somebody on call waiting for him. MacFee was nothing if not a planner.

I tear a name sticker off the roll in my bag, fold it in half so it sticks to itself. The number of my phone and the two new burners goes on it. I place it onto the cooler, and quietly leave her to mourn.

I walk through the portal out into the Forum parking lot, the sounds of haggling and arguing are an assault on my ears, the sunlight hits my face and my sunglasses do fuck-all. I collect my Walmart bag full of stuff that all seems inconsequential now.

Something needs to be said. A good man has

passed and something needs to be said. I turn my face up to the sky, stare into the hazy blue. I have a message for the gods, a request to take care of MacFee, make sure he's safe.

"You arrogant, monkeyfucking asswipes," I say. "Whichever one of you bloated, maggot-assed fuck-nuggets he goes to, you treat him right. Because if you don't, I will burn you. I will burn your kingdoms, your palaces, your shrines, and every limp-dick, piss-headed demigod in your whole pantheon to the fucking ground. I'll make what Darius did to the Aztecs look like toddler fucking teatime. You know I'll do it. And you know I can."

Good a prayer as any, I guess.

———

I steal a car on the edge of the lot and drive out of there like my ass is on fire. I make a hard turn onto Manchester, hitting a pothole and sending a rear hub-cap rolling off across the street.

They say don't drive angry. But this isn't anger. It's burning fucking rage. Yada yada death is just a transition bullshit bullshit bullshit. I get it. I know it. I've seen it. I've watched the dead file through the afterlife and for the last five years I helped them do it. I guided souls looking for peace at the end of the road.

I helped ease MacFee's pain. I helped him move on in a way not a lot of other people could. So what? He's still gone. His family, friends, customers, the random people who knew him for good or ill, they've lost someone.

MacFee's lost everyone. A soul is the person. Every detail, every belief, love, hate. And fear. The souls I helped in Mictlan, most of them didn't know what was happening. They were terrified. It's the universal state for everyone coming into this world and moving onto the next.

And I hate it.

I've heard some people call death the Grandest Adventure. Ya know what? Ask anybody which they think is a better adventure, dying or looking for parking at a Trader Joe's on a Saturday afternoon and I guarantee the answer ain't death.

I can only hope that MacFee's soul is being taken care of. I'll have to look around, see if there's some way to check on a soul after it's gone. It's not something Mictlantecuhtli knew, or I'd have it in my head already. Santa Muerte might know, but if she does, she's never talked about it.

I don't really want to look up any other gods. Baron Samedi or Maman Brigitte, maybe. Haven't talked to them in a few years. I probably won't, though. I've got enough trouble as it is. And from what Muerte was telling me, I'm not exactly popular in god circles right now, what with my double deicide and all.

I manage to drive all the way into Playa Del Rey, the smell of the ocean pushing out the airplane fumes from nearby LAX before I lose it. I pound the steering wheel, scream at the air, the sky, the gods, the whole fucking system. The car swerves dangerously, almost takes out a stop sign as I barrel through the intersection. What do I care? It's all pointless anyway.

I'm pissed off and I want the world to know it. I want to tear everything in two. Burn everything down all over again. I know it's stupid. I know he's not gone. Not really. But my brain keeps telling me he is, no matter what's happened to his soul. He's gone. I will never see him again.

I want something to hurt. I want to blame something, someone, for a random roll of the dice. For some biological twist that turned a man's body against itself. I want someone I can punch, kick, shoot, anything to make it better. To make it hurt less, but I know there isn't anything. There never is.

I tell myself I helped, and on some level I know this is true. But another part of me is screaming that I should have done something else, something to cure him, make him whole. Keep him from dying.

I preferred being dead. Dead was not caring about the living. Dead was understanding how it all worked and being okay with it. Dead was being reconciled with the inevitable. Dead was not feeling this sort of pain and anger. Life has stolen that peace away from me, and goddammit I would like nothing more than to get that back.

I'm meat now, and meat hurts. Grief, anger, regret. You'd think spending a few years as a death god and I'd be over it. But I don't have the detachment. I don't have the distance. This was a friend. He suffered.

He died with his granddaughter holding his hand. He was ushered out of the world as quietly and peacefully as it's possible to go. So fucking what? I've seen enough of the dead to know that despite appearances, there's no such thing as a peaceful death.

He hurt living through his cancer, and he hurt dying from it, too. I did what I could, but if I was still Mictlantecuhtli I could have done more. One more reason to find who did this to me and beat the shit out of them. They brought me back from somewhere I didn't want to leave, made me feel pain and grief all over again, and I will never forgive them for that.

I wind my way down to Vista Del Mar and park. The Pacific Ocean is a vast blue stretching away into the distance. A few oil tankers unloading at the nearby refinery, a Coast Guard ship. But the beach is empty. There is no one between me and the horizon.

I head down a path from the bluffs to the beach. The sand is like walking through wet cement, each footstep sinking in just enough to make it a pain in the ass.

I want to curse the gods, and the irony hits me and I start laughing. You'd think a death god would know a thing or two about dying, but even they just know bits and pieces. There's all sorts of shit they don't know. What happens to nihilists? The people who've questioned the faith they grew up with and don't know what to believe anymore? It's as unclear and filled with pain and loss for me as it is for anybody. I just know a little bit more about some of the mechanics.

I sit on the edge of one of the empty blue lifeguard huts that run all up and down the beach. I don't think I've ever actually seen a lifeguard on one of these things. I'm not sure anyone even uses them anymore. They feel like relics of a different time when people went on family road trips along the Pacific Coast Highway or out along Route 66 to stop at cement dinosaurs and giant balls of twine.

It's a lie. I know it is. But it feels like a more innocent time. Maybe I'm just missing my own innocence. Or my own ignorance. I still play what-if games in my head. What if I didn't have magic? What if I couldn't see the dead? What if I hadn't killed my parents' murderer and left L.A.? Would I be any different? Probably not. I was even more of an asshole before I'd ever killed anybody.

I run through all these thoughts knowing that the only reason my mind is wandering like this is so that I don't have to think about MacFee. And more, so I don't have to think about Alex.

When I came back to L.A. and reconnected with people here, it was Alex who I saw first. He and Vivian had hooked up. He was doing well for himself running a bar in Koreatown and selling dangerous magic on the side.

My coming back not only got him killed, it destroyed his soul. MacFee might be dead, but Alex is gone. I have a string of corpses and murdered souls going back two decades. I've never really thought about most of them. But now, I can't seem to get any of them out of my mind.

"Soul searching, Mister Necromancer Man?" My shoulders clench and my fists tighten.

"Hank," I say, not turning around. "Funny you should put it that way. You following me?"

"A little bit. You're pretty fucking boring, you know that?"

"Last time you were following me around you said the same thing. So, what gives? You here to 'convince' me to open the bottle?"

"Nah. I'm here to remind you that he's paying attention. You can get him out and he can give you anything you want. Money, power. Your family. Friends."

"He also tell you the message I left for you?"

"Yeah. Kinda funny, you wanting to kill me," he says. "You really think you can take me down?"

"Yes," I say, turning ready to fire off a spell, but he's gone. The only footsteps I see are my own. He laughs behind me. Fucker's not even here.

"Well, tiger, I'm looking forward to it. But until then, Darius would like you to know that he always has your best interests at heart."

"I'm sure he does." One of the burner phones rings. Letitia. "Excuse me," I say. "I have to take this." Even though he's a projection I can feel his anger at being ignored.

"Hey," I say. "How's it going?" I look over my shoulder and sure enough there's no Hank.

If he'd actually been here I'd have buried him. I'll run into him again. At some point Darius will see me more as a liability than an actual asset, and Hank will pop back into my life. And then I'll kill the sonofabitch.

"I'm all right," she says. "Concussion, contusions,

some scrapes and bruised ribs. Nothing new for me. How about you?"

"Having an existential pity party. It appears that being cut off from your own divinity kinda does a number on your own sense of self."

"I have absolutely zero frame of reference for that," she says.

"It doesn't matter," I say. Nothing really matters. I wipe tears out of my eyes I didn't know were there. Goddammit, MacFee, I don't have time for this shit.

"I didn't tell Vivian you're back."

"She'll find out eventually."

"Not from me," she says.

"Appreciate it. What's up?"

"You find anything else out?"

"Couple things. I am now on the market. Seems once I got split apart any and all marriage claims on my particular piece of soul were rescinded."

"You got an annulment from Santa Muerte?"

"That would imply we never consummated."

"I did not need to know that," she says. "I don't even want to know how that works."

"Well, you know, birds, bees, Aztec death gods. It all pretty much works the same way. Anyway, not an annulment. Think of it more as an amicable divorce. Only she's seeing a bigger, better, more well-endowed version of me. It's nice to know I'm somebody's type, at least."

"Frame of reference," she says. "Still don't have one."

"Not important. Hey, you know Jack MacFee?"

"Yeah. Everybody knows him."

"He's dead."

Silence, then, "Shit. When?"

"About an hour ago. I was with him when he went. You know he had cancer?"

"Yeah. Word's been going around. Didn't realize it was that bad. Goddammit. Fuck cancer, man."

"Yeah, fuck cancer. I need to track down Gabriela. I need information. She still as connected as she used to be?"

"Probably. Like I said, I don't talk to her much. I gave you her number, didn't I?"

"I haven't called it. Feels weird."

"Right," she says. "Because a phone call from the dead might be a little more awkward than just showing up at her door."

"Worked for you," I say.

"I punched you and stuck you in a jail cell."

"I don't think she has jail cells."

"Fine. Her community center is at the old site of the Edgewood in Skid Row. You know. The one you burned down."

"I didn't burn it down," I say. "Demons burned it down. I just happened to be there at the time."

"Yeah. Sure. Look, I gotta go. Annie's in the other room all pissed off at me for getting beat to hell again."

"Hey, one last thing," I say. "Stay away."

"The fuck? You don't get—"

"I know I don't get to tell you what to do, but I'm doing it anyway. You've got a fucking concussion. Get some rest. I got it from here."

"Oh, no, you don't," she says. "I'll—"

"If you don't stay out of this, I'll tell Annie all about what happened. In detail. And then I'll have to explain demons. And you really don't want me to explain demons to her."

"You bastard," she says.

"Nobody ever said I wasn't," I say. "Go take care of yourself. And tell your wife you love her." Never know when you won't have that chance anymore.

"Fucker. Fine. Yes. I'll stay away. And thank you."

"For what?"

"Kicking me to the curb. I don't know that I'd have been able to do it on my own. Annie'll appreciate it. But what about you? You gonna be okay?"

"Not even a little bit. I'll talk to you soon." I disconnect and head back to the car, hoping Gabriela might have some answers for me.

Chapter 11

The world is filled with monsters. Most of them are human.

The ones everybody calls monsters, though, are few and far between, and of those a good ninety percent are decent people just trying to get by.

It's a toss-up whether it's an easier life for the ones who look human or the ones who don't. It's the difference between trying to blend in with a population that will murder you and parade around your corpse as the latest scientific discovery if you fail, or just saying fuck all that and going off to live in a hole in the ground. My money's on the one in the hole. They don't need bank accounts.

Most normals don't know about them, obviously. It'd be bad for everybody if folks found out that your local butcher was a ghoul who kept scavenged corpses in a freezer in the basement, or that the junkies strung out in a crack house are all vampires shooting up blood chasing a high they lost a hundred years ago.

Last I heard, an average of twenty percent of the homeless population in any city is supernatural, though L.A. and New York skew the numbers. These are the ones that don't fit in anywhere else. They look just wrong enough, or they've got dietary restrictions that make it tough to hold down a job, or they can't control certain aspects of what they are. They're afraid, hungry, living minute to minute, always hiding. They've got nowhere to go, no one to help them.

It's bullshit, and Gabriela Cortez—sorority sister, Bruja, ruthless crime boss, and fan of sparkly shoes and being underestimated—has made it her life's work to help them. She sees them as people, a rare thing for a human, even rarer for a mage. Most of us look at them like vermin at the best of times.

Hiding the monsters who live under the stairs is in every mage's best interests. The fewer who know about them, the fewer learn about us. Most mages treat them like they would any pest: extermination. But Gabriela is one of those rare mages who believes in a better world. She also believes she can solve most of her problems with a machete, and to be honest, I can't really argue with her.

She bought the old Edgewood Arms hotel in Downtown, turned it into a haven for her "hidden homeless". The Edgewood was one of L.A.'s more notorious murder hotels. It's like the nearby Hotel Cecil but not as upscale. Hers only had one resident serial killer and half as many suicides. The Cecil has more ghosts in it than rats, and the Edgewood Arms would, too, but Gabriela knows her shit. She got rid of them all, warded the place up tight against them, and made it safe for her people.

Then I showed up and it all went to shit. Place burned down by demons who were either sent to get me or get her. Still not entirely sure which of us they wanted out of the picture.

I'm thinking about all this while I should be paying attention to driving. The car I've snagged is a gold SUV with tinted windows, so I think I can blame some of what happens next on those. Probably not most, but I'll take it anyway.

A white panel van cuts through an intersection, and though I swerve to get out of its way, it's too little, too late. The van slams into the front end of the SUV. A jarring crunch, airbags deploy, and the SUV goes into a short spin. I black out for just a second, but it's enough time for whoever crashed into me to get out of the van and over to my side of the car. My vision's still swimming, but I can tell it's one of those fucking clay dolls, and it's pointing a gun straight at me.

It pulls the trigger a split second after I hit the car door with a spell that blows it out of its frame to bounce into the street. The force is enough to knock the thing down and scrape it along the pavement. It loses enough of itself that it crumbles into clay.

But I still have problems. There are five more already getting out of the van. Bland coveralls, ugly-looking submachine guns. Even if I couldn't feel the magic, I'd know there was something wrong with them. They all look the same. Not a detail on one that's missing on the others.

What the hell did I do to this guy? I don't even bother trying to take them on. I'd lose, and fuck if I'm dying at the hands of a goddamn mannequin.

Instead, I slide over to the twilight side and leave them in the land of the living. It's only a temporary respite. Too long and I'll die, the energy sucked out of my body, and my soul eaten by ghosts.

I head a little past where I think the van is. I can see older buildings, and hazy halos of people, but more ephemeral things like the van are completely invisible. So are those clay motherfuckers waiting to gun me down. Guess they don't have enough of a soul for me to see.

I slide back to the living side. I've misjudged the distance to the van a little bit, but at least I'm behind it. The five have fanned out and it looks like they're doing a coordinated sweep of the area. None of them say a thing, or even look at each other, but they all stay in their zones. The benefits of all being run by one person, I suppose.

I ease the passenger side door of the van open and slide across to the driver's side. Keys are still in it. Dude, if you're gonna use clay dolls instead of hired muscle, be a little smarter about it. I duck down, start the car, and slam on the gas.

Immediately there's gunfire, but it turns out they're pretty bad shots. Most don't even hit the van and the ones that do are just punching holes into the back compartment. I swerve, keeping my head down, and head straight for them. Their shots are a little better, but now I've got the engine between us.

They keep firing as I get closer and closer. Not moving, not making noise. Not even when I plow through four of them and turn them into mud under my wheels.

I can see the fifth in the side mirror. It suddenly gets a lot more animated. Interesting. I wonder if it's because the more dolls being controlled, the rougher the connection. I have no idea how I could use this, but I file it away for later.

I hit the brakes, tires smoking, and throw the van into reverse. The doll looks terrified, tries to get out of the way, but it's too slow. I hit the brakes right before impact, and instead of flattening it, I bounce it off the back of the van. It flies about three or four feet, but this one doesn't disintegrate. I get out of the van, gun drawn and run over to it. Going to have to make this fast. Even with the city reduced to ash the police still seem to think that gunshots are something to pay attention to.

The doll's legs are bent at a weird angle and no matter how it tries it can't get up. One arm is twisted behind and under its body, and the other is having trouble figuring out how to move.

The impact from the van knocked its gun out of its hands, but it's close enough that I kick it aside. When the gun gets about three feet away, it disintegrates into clay. I place the barrel of the Browning against the doll's forehead. It goes very still, its eyes locked with mine.

"I know that shooting you won't do much, but given the look on your face, I get the feeling it's gonna hurt. Now I'm going to ask questions, and whoever's on the other end of this Ken doll's gonna give me answers."

"I'm not telling you a goddamn thing." It's a boy's voice, cracking with puberty. A quick look and I can see that it isn't the same soul as the ones that attacked me earlier.

"Oh, I get it. You took Daddy's toys out for a spin without telling him. He's gonna be mad when he finds out, won't he?"

"These are mine. All mine. He thinks I'm not ready."

"Ready to do what? Kill me? Because if that's the case, I gotta say I'm on your old man's side on this one."

"Ready to run an army." The doll sneers at me like I should be impressed. I kinda am, but mostly at how green he is.

"Last question."

"Then you let me go?"

"Okay, second to last question, then. Why don't you just stop running the doll? Break the connection? Snap the cord?" Then I get it. "Oh. Of course. All of these things have pieces of your soul in them, and you don't know how to pull them all back. So instead they all collect in the remaining ones. Wow, you are bad at this." He tries to spit at me, but the doll doesn't have any saliva so it's a pretty stupid gesture.

"Okay, I'll make you a deal. You answer my last question, I walk away. You do whatever mojo it is you have to do to get out of that thing, and we're all good until the next time your family tries to kill me. Deal?"

There's a long pause. Kid's worried. What is it about these pieces of soul? I focus and then I see it. The other dolls had tiny slivers of soul in them. Little pieces that he may not even notice, pieces that will grow back to fill the chips in. No big deal. But Mister Can't Drive His Car Yet here has a hell of a lot more than little slivers invested. There's a big ol' nugget of his soul sitting right there in front of me.

"Deal," he says.

I was going to ask him why his old man's after me, but now I'm going for something different. And he'll either answer and he'll be fucked, or he won't and he'll be fucked. From what I can tell this is win-win for me.

"What's Daddy's name?" His eyes go wide and I get the feeling that if this thing could go pale it would.

"I can't tell you that."

"Sure, you can. So far you've been able to make lots of mouth sounds. What's a couple more? His name."

"He'll kill me."

"I'll do worse."

"The fuck you think you can do to me worse than that?" Panic has flipped around into a smile. He thinks he's won. Daddy's probably the scariest thing he's ever seen. He can't imagine anything worse than what he can do. But he's never met me.

"I'll do this," I say, and reel in that nugget of soul. He starts to scream and beg, but I keep pulling, slowly gathering it inside myself, reeling him in like a fish.

"Need a name," I say. He's fighting back, trying to hold onto what I'm taking away.

"I can't. I can't. I'm sorry, but I can't. Please don't do this. Please don't eat me. Please." It's clear I'm not getting the guy's name.

"Oh, stop. I'm not gonna eat your soul," I say. "I don't know what losing this much of yourself is going to do to you, but I'm hoping you're not too much of a vegetable that you can't give your old man a message."

"Anything. Anything. Please give it back."

"Tell him I've got the rest of your soul in a jar, and if he wants it back then he and I need to end whatever the fuck this is in a way that doesn't end with me dead."

"Yes. Yes, just don't eat it. Please don't eat it."

"Give the message and I won't have to." I yank the last of it free from the doll. Its face goes smooth, all the emotion gone. And then it disintegrates into clay. I rummage through my bag and pull out a glass jar. It's partly filled with herbs. I get the lid unscrewed with one hand, dump out the contents while the piece of soul is trying to escape in the other.

After a few minutes struggling one-handed I manage to get the top off, will the soul into the jar, and close it up, mumbling an old Aztec spell that I learned from Mictlantecuhtli. It's one of the locks that he put on Darius's bottle.

If Daddy wants his little boy back, Daddy's gonna have to come get him.

Chapter 12

Souls are funny things. Like the ghosts that come from them, they raise more questions than they answer. Like what the hell are they? Are they the accumulated experiences of a person's life? Their memories? How do they remember anything if there's no meat to remember? What happens if you don't believe in a soul, do you not have one?

Try not to dwell on it too hard, it'll only give you a headache.

I'm in a rare position in that I know souls are real. No question. I've talked to the dead. I've fed souls to pissed off ghosts and even eaten a few myself. I've almost had mine torn out a time or two. Twice today I've held one in my hands.

Beyond that, there's not much I know. Guess, sure. But know? I don't think anybody does, to be honest, not even the gods whose jobs are to safeguard them in their afterlife, or torment them, or whatever. I know I didn't, and I was Mictlantecuhtli for five years.

I've never run into one that was like any other. I don't know if that holds for everyone, but it seems pretty likely. We're shaped by our life experience, dreams, ambitions, fears, and they all get rolled up into a glowing little package. I think. Like I said, I'm really not sure.

There is definitely a difference between MacFee's soul and the kid's. It's like trying to compare battleships to elephants. Beyond the fact that they are both things, they simply have nothing in common. The feel of them is different, the smell, the weight. Like it or not, we're all unique. We're all alone.

I stop on my way Downtown and look through all the necromantic bric-a-brac I have stashed in my messenger bag. I find a half-drunk bottle of Stoli I trapped a ghost in a few years back and forgot about. I should probably let him go. Not out here, of course. Ghosts on this side of the veil are a disaster. Like a bunch of people have their souls eaten sort of disaster.

This ghost is one I'm still not sure I understand. This guy died in Darius's bar and his ghost started haunting the place. It didn't act like a normal ghost. It didn't try to eat anyone, didn't attack anyone. Mostly it was just a memory of some sad guy who got really drunk and wouldn't leave. For some reason Darius couldn't get rid of it. Or maybe he could and he wanted me to think I was doing him a favor. Who the fuck knows?

So I trapped him in the closest thing I could get my hands on, a half-drunk bottle of Stoli. And then I forgot about him. I tap the glass and get a wave of hungry rage off of it. Okay, not the sad sack drunkard I put in there anymore. Definitely not opening it up out here. I see a smoky presence inside swaying back and forth, but otherwise nothing unusual. I really need to kick this over to the other side and let him go. Somebody might actually drink him. If they survived unscrewing the cap.

Eventually, I find something a little more appropriate for the kid's soul. The difference between a soul and a ghost is like the difference between cold hard cash and Monopoly money. I've actually got the essence of the kid right here. A chunk of it, at least.

It's a small spirit bottle made of thick, leaded glass. Really, the thing is a piece of shit. The wards on it are garbage, the cork doesn't seat properly. This thing wouldn't even hold my buddy in his bottle of Stoli.

So, I just have to put better wards on it. I spend a few minutes making it as bulletproof as I can, laying down seals, wards, traps. The seals aren't nearly as good as the ones on Darius's bottle, but they're similar and they'll do.

I need to make sure that if someone comes after the kid they can't get him out without breaking the wards and setting off the traps. I'm not really worried about someone opening it, since I used a type of Aztec magic that no one's seen in a few hundred years.

When it's ready, I uncap the herb jar and hold the soul in place by sheer force of will. It wants to get away. Wants to be back with the rest of itself. Back to where it belongs. Back home. Yeah, don't we all. Get in line, kid.

I get a firm mental hold on it. Though I'm using my hands, that's just a convenient metaphor for me. I'm using my magic, my willpower. It's strong, stronger than I expect, but I manage to shove it into the bottle, close the lid, and activate all the spells. Once it's locked inside the bottle starts bouncing around the car seat, trying to get through the windshield.

If the kid gave his message, great. Daddy will come looking for me. I should be able to lay a few obfuscation spells to muddy things. Once he runs into those my money's on him thinking I'm trying to run away.

Spoiler alert: I'm not.

The bouncing of the bottle gives me an idea. I get hold of it, feel it pulling, trying to hop its way out of my grip. I find some twine in my bag and tie one end around the rearview mirror, make a little macramé harness with the rest to hold the bottle so it doesn't get free. And they said all those second-grade art projects were bullshit.

When I let it go, it pulls in a straight line to the west. Now I know what direction the rest of the kid's soul is. Probably. Maybe. In theory I just have to do some triangulation and I'll have a location. And then I'll go pay Daddy a visit.

The last time I did something like this was when I was hunting down Quetzalcoatl's cartel assassin. Led us right into a trap. I'm not planning on doing that this time.

Driving around to get a fix is a lot more difficult with chunks of the freeways missing or streets leading into the middle of the wasteland. I narrow it down to "somewhere on the Eastside". I should have given up hours ago, called it a day, but I don't, and then I realize why. I'm avoiding seeing Gabriela. Shit.

I wrap a pair of socks around the kid's bottle and shove it into the bottom of my messenger bag. Head up toward Skid Row. I'm arguing with myself all the way there. Go. Don't go. What would be the point? Why would she even want to see me? By now she already knows I'm back. If I see her, am I going to get the same sort of reaction I got from Letitia? Knowing Gabriela, it would be one that involved bullets and machetes.

But is that what I'm really worried about? She and I have been through a lot together. Is that going to count for anything if I show up on her doorstep and try to convince her that I'm me? Hell, I'm not even sure that I'm me.

Back and forth and back and forth. Before I know it, I'm parking the car in the lot across the street from her shelter. I guess it's time go see her. I get out of the car and stand there a minute just taking it all in.

This is a homeless shelter the way the Moon is a

hunk of rock. Sure, you could call it that, but that doesn't come close to describing it.

It takes up the entire block, replacing the old hotels, apartments and shops that Firepocalypse took out. It's a sprawling complex of attached and unattached buildings with wheelchair ramps, wide spaces, a lot of lights. The tallest buildings are five stories, the shortest two, all sweeping curves and wide corners. It puts me in mind of a community college with a killer architecture department.

I would hate to have to ambush somebody here. There are no places to hide. There are no blind corners. There are lights everywhere. The paths and walkways are separated by difficult-to-navigate greenspace, forcing people through choke points with security doors on either side, but no roofs, leaving them exposed to the windows of at least two buildings at a time.

Holy shit. This isn't a homeless center, it's a killing ground. Anybody who tries to come at her in force here is going to have a really shitty day.

And there's the magic, of course. I can feel it around the buildings, the protections as I pass through them up the stairs to the main building. There's a landing that splits off to a smaller building that my eyes want to slide on past. It tries really hard to not let me notice it, so of course that's the direction I want to go.

The path leads down a ramp out of sight from the street to a building I hadn't noticed even though I had walked right past it. The magic that's telling me I should leave and that I really don't want to be here is stronger than I'd normally expect from wards. But this is Gabriela we're talking about, so the watchword here is 'overkill.'

I'm thinking that this is where the supernaturals get shunted off to. You don't want them mixing with the humans, and you don't want the humans asking questions or getting too curious.

So of course this is where I need to be. It takes an act of will to set foot on the path. Walking is almost as bad. I'm feeling nervous, jittery. I don't want to be here. It's nice work. Gabriela's a pro, all right. But I don't have all night.

I stop about five feet in and cast a shield with a spell with an added sprinkle of magic blocking. It'll still stop a fireball, but it'll stop magic from interfering with me, too. It's straining against the wards, but it'll get me to the building.

And of course the double doors are locked and warded. Jesus fucking Christ. I got shit to do. I hit the lock and the chain on the other side with an unlocking spell and the doors slide open. Good thing I still have my shield up, because somebody's put an acid trap above the door. It pours onto the shield and rolls, breaking against the floor. Another spell and I've collected the pieces of the trap, a large vial of glass, and put it back together. It's not good as new, but then, that's not my knack. It's the least I could do, since they went to so much trouble to try to kill me. I leave it on the pitted and smoking floor.

The short hallway goes to another pair of double doors. I don't see guards, but I can feel more wards, and there's a trap or two. If I was a normal who somehow managed to get this far I'd walk right into them and probably get turned inside out or something.

As a mage it's just as bad for different reasons. I have to dismantle the traps and that takes time. Enough time for somebody to show up and start shooting bullets in my face.

"I assume you can hear me," I yell at the ceiling. I assume somebody, if not Gabriela herself, is watching. "I'm tired and cranky and really not in the mood so I'm gonna do this the messy way. Sorry in advance."

I push out a wall of scouring force that hits each of the wards, burning them out of the walls, tripping the traps, and then taking a second and a third pass just to make sure I didn't miss anything. Alarms sound, sprinklers go off, water sluices off my shield to puddle on the floor.

When I'm done, I walk across steaming water in the black and smoking hall to the pair of double doors at the end. Before I can get to them, they open. A young man built like a boxer, wearing a polo shirt and khakis that are a size too small for him, stands there, scowling in all his business-casual rage.

"Those wards weren't yours, were they?"

"They were," he says.

"If it helps, they were really good."

"They took me days to get in place."

"Shows. Quality craftsmanship." He's not sure if I'm being sarcastic or not, so he spins on his heel and heads into the room.

"Come on. She's waiting for you."

The lobby looks a little like a bank. There's a front desk like a teller's window with two men and a woman sitting behind four-inch-thick bulletproof glass. Three cameras cover the lobby, a single metal door with a panel of inset wired glass is over to the right of the booth. A rent-a-cop stands next to that door. He's built wrong for a human. Shoulders too wide, throat too saggy, arms a little too long. He's a ghoul.

And then I recognize him. "Fred?"

"Holy shit," he says. "I heard you were dead."

"Yeah, I heard the same thing. I thought you were in New York. Problem with the shop?" Fred, like a lot of ghouls, likes his meat seasoned. And so, also like a lot of ghouls, he owns a butcher shop with a freezer he can hang corpses in.

"The city's going to shit," he says. "Scraps are getting harder to come by. Why, yesterday I—" Business Casual stops and clears his throat, staring at us.

"I take it you know each other?" he says.

"What tipped you off?" I say.

Fred chimes in. "Eric and I met in New York, Mister Meduro. He helped the supernatural community out of a jam nobody else wanted to touch. He's good people, sir. I vouch for him."

"Don't let that get around," I say. "I'll have to murder some more people just to maintain my reputation."

"So long as I get the bodies afterward," he says.

"Deal."

Business Casual's scowl gets even deeper, showing impressive muscle control. He turns, opens the door, and goes through, slamming it shut.

"You were saying?" I say.

"Oh, right," Fred says. "I don't know what it is but there are fewer and fewer corpses to scavenge. You know, sewer homeless, people like that. Some of us are having to go all the way down to Baltimore just to pick a couple up. And it's not like the murder rate has dropped, or anything. Weirdest damn thing."

The door yanks open and Business Casual glares out from it. "Are you coming?"

"I'm not even breathing hard," I say. Confusion, anger, resignation all blink across his face like a malfunctioning neon sign.

"Follow," he says. "Me."

"It was good talking to you, Fred. We'll hook up sometime when everything isn't going to shit."

"So never, is what you're saying."

"Pessimist." To Business Casual, Mister Meduro, whoever the hell he is, I say, "Lead on, my good man. The Queen awaits hither!"

He really wants to hit me. He looks like he spent a lot of time hitting people at some point in his life. I can see gang tattoos poking up over his collar. I wonder if he's hitting people for Gabriela. Probably. His people skills suck.

The hallway through the door is different. Carpeted. Muted colors. Piped-in classical music. It's not even Muzak. Very relaxing. This is probably the main intake for the supernaturals who come in looking for a hand. They're sketchy, probably terrified. Anything soothing is good. The calming spells etched in the walls can't hurt.

We turn a corner and he points to a door. "She's in there," he says, none of the calming magic radiating down the hall seeming to do a thing for his sour mood. "I hope you get murdered."

"Wouldn't be the first time," I say. "Thanks for the tour, Mister Menudo, much appreciated." He stalks off, grumbling to himself.

I look at the door too long for it to not be awkward. I don't know if I'm doing this on purpose or if I'm really just freaking out over seeing Gabriela. Why the hell should I? By now she's knows I'm me. Taking out her wards and traps the way I did should convince her if nothing else will. Tish has probably already told her. Or one of her people.

I reach for the door and its yanked open out of my hand. Gabriela, all five foot damn near nothing standing in a skirt, blouse, and pearls. Hair's short, very black. Not a hint of sparkly anywhere. In fact, she looks a little like a corporate executive. A parade of emotions flicker across her face before it turns into a mask, too fast for me to see what they are.

"Hey," I say. What the hell is wrong with me? I'm almost shaking.

"You're late," she says.

"L.A. traffic," I say.

She pulls me into a hug. I'm so surprised that I hug her back. The burning need to reassure myself that I'm real and not some cast-off Pinocchio left in the trash punches through everything else and I hold on tight.

"You motherfucker," she says, her face buried in

my chest. "I don't have a lot of friends left. You don't get to die again."

"If I point out that that's not technically possible is it pedantic or mansplaining?" I say.

"Mansplaining starts with 'Well, actually,'" she says.

"Noted. It's good to see you, Gabby."

"I told you to never call me that again or I'd kill you."

"Look, make up your mind. You can't have it both ways."

"Smartass." She moves back into the office, heading for a chair at a small, circular conference table. "We need to talk."

"No shit," I say. "Not sure I have a lot of ans—" I freeze as I see who else she has in the room with her.

"Hello!" the Indian woman says, standing up, her bright smile as terrifying as the first time I saw it. The man sitting next to her is an unmoving rock and I can tell right away he's dead, but he's still walking around in his own corpse, which I would probably find interesting at any other time. Instead my brain is spinning around wondering what the hell this woman's doing here and my vision goes red and before I know it, I've drawn the Browning and pulled the trigger.

The dead guy is on me in a flash, knocking me back out the door with the force of a speeding bus. The shot goes into the ceiling, and he knocks the gun out of my hand, sending it bouncing down the carpeted hall.

I push this gorilla off with a spell and slam him into the ceiling, pinning him there like a bug in a collection. Letting him fall would just mean I need to deal with him again. Since he's dead I could probably do something a little more drastic, but I don't know for sure that would work. Better I just keep him out of the way and deal with him later.

I take a run into the office, straight razor in my hand. I might not be able to shoot her, but there are lots of places I can cut her. Gabriela stops that line of thinking when she tackles me like a linebacker. You'd think somebody who couldn't be all of a hundred twenty pounds soaking wet wouldn't have much of a punch, but she's got magic bolstering that. I've been on the receiving end of that once. It hurts just as much as it did back then.

"Get out of my way," I say, trying to stand up in a tangle of limbs. "Do you know what she did to me? Do you have any idea? I am not supposed to be here, Gabby. I'm not supposed to be alive. She tore me into pieces and shoved me into some random piece of meat and now I can't go home. And yes, it was home."

I hadn't realized that was true until just now. There's a memory of a feeling, like seeing the reverse color of a shape wherever you look after a flash bulb goes off. I don't want to think about it, but it hits me almost as hard as Gabriela did.

It's a memory of being happy.

In that split second that I pause, she makes her move. Force slams me into the floor, an inexorable weight presses down on me. She's using the same sort of spell I used to pin the dead guy to the ceiling to keep me pinned to the floor. She's straining against my counter-spell trying to push her away.

"Goddammit, Eric. Stop. It's not her fault."

"Bullshit. I woke up puking, with her face hovering over mine. She fucking told me she'd done it. Don't tell me it's not her fault." She hits me with an even stronger punch of magic that knocks the wind out of me. I can barely breathe.

"It isn't her fault," she says. "It's mine."

Chapter 13

The conference room is empty save Gabriela and me. She kicked out the zombie and the woman. The woman was slightly amused, like this was all a game, which to her it could be as far as I know. The zombie wasn't happy about it, though. Didn't push it when Gabriela ordered him out the door. He walked past giving me this look that says 'You do anything and I'll kill you.' Yeah, try it, dead man, let's see which one of us wins.

I sit on the other side of the table from Gabriela. I don't want to go near her. I don't trust myself not to try to kill her. Because if we start that business it's only going to end when one of us is a corpse.

She matches my glare with a calm, cool gaze. Gabriela does what needs doing and meets everything head on. She does not flinch. She does not crack. I've only seen her at the edge of that once before. She almost died then, but she did it knowing full well she might, and the stakes were too high not to do it.

We sit in silence like that for a full ten minutes before she says, "You gonna keep being a fucking drama queen about this or are we gonna talk?"

"By all means," I say. "Please. Talk. Tell me why you decided to shear me into pieces and cram all the really choice bits into somebody else's dead body. Tell me the rationale. Tell me why you thought it was a good idea. And tell me why you thought I would even be remotely okay with it."

"I knew you wouldn't," she says. "I knew it would piss you off. I knew how it was going to work and what it was going to do to you. I was pretty sure it was irreversible and that if it did work whoever woke up in that circle might not even be the person I was trying to get back."

"And am I who were hoping for?"

"The fact that you tried to kill Pallavi back there tells me I got it right."

"Am I that predictable?"

"Sometimes," she says. "Yes." Gabriela may not always have a plan, but she always has a reason. She doesn't do anything without considering multiple angles, possible outcomes. I push aside my anger as far away as I can and start using my head.

"Whether I like it or not, I know that you wouldn't have done this unless you needed something that only I could do," I say. "Which is why I'm sitting here and not murdering you. It also tells me that it's about Darius. Nobody else can touch those wards on his bottle except for Mictlantecuhtli."

"And since you're Mictlantecuhtli—"

"Except that I'm not," I yell, and I can feel my eyes turn black. "Or did you not hear that bit about splitting me into pieces? Mictlantecuhtli and I are now officially and on some fundamental cosmic level no longer the same person."

"Huh," she says. She bites her lower lip when she's thinking and from the way she's currently chewing on her own flesh I'd say the mental wheels are spinning like a turbine at Hoover Dam.

"That's it?" I say. "That's all you have to say about this? 'Huh'? What the actual fucking fuck?"

"Okay, so you've been split. Does that mean you can't affect the wards?"

"Haven't the first goddamn clue. I'm not a god, Gabby. I'm human. I eat and sleep and shit like everybody else does now. All I am is meat."

"Fuck, Eric. I have to know. Can you do anything to the fucking wards?"

I'm about to keep yelling, but I know that's not going to do anything useful. "I can do some of the smaller ones. I remember how to do the rest. I remember everything."

I let that sink in. Everything Mictlantecuhtli did. I remember trying to sacrifice myself so I could take over Eric's, my, body. I remember Quetzalcoatl's betrayal, and the battle with Darius. I remember being imprisoned in jade.

"Then you should be able to do something with the wards."

"Darius seems to think I can do something. But I haven't seen the bottle since before I died, and that thing's a hell of a lot more complex than the few I've spun since I've been here. Just because I remember something doesn't mean I have it at my fingertips. I don't have his power. Not sure I can even still see them."

"You've spoken with Darius?"

"You're gonna chew a hole through that lip you keep going like that," I say. "Yeah. Though 'spoken at' might be more accurate. One of his associates hit Tish and I with a flash-bang, stuck a bag over my head and took me to have an audience with his Lordship."

"What did he want?"

"The usual," I say. "For me to open the bottle. I told him I'd think about it."

"Shit," she says. "I was hoping I'd have a little more time before he found out about you."

"We are talking about Darius here," I say. "He tried to bribe me with power, riches, bringing my family back to life. Kinda cliché, if you ask me, but I guess he's a traditionalist. You want to tell me what exactly is going on that you had to run my soul through a woodchipper to bring me back?"

"The wards are failing."

"Yeah. I know." This is not news. Darius told me that himself once. I've seen the cracks in them. "But at the rate they're going it's gonna be another five hundred years until they break."

"We've got a week," she says.

"Excuse me?" Wounded pride over a memory that isn't mine. "That was quality craftsmanship."

"It was," she says. "But that was a last-ditch effort, wasn't it? You put them in place because Darius was kicking your ass. Or did you stick yourself into a jade prison for five hundred years for shits and giggles?"

"That wasn't me," I say, but I can hear the uncertainty in my own voice.

"Bullshit. That was you in all the ways it needs to be you. You remember. Tell me those memories aren't etched into your brain more vividly than the first time you got laid."

"Still doesn't change the fact that I don't have his pow—" I say. I feel my own identity struggling between Eric Carter's memories and Mictlantecuhtli's. I hear Gabriela start to say something and I put up my hand to stop her. The room is spinning, my vision is blurring at the edges and then everything snaps into a focus that's much more than vision.

Gabriela is watching me, wary. "You all right?"

"Existential crisis," I say.

"Is it over?"

"Something tells me it's just getting started. But I'm all right." I can feel Gabriela sitting across the table from me, Pallavi in the hall. Interesting. She's not human. How do I know that?

She's not the most interesting thing, though. The

zombie has my attention. He's dead, all right, but there's something anchoring his soul in place. A stone in the center of his chest. It pulses like a heartbeat, entwined into every part of his being like a cancer. He loses that stone, he's gonna be real sad, real fast. I suspect he already knows this.

"Who's the stiff?"

"His name's Joe Sunday. Met him a few years back. You know Sandro Giavetti?"

"Fuck, is he still alive?" Sandro Giavetti was kind of a legend in necromancer circles. Not that he was one, necessarily, but he'd managed to keep himself alive for, fuck, I don't know how long. Five hundred years, easy. Was obsessed with immortality.

"No, thanks to Joe. Same with Neumann."

"Joe's the one who ate the Nazi?"

"Head to toes."

"I'll buy him a fruit basket. Guy was an asshole." Neither of those mages were slouches. Neumann and I were easily on par with each other. If I'd stuck around L.A. one of us would have killed the other eventually.

"And Pallavi?" I say. "She's not human. Not by a long way. I don't know what the hell she is. I can't quite get a read on her. She's something, but she's evasive, knows I'm looking. She's very good at hiding." So good she can even hide from the echo of a god's sight.

"She's a rakshasi," Gabriela says.

"I thought it was rakshasa." Rakshasas are demigods? Shapeshifters? Demons? I've never been able to really parse out what they were supposed to be. I also didn't know they actually existed.

"Rakshasa is the name for the males."

Once things started to kick off in my vision, I caught a glimpse of Gabriela and looked away. Something there I didn't want to see. I give her my full attention.

She's all heat. Flames in her veins, her heart a smoldering steel trap. It's locked closed but I can see that when it opens and snags someone, they stay there forever. I can't see what's inside the trap; an old lover, a memory, a place, nothing at all. But I can see that it hurts, and its hinges aren't opening up any time soon, if ever.

I want to tell her this. Tell her, I don't know, that it's not healthy? That she doesn't need to lock herself away like that? That doesn't sound like me. But oddly it sounds like Mictlantecuhtli. The old god wasn't intentionally cruel, regardless of what he and his wife did to me and my family. I've felt his compassion, his empathy, as I helped souls through Mictlan.

Instead I say, "Your cholesterol's a bit high. Might want to look at that."

"Excuse me?"

"Your cholesterol. You'll want to get it looked at. You're getting some arterial plaque."

"I know. My doctor has told me the same thing. How do you know?"

"I'm not sure. I think it's a sort of god hangover. But to your point, yes, I'm Mictlantecuhtli enough to do something about the wards. It will take me a while to strengthen them, and honestly I don't know if it will work. These are memories that aren't mine."

"Your eyes went black," she says.

"They do that. Seems to be a death god thing." I will them to change and I feel them shifting back. I blink and my sight goes back to normal. She seems a little shaken, like she's worried I saw something I shouldn't have. Maybe I did.

"Your zombie boyfriend out there needs to do something about that stone in his chest," I say. "Much as he's afraid of dying he's not gonna want to stick around forever."

"What? Sunday? No, the stone's gone. It was destroyed. He keeps the rotting away by eating hearts I get for him from pathology labs."

"Uh huh. If you say so," I say. "But you might want to talk to him about that. Because whatever's holding his soul in place, it's not hearts."

"I'll do that." There's an almost worried look in her eye, the confidence slipping a bit, uncertainty. She's rattled. I don't want to tell her, but if she's rattled now, maybe I should rattle her some more. Right now I don't know what to think about her.

"And I can see that steel bear trap in your soul. You're holding onto something fierce." The reaction is immediate. There's real fear in her eyes, not something I've ever seen before.

"What did you see?"

"Not much," I say. "Someone. A person. Maybe a memory. Can't see who, though. You've got that thing locked up tight."

"Stop it," she says.

"I did. I don't even know how I started it or why it stopped. So, there's no point in telling me not to do it again."

"Are you lying to me?" she says. "Did you really not see?"

"No, I'm not lying. And I really did not see what you've got hold of in there, but I get you're not letting go of it any time soon, whether you want to or not."

"Goddammit," she says. Her composure is beginning to fray.

"You're off your game," I say. Not something I've seen a lot of. "There's a lot more going on here than you're telling me, isn't there?"

"Tell me exactly what you saw," she says.

"Unh-uh," I say. "Besides looking at the bottle, which I'm hoping you have here so I can get this shit over with, I don't owe you a goddamn thing. And before you say something stupid, no, friends don't bring dead friends back to life."

She puts her head in her hands and I can see how tired she is. She puts on a brave face so well that it's impossible to tell it's a mask until it falls off.

"I'm sorry," she says. I'm not sure I've ever heard those words come out of her mouth before. "I need your help, and I can't regret what I did, but I'm sorry for what it did to you."

I don't say anything for a few moments. "How about we fill each other in on what the hell's going on? I'll start. Feel free to jump in any time. So, I wake up puking up all this black shit onto a concrete floor . . ."

It takes three hours to get through everything. Gabriela fills in a few blanks along the way.

"That was you calling me at the motel?"

"I was trying to warn you to get out," she says.

"Well, it worked. Motel phone calls are always bad. So, you know who the clay guy was who came for me?"

"Calls himself the Dollmaker," she says. "Self-righteous asshole thinks he knows what's best for everybody."

"Huh, I don't know anybody like that."

"Fuck you. Nobody I've spoken to likes him, or wants to talk about him. I can't get a name out of anybody, though it's clear some of them know him. Makes these simulacrums, sends them on errands, the occasional hit. Thing is, he doesn't seem to do it to gain anything. Everybody he's taken out has been an asshole that everybody's happy to see gone. But when he does it, he doesn't take anything. Lets the vultures swoop in and fight over the leftovers. Lots of little power vacuums popping over the city the last few years."

"He's got a kid," I say.

"I hadn't heard that. You sure it's his kid?"

"Maybe an apprentice. He sounded terrified of the guy. Came after me before he was ready hoping to score brownie points with the old man." I reach into my messenger bag and place the jar with the chunk of soul in it on the table. "I got half of him right here." I tell her the story about the last attack.

Gabriela picks up the jar, turns it in her hands, inspecting it with the care of a jeweler examining a diamond. "I don't get it. Why did you do this?"

"Bargaining chip. If I read the situation right, Daddy's gonna be awful interested in getting this back. It also makes a nifty little compass to find the rest of itself."

"Which you're hoping will lead you to him."

"I've had worse ideas," I say. She raises an eyebrow at that. "What? I have totally had worse ideas than that. You've even been there for a few."

"Nobody knows what the hell that guy is thinking," she says, ignoring me. "I got word that he was sending a car to your location. I tried to warn you. I sent some guys but by the time they got there, everybody was dead and you were in the wind."

"I'm good at that. So, what's Pallavi's deal?" There's something about the name Pallavi and her being a rakshasi that's poking at the back of my mind. Something I read a long time ago.

"We met in London a few years ago," she says. "Been with me trying to piece together how to bring you back. Something's been chasing her for about, I dunno, few hundred, maybe thousand years now? She won't say what, other than he's a rakshasa and is kind of related?"

"That doesn't sound good."

"It isn't. He gets close, she gives him the slip for a few decades, and then he's back like a bad herpes outbreak. Pretty sure he wants to kill her. And one of these days he's going to catch up to her."

"But you're not certain."

"You might have noticed that Pallavi has a certain . . . quality about her."

"I'd say that she's off her fucking nut. But I don't know if that's a rakshasa thing."

"It's a rakshasa thing. They're expert hunters. Predators from head to tail. Pallavi's no different. Though she's not as bloodthirsty as she tells me others are. But watch yourself. If she starts to come on to you she might try to eat you. Or fuck you. I think she sees both as pretty much the same thing."

"That sounds fun."

Gabriela gives me a sour look. "I wouldn't advise it," she says. "She clawed the shit out of one of my guys. Put him into the ICU. He's just lucky she didn't eat him. She did get one of his kidneys, though."

"Still sounds fun. You figure this other one is just as much a predator?"

"The way she tells it, yeah. And then some."

"So, why her? Why bring her into this?"

"I don't really understand her magic. It's hard to detect when she's using it. And if there's a lot of magical noise around it's almost impossible. She does things that seem to be inherent to her species, but she doesn't pop off spells the way we do. And her understanding of ritual magic is so much more advanced than anyone I've met. She had some ideas I hadn't considered because I hadn't thought they were even possible. It actually took us a couple tries to get it to work."

"She sounds scary," I say.

"She is. But I've never had a reason to distrust her."

"There's a story there," I say.

"For another day," she says.

"Okay. Different question, then. Where'd you get me a body? Did you dig up a dead hobo?" I show her my new tattoos, my lack of scars. "I'm still trying to figure out why I've got one but not the other."

She looks away, more uncertainty. Then she stands up, starts to pace. "I'm waiting for somebody else to show up. You should probably hear it from her."

"Is this gonna piss me off more?"

"You really need to hear it from her." In other words, yes, it's going to piss me off more.

"So, what now?" I say. "I can't see how I could lock the bottle up any tighter than it is, even if the wards are degrading."

"I don't want you to lock it up," she says. "I want you to open it."

Chapter 14

"I think I'm losing my hearing," I say. "Because it sounded like, 'Eric, let's pop the seal on a pantheon-destroying djinn who could probably snap the world in two just for shits and giggles,' and I know you wouldn't say that because that would be fucking insane."

"Hear me out," she says.

"No. I will not 'hear you out.' Jesus, you've got me doing air quotes. We hand the bottle over to Santa Muerte and Mictlantecuhtli and they deal with it. They just need to refresh the seals on the bottle. Bam! Five hundred more years genie-free."

"Do you think I haven't thought of that?"

"Yes. Clearly. Or else you would have done it already."

"They can't fix this, Eric," she says, slamming her palms on the table. With her diminutive height it'd almost be comical if she didn't also have thin strands of lightning running across her body.

"Then what the fuck makes you think you can?"

"I can't. That's the whole fucking point. If I could, you wouldn't fucking be here." She closes her eyes, forcibly pushing down her anger until the lightning fades from her skin. "They've grown too weak. You know this. You might be in denial, but you know this."

I want to argue with her, but she has a point. I'm—dammit. The new Mictlantecuhtli is only five years old. He's still learning the ropes. At the height of their powers they barely survived the fight with Darius and Quetzalcoatl, and the only reason Santa Muerte won against Q was that he was in even worse shape than she was.

Worse, they're gods. Gods need belief. The amount of power they've got from belief these days is like one kid in the crowd clapping for Tinkerbell not to die. Darius, however, doesn't depend on belief. He simply is. They won't be able to take him down.

"Yes," I say. "Okay. But how is opening the bottle going to help?"

"It's a long shot."

"You don't know, do you."

"It should work. There are some things I still need to work out. We need a better prison than that bottle. Something else that will hold him better."

"And that would be?"

"That's what I haven't figured out, yet."

"Jesus H. Monkeyfucking Christ. Seriously? You've been planning this for a while. The magic that yanked me into this skin suit is not something you just pull off the shelf. How long have you been trying to get me back?"

"Four years," she says, voice a whisper. She won't look at me. "Give or take."

"So, pretty much the whole time I was gone. And you couldn't come up with a better plan? His prison is that bottle for a reason. It's its own pocket universe. So, unless you've got one of those lying around, I think you've got yourself some problems."

"This is why I needed you back. I need help figuring out how to pull this off and you are the only other mage who has dealt with him as much as I have. I need your help figuring out what to do."

"No, you needed Mictlantecuhtli. You might not have been able to bring all of him here, but fuck, you could have contacted him. Or Muerte. It's not that difficult. The world didn't need me back."

"I needed you back," she yells.

I don't know what to say to that. Or what exactly that means. The silence between us stretches.

"Just because we don't have a solution yet, doesn't mean we won't have one in time," she says, pulling us back to the matter at hand.

"Right," I say. "Okay, yeah. Yes. Where's the bottle? I want to see what you're talking about. If the wards are that degraded, I should be able to tell. Maybe I can't shore them up, maybe they're unraveling as fast as you say they are. But I won't know for sure until I take a look at it."

"That's the other problem."

"You lost it, didn't you?"

"Fuck you. No, I didn't lose it. It was stolen."

The first time I met Gabriela she'd had an obsidian knife that could skin a person, allowing the wielder to take the victim's form, memories, abilities, everything. I wouldn't have cared except that somebody had tried to use it on me not long before then. When I traced it to her I found out somebody had stolen it. She wasn't happy about it.

"This happens to you a lot, doesn't it?" I say.

"Twice. This has only happened twice."

"Considering the things that are getting stolen I'm gonna say that's two times too many. Do you at least know who has it?"

"I've got people working on that. It happened last night. Someone walked right through the protections where I had it stored like they weren't even there. Didn't trip anything, didn't raise an alarm, nothing.

The only person who should have been able to do that is me."

"Are you sure you didn't?" A glare that could punch through steel is all the answer I get. "Hey, up until I was sitting in one of Tish's holding cells I thought I was just having a weird-ass blackout, so lighten the hell up."

"I've checked," she says after a pause that I don't like. "My rooms are even more heavily warded than the rest of this place. A flea so much as farts in there and I know it. I didn't leave bed last night and I didn't go on any astral walkabouts, either."

"I hear a 'but' in there," I say.

"No, I'm not sure, okay? The wards I have on the vault show that I'm the one who went in there last night and walked out with the bottle."

"Can they be fooled?"

"Anything can be fooled, I just don't know how."

"One second." I open the door and see the dead guy standing there with a stillness even statues can't achieve. "Hey, zombie man, do me a favor and sweep the grounds for anything that looks like a pile of discarded clay."

"Do it yourself," he says.

"I'm in conference with your boss," I say, "Or I would. No, scratch that. I'd still have you do it because I don't know how you tick and I don't like dead shit that I don't understand. Now get going. We don't have all day." I close the door and sit back down.

Now that I know what I'm looking for I can see him out there. I shift my focus and he blazes in my vision like he's on fire. After a moment, he turns around and walks away.

"You think he's actually gonna do it?" I say.

"I think he might, but I know he'll definitely try to beat the crap out of you as soon as he gets the chance."

"Looking forward to it," I say. I'm curious to see just how dead he really is.

"You think it's the Dollmaker who stole it."

"I'd bet my left nut it's the Dollmaker. I don't know all he can do, but after seeing his apprentice last night I get the feeling he can be whoever the fuck he wants to be. Dude's made out of clay, after all."

"Shit. I hope you're wrong," she says. "I really don't want to tangle with him right now. My tolerance for stupid bullshit has dropped in my old age."

"Yeah, you're a real old lady over there. You get your AARP card yet?" I stop and take a good long look at her. It's not just the hair and the outfit that makes her look professional and respectable. It's not wrinkles or any shit like that. It's years, wisdom, bad ideas and worse solutions.

When I came back to L.A. after fifteen years it was like everybody had grown up and I stayed stuck. This is like that, only worse. Sure, five years is nothing, but it feels like Peter Pan watching the Lost Boys turn into teenagers.

"Why are you looking at me like that?" she says.

"You're not well," I say.

"Yeah, no shit."

"Talk to me," I say. "What's going on? You. What's going on with you?" She tenses and then her shoulders sag.

"I'm tired. I've got this place up and running and it's harder than when I was doing it in a rundown hotel as the Bruja. I've always been in charge, but never like this. Bureaucracy, licensing, fundraisers, politicians to convince, pay, or blackmail."

"And then there's all this crap," I say.

"And then there's all this crap. It doesn't help."

"Why are you dealing with this? You can't be the only other mage in this town who knows this is a problem."

She laughs. "Are you kidding? You know what we're like. We work together about as well as rabid wolverines. Everybody knows something's coming. They can feel it. But I haven't told anyone I have the bottle. Not that some of them don't already know, and even more suspect."

"You think if you approach any of them they're gonna try to snipe the bottle and do something stupid with it."

"Of course. I've even gotten an offer from Werther to buy it from me. We both know his getting ahold of this would be a bad idea." I haven't thought about Attila Werther in a good long while. We were loosely what you could call allies for a good five or six hours one time. There are only a few big mage families in L.A. He's all that's left of his after his daughter was murdered.

"I don't see that going well."

"Yeah, I told him the same thing. He shrugged and put his house on lockdown. The other big families did the same, or just up and left town altogether. Figure they'd ride out the storm and see what's left standing afterward."

"Yeah, I get it. Typical. But even without that, there's something wrong. This been going on a while?"

"Couple years. I turned thirty-four a few months back. And feel like I'm fifty. I don't sleep. My appetite's for shit. I can't walk out of this place without feeling like there's a target on my back. I feed four hundred people a day, have beds for two hundred and fifty, and that's just the humans. There aren't as many supernaturals, but they're harder. Some normal who comes in with schizophrenia I can handle. You ever seen a schizophrenic boggard? It killed three of my staff before we could get it sedated."

"You're doing good things," I say, knowing that's a weak argument.

"But why? Does anybody even fucking care? I've

built myself a goddamn prison. You know I haven't gotten laid since college?"

"I do now," I say. "Not something I've ever really thought about."

"Yeah, well. You've been dead."

"That is the excuse I'll be using for the rest of my unnatural life," I say. "Look, you clearly need a break. World's not gonna end in the next day. Okay, maybe in the next couple of days, which is all the more reason to cut loose while you can. Get really fucking drunk. Take a shit-ton of drugs. Have regrettable sex. You're gonna die eventually and take it from me, you're gonna miss being able to get drunk."

"But not miss having regrettable sex?"

"Nah, we're all banging each other in the afterlife." She laughs like she means it. I'm not sure I've ever heard her laugh like that.

"When did you get all enlightened and shit?" she says.

"Oh, this isn't me. This is just leftover death god. I'm nowhere near this chipper."

"Fine," she says. "Let's get a drink. I'm sure somebody around here has some tequila or something. Like you said, nothing's gonna happen right now." The door opens and Joe throws a plastic shopping bag filled with clay onto the table.

"Hey, asshole," he says. "Found this a block over. And Meduro. Stuffed in a dumpster. At least two days old."

"Meduro's the guy who escorted me in here, isn't he?" I say.

"Yes," Gabriela says and suddenly she's all vengeful warrior witch queen. Now that looks like the Bruja I remember. "Get everything locked down. Find whoever is pretending to be Meduro and check everybody else. If this fucker can look like anyone, we can't trust anybody."

"Already on it," Joe says. He marches out the door, closing it behind him. Gabriela turns to me and I answer before she can ask the question.

"Yes, that's really him," I say. "He's still dead, his soul is still stuck to his body like some guy with his dick superglued to their nuts."

"That sounds painful," she says.

"Trust me, it ain't fun. Raincheck on that drink?"

"Deal."

———

The lockdown is quiet, efficient. Only one half of the place is sealed up. All of the exits from the supernaturals side and any corridors leading into the human side are strung with alarm wards that will pop at the first sign of magic.

And I mean every exit. Doors, windows, plumbing, conduits, loading bays, trash compactors. Between the time the theft happened and it was discovered, only me and the zombie came through any of those points. Meduro went through three days ago on his way out, and the Dollmaker came back in his place three hours later. He hadn't left since then.

So, unless there's a hole somewhere Gabriela doesn't know about, the Dollmaker and, more importantly, Darius's bottle are still inside. The trick is going to be finding them.

"I think we should do that blood test like in *The Thing*," I say. We're walking together down a long hall toward a cafeteria / auditorium. By the time we get there everyone else should be accounted for. "You know when they get some blood and try to burn it, if it jumps up and screams it came from the monster."

"Do you have any idea how many people we have here whose blood would scream if you tried to burn it?" Gabriela says. She's walking with purpose, long strides on short legs. She has places to be, shit to do. A walkie-talkie is clenched tight in her hand.

"Good point," I say. "So, what's your plan?" We stop about thirty feet from the auditorium doors next to a firehose in the wall. She unhooks a hidden latch and the whole assembly swings out, revealing a cubby in the wall holding a couple Benelli military M1014 shotguns, a box of 12-gauge beanbag shells, and a row of gas masks. She tosses me one of the masks, while putting on her own.

"Grab a shotgun," she says. "But be careful, they're already loaded with one in the pipe." I do and check it. As she says, there's a beanbag shell already in the chamber.

"Nice hardware. In case the residents get rowdy?"

"It happens," she says.

"I can never remember," I say. "Are these five in the tube and one in the chamber, or is it seven and one?"

"Does it really matter? If you run out of shells you've got bigger problems." She hits the talk button on her walkie-talkie a couple times to signal whoever's on the channel to listen. "Joe, you got me?"

The gravelly voice of Zombie Joe answers. "Five by five. Tell me when."

"Hit it."

The sprinklers all up and down the hallway go off, only they're not spraying water, they're spewing gas. Screams and yells sound inside the auditorium, followed by dull thuds as bodies hit the floor.

"The hell is this stuff?"

"Some valerian root, ground-up mandrake extract, basilisk liver. But a lot of it's aerosolized fentanyl," she says. "Got it off some Russian mobsters. Made changes to take into account different body weights, species, and so on. It shouldn't kill anybody, and they should wake up relatively hangover-free, so long as we get this handled fast."

Of course, the Dollmaker's mannequins are clay.
They shouldn't need to breathe. So if anyone walks
out of there, they're not who they say they are. We
wait.

"Your residents are gonna be pissed when they
wake up."

"They signed waivers," she says.

A minute goes by. Gabriela's getting antsy. A few
more and we hear footsteps inside getting closer. The
auditorium doors kick open and the only reason I
don't fire is that I don't want to waste a round on
somebody who's probably not going to notice. A gasmask free Joe, with all his swagger and undead atti-
tude, steps into the hall.

"We're clear in there," he says. "Everybody's out."

"Shit," Gabriela says. "Is anybody missing?"

"I'm gonna double check against the roster. There's
another copy over near intake." He starts to walk away.

I shoot him in the back of the head. The beanbag
hits him at damn near point-blank range and his head
explodes like a melon from a hundred-foot drop.

"The fuck, Eric?"

"That's not him," I say.

"He can survive the gas, you dumbass," she says.
"He doesn't breathe."

"Yeah, I know. But can he survive being made out
of clay?" Gabriela follows my gaze to the body. Blood,
brains and shattered bone should be caking the hallway, but instead it's a spray of rust-brown clay.

Gabriela thumbs the button on the walkie-talkie.
"Where are you?" she says.

"Where I'm supposed to be," Joe says. "I heard a
blast. You get him?"

"Yeah. Almost got away. He came through the doors
as you. Eric blew his head off."

"Now what?" he says. If he has any opinion on the
matter, it doesn't come across the radio.

"Get in there and help people before somebody swallows their tongue."

"On it."

She looks down at the clay corpse, looks back to me. "How'd you know?"

"I could tell you that I could see that he didn't have his soul sewn to his body like a fifth-grader's first assignment in Home Ec."

"But?"

"I really just wanted to shoot him and see what happens."

"I—Ya know what? No. I'm not touching that," she says. "All right, we got the Dollmaker out of the picture. Now where's the bottle? Meduro's room?"

"Closer than that," I say. I bend down to the body and start pulling off chunks of the corpse that change from flesh and cloth as soon as they're torn away. "Every time I've killed one of these things they've disintegrated into blobs of clay almost immediately. But this one hasn't."

Gabriela drops to the floor and helps me dig. We're throwing clods of the stuff all over the place, digging like frantic dogs who can't remember where they buried a bone. We've got a nice pit in the mannequin's back before my hands get purchase on something that isn't clay. I pull. With a little effort Darius's bottle comes free of the clay with a wet, sucking sound. The moment it's outside the body, the corpse crumbles back into clay.

We fall back against the hallway wall, our clothes smeared in clay, our masks fogged up with steam. I hold Darius's bottle tight in my fist. I tap the faceplate of the gasmask. "When can we take these fucking things off?"

"About an hour," she says.

"You're fucking kidding me."

"Yes," she says and pulls her mask off, laughing. I

can hear people getting up, bewildered, not sure what just happened. I wonder how they're all going to feel about this place now that Gabriela just knocked them out with riot gas.

I pull off my mask and throw it at her. "We got the bad guy," I say. "And this time nothing burned down. Is it just me or have we grown up a little, today?"

"It's just you."

"Nice to know I'm alone in my delusions. Makes me feel special. What now?"

"Now," she says, "I put that back where it belongs, wake people up, and then try to explain to them what the hell just happened."

"If it helps you could always blame it on me," I say. "I have been the scapegoat for some of the best people."

"I was planning to."

Chapter 15

I step into the locker room wrapped in a towel, steam from the showers following me. Took hours before I could get all that shit off me. Too much to do to make sure nobody was asphyxiating or having an allergic reaction. Easier than I expected it to be but that doesn't mean it wasn't a pain in the ass. Whatever Gabriela had loaded in that gas worked great. Almost everyone snapped awake inside of ten minutes without a problem. It took longer to wear off for some, though. A couple didn't wake up at all.

Gabriela had her people scrape up as much of the Dollmaker's clay as they could find and dump it into a warded box, then had them scrub the shit out of the hallway. If he could somehow use the clay to build a new mannequin, we didn't want to find out the hard way.

I looked for the glimmers of his soul I'd seen in the earlier mannequins, but there was nothing. He's either gotten better or smarter. I've already eaten part of him, and if he's seen what happened to his apprentice/son/whatever, he's going to be a lot more careful.

"Hello, darling!"

I lift the towel I was drying my hair with so I can see, but I already know who it is. Pallavi sits cross-legged on one of the benches in front of a row of lockers. This is the first time I've gotten a really good look at her that wasn't while I was puking my guts out or trying to kill her.

She appears to be a young Indian woman. Supermodel-thin with looks and long legs to match, in a cream-colored blouse and silk pants. Long black hair falls over her shoulders, eyes track everything with a predatory gleam.

"Pallavi," I say. My gun is in my bag, and that's stashed in a locker. Fortunately for mages, nude doesn't equal helpless. I get ready to throw up a shield or lash out with something if I need to. I'm not quite so pissed off at her anymore. That was a heat of the moment thing, and honestly, I didn't expect I'd have such a strong reaction. I knew I was pissed, I just hadn't realized I was that pissed.

"How are you feeling?" she says. "Well, I hope? I see you've already put your body through some practice runs." She points to my eye where one of Letitia's cops gave me a nice fat shiner and the big purple bruises just below my rib cage.

"It's like scratching the paint on a new car. Breaks it in."

"Ah, yes. I see. All your bits and bobs working as expected?"

"Near as I can tell," I say.

"Good, good. Still, if you don't mind I'd like to check a couple of things myself."

"Is this a come on?"

"Oh, darling, please. You're not my type."

"I can tell you right now I don't have a hernia so you don't need to do the turn your head and cough thing."

"Noted." She stands up and pulls a stethoscope from around her neck that was hidden by her hair. She presses it against my chest. "Deep breath, please. And release." She taps my chest a couple of times while listening.

"Aren't you a Vedic goddess or something?"

"Oh, dear lord, no. Godling, maybe. More like a demon is how your kind paint us. Though from what I've heard you're not quite so bigoted for a mage."

"Oh, I dunno, I hate demons as much as the next guy."

"Yes, but you're not calling everything you don't understand a demon, are you? Open your mouth and say 'aaah,' please." She shines a penlight in there. "Very good. Excellent teeth, good color. How do you feel?"

"Confused," I say. "Angry. Human."

"Well, I can allay your fears about number three. You smell wonderfully of death god. All right, all good aside from the bruises and confusion."

I push aside the warning bells going off in my head and half expect her to claw my head off as I step past her to the locker. My clothes and messenger bag hang from a hook in the back.

"I'm not Mictlantecuhtli, anymore."

Getting the clothes clean was easier than getting all the clay out of my hair. One of Gabriela's people knows some good cleaning spells for lifting stains. Great for clothes, not so good on people. Tends to rip the skin right off.

"Oh, yes, you are." She closes her eyes, lifts her nose in the air and takes a big whiff. "Mmmm. I can smell it on you. I must say, death god is quite the heady scent."

"And here I thought I used the good soap."

"Do you remember being Mictlantecuhtli?" she says, and goes on before I can answer. "Remembering is most of it. You know his victories, his defeats, why he did what he did. And best of all how he did all the things that he did. Even if you're no longer the same person, godhood isn't something you shed easily."

"I don't see me guiding the dead through Mictlan anytime soon, thanks."

"Ah, but the point is that if you really wanted to, you could."

"You can leave now."

"And miss this conversation? Hardly. Go on. Get dressed. You remember I saw you naked as a babe not long ago, so no need for embarrassment for my sake. Which reminds me, are all the tattoos how you expected them?"

"They're a little more colorful than I remember, but besides that, yeah."

"Fascinating. Have you puzzled out why?"

I toss the towels into the locker and get dressed. It's one thing to have a hot woman watching your ass, but it's totally different when she literally wants to eat you. Not saying danger doesn't have a certain appeal, but time and place, you know?

"What do you want, Pallavi? If it's to shoot the shit, I'm too tired. If it's to talk shop, hit me up after I've gotten some sleep and don't want to kill you quite so badly. That'll involve large amounts of coffee, by the way."

"Oh, come now. Even if you won't give me answers, at the very least you must have questions."

"Do you eat human flesh?"

"Oh lord, not in years. Like I said, remembering is most of it. When I took this form I forgot myself. Took me years to remember. It's what you call a feature, not a bug. If I don't know who I am I'm much harder to find. Going vegan didn't hurt, either."

"But you used to," I say.

"Of course. I am a rakshasi, you know. Little hard to go through life without a little nibble here and there."

"What do you want?"

"Truly, I came to ask how the new body is holding up. One does care about one's handiwork, you know."

"Seems to be holding up just fine. So you can go now."

"I was also wondering if you'd seen a particular someone recently. Someone who maybe makes you feel a little uneasy."

"You mean besides you?"

"Yes, but very like me."

"This rakshasa who's chasing you. Gabriela told me about him."

"Just so."

"I wouldn't even know what to look for." I remember what I was thinking about her name earlier. "You're Hidimbī. From the *Mahabharata*."

"Oh! Delightful! A fan."

"I barely remember a bit of it." The *Mahabharata* and the *Ramayana* are two sacred Hindu epics. One, the *Mahabharata*, tells the story of a war, some sort of family tiff. The *Ramayana* tells the story of Rama, a prince who, and I've never been real clear on this, becomes or already is a Hindu god. It's very confusing.

"Still," she says. "My starring role. The *Mahabharata*, the story of the tragic and beautiful Hidimbī, a rakshasi who also happens to go by the name Pallavi, in case you were wondering."

"Yeah, I figured that part out."

"Shush, I'm having a moment. That's actually part of why Vibhi is looking for me."

"Vibhi?"

"Vibhishana. Appears in the *Ramayana*. He betrays his brother, Ravana, because he's Oh So Fucking Pure and has a problem with the fact that his brother has kidnapped Sita, the wife of Rama, who is an Official God, who you may have seen as a blue-skinned bloke. Vibhi then tells Rama all of the secrets of Ravana's army, ensuring his brother's death. Conveniently, he takes the throne of Lanka, which should have gone to Ravana when their father died."

"Got it. Pissed off gods beating the snot out of each other."

"Oh, and then some," she says. "Then there's the *Mahabharata*, wherein the stunningly beautiful Hiḍimbī does pretty much the same thing to her brother Hiḍimbā that Vibhi did to Ravana. Only for me, it wasn't righteousness, it was love. I fell for a handsome young man named Bhīma, who simply did not get along with my brother.

"So, I helped Bhīma kill Hiḍimbā and then we made mad, passionate love in the forest, resulting in the birth of my son, Ghatotkacha, who is a right shit, let me tell you. Dumb as a sack of hammers. Truly embarrassing."

"How much does that jibe with the truth?"

"Almost none of it. The gist is there, but the details are all wrong. I didn't betray my brother. Bhīma used me to get to him and then told me someone else had killed him and hey, would you like to go shag in the bushes?"

"And Vibhi?"

"He did betray his brother, but not because he wanted to return Rama's wife to him. He wanted Rama all to himself and used Sita as an excuse to jump ship and play hide the sausage with Rama, which they did with great gusto the way Sita tells it."

"Okay. You both made questionable relationship choices. Congratulations. I'm not seeing the connection."

"The connection is one you won't see in either of those texts. Vibhi and I are cousins. I am related to him because his brother couldn't keep his dick in his pants. Through a fascinating little hole in cosmic logic that I've never fully understood, I am the rightful Queen of Lanka, and Vibhi is—well, 'bootlicker' is too kind a word for him."

"And he wants you out of the picture so he can maintain the throne?"

"At this point I think he just wants to tie up a loose end he's been worrying at like a broken tooth. Everybody thinks Lanka must be Sri Lanka, but it isn't. It's gone. Slipped beneath the waves like Atlantis."

"If there's no kingdom, then there's no throne, so what the fuck is his problem?"

"He's a shit," she says.

"There's always more than that."

"Yes, well. We might have had words once or twice. And a fight or two. And I might have burned down most of the countryside and killed the rest of his side of the family, but in all fairness they really had it coming."

"So, this really has nothing to do with the throne at all," I say. I finish tying my shoes and start on my tie.

"You're all uneven," Pallavi says. "Let me do it." She stands and begins tying my tie for me. It takes everything I have not to flinch. "It actually does have to do with the throne. If it wasn't for the throne we would never have been fighting each other for control of it in the first place and I wouldn't have gone and killed anyone. All I needed was to finish the job with Vibhi and everything would be right as rain."

"But you missed," I say. I have a momentary panic that I've just given this woman/monster something to garrote me with if she doesn't like the look in my eye. But then, if she wanted to kill me, she's had ample opportunity, so I relax and let her do her thing.

"I did, yes," she says. "Mostly on account of the fact that Vibhi sunk the island beneath our feet. By the time I finally made it back to shore I couldn't find him, and I didn't particularly want him to find me. I'm no match for him in a fair fight, and I've never had a good enough opportunity to stab him in the back. I've been running ever since. I lost him for a few decades after I came back to Earth in the 1870s and settled in Britain as a translator."

"Good money?"

"Shit money, even by 19th century standards. He found me again, of course. San Francisco of all places. It was an ugly, ugly fight. Took the whole city down."

"The quake?"

"Hmm. Just so. Though I don't think we can really be blamed for it. I certainly didn't know anything about a fault line. I doubt Vibhi could even comprehend the word."

She moves the knot of the tie just below my chin. It's snug, but not tight. And it doesn't look like she's going to pull on it until my head pops off, so that's something.

"Families, man," I say. "They're the worst."

"That they are," she says. "I've been on the run from what's left of mine for almost two and a half thousand years."

"And you're worried he's here?"

"Not yet. But he almost caught me in London a few years back, so I know he's back on the playing field. I have no idea how he found me." She steps back to admire her handiwork. "There you go. All prepped and ready to go like a pig into the oven."

"Thanks," I say. I loosen the tie a little, but I have to admit, she ties a mean Windsor. "You think somebody gave you up? Who knew you were in London?"

"That's the thing, I'm completely stumped. Over the last twenty years I've been in the role of a wealthy socialite who sadly has not married, for her true love died in a horrific boating accident, so she spends all her time moving from property to property throughout Great Britain, France, Greece, Spain, Monaco, and the Netherlands. So I don't have a lot of time for friends."

"The Netherlands?"

"Yes, I just love their pastries. So I don't know who could have, as you so adorably put it, given me up. And here the only ones who know are Gabriela, Joseph, and you. Everyone else here just thinks I'm crazy Pallavi, a mage hired for my expertise with dead people. And that's only Gabriela's staff. Everyone else thinks I'm a counselor. I'd like to keep it that way, if possible. I suspect the cat's already out of the bag, though. Modern travel leaves far too wide a trail to follow. I've been on Earth in this form for almost twenty-five years. I should have switched it about sooner."

She brushes some non-existent dust off my shoulder. "Thank you," I say. I step back, pull my coat out of the locker, and slide it on. The Browning goes into the holster at the small of my back.

"You look good enough to eat," she says.

"Last time a woman said that to me she actually tried to eat my soul."

"I imagine it would be tasty," she says.

"She said that, too."

———

I find Gabriela in her office. She's changed into a pair of jeans, purple Doc Martens, and a t-shirt with the words JUST FUCKING DIE ALREADY in a glittery flowing font. This is a lot more her style than Business Lady Pantsuit.

She's not alone. A woman sits next to her at the conference. Young. Early twenties, maybe? Long brown hair, unearthly blue eyes like chips of glacial ice. And then I catch that vibe. She's not young, she's just not human.

"Hello, Eric," she says. I stop in the doorway, trying to piece together where I've seen her. And then it comes to me. Last time I saw her was in Union Station and she had a glamour that made her look like she was in her nineties.

"Miriam," I say. "Had no idea you two knew each other."

Miriam and my grandfather had been a thing from back in the late 40s until he died sometime in the early 80s. She's a lamia. Lamiae eat souls, usually a bit at a time, but sometimes they'll go whole hog. Relationships between humans and lamiae aren't unheard of, but they almost never do as well as she and my grandfather did.

"Everyone in the supernatural community in L.A. knows Gabriela," she says. Of course they do. They'd be stupid not to. Gabriela's probably the best ally they could possibly have.

"Makes sense. But this isn't a coincidence, is it? You showing up here now."

"It isn't," she says. I wait for her to go on, but she doesn't. The silence drags until it starts to feel very awkward. And then I start to get what this is about.

"My body," I say. "Whose is it?"

"Well," she says, pausing just a touch too long to not be awkward. "The spell to bring you back required your body, or as close a match as could be found."

"Everybody in my family was cremated, including me," I say. "So, how— Granddad bucked another tradition and was buried, wasn't he? And you went and dug him up."

"Yes."

"Okay. So . . . Mictlantecuhtli gets poured into my grandfather's embalmed corpse, and before it can overflow with god juice the tap gets shut off and what's left in the bucket is me."

"Yes."

"And the spell that did all that added my tattoos and got rid of all my scar tissue, or at least Granddad's scars?"

"That was all you," Gabriela says. "Once the spell was complete your soul reshaped the body according to how you see yourself. Late twenties, early thirties? No scars, covered in tattoos."

"I have a very positive body image," I say. I pull out a chair and sit. "How'd they rope you into this?"

"You came up in conversation, though I honestly don't remember how. Gabriela found out about Robert and me, and that he'd been buried. Things snowballed from there."

"Just goes to show you can kill a Carter but not keep 'em down," I say. "Whether they want to stay down or not."

"Eric, we didn't have any other options," Gabriela says.

"Oh, I get that. Hate to wind up in the body of some murdered hobo. It's kind of ironic, really, don't you think, Miriam? I mean, Granddad did try to kill me as a child, and now he's given me a second chance at life."

"You know it wasn't like that," Miriam says.

"I really don't," I say. "Because I was too young to remember it. Or I suppressed it. Who knows? And it doesn't matter anymore because we're both dead and we can move on. No, wait. We aren't."

"Fine," Miriam says. "Be angry. But be angry with me. I came up with the idea to use Robert's body to host your soul. I offered up the body of a man I loved for forty years. I know I'm not your blood, but I knew him. And he did what needed doing no matter the cost."

"Hence the PTSD," I say.

"Oh, like you're any different," Gabriela says. "Vivian told us about all those knocks to your head. Multiple TBIs, brain bleeds. She was surprised your head didn't just pop off the top of your neck. So, spare us the victim routine. We all know it's bullshit."

I close my eyes, count to ten, and say, "You're right. I'm sorry, Miriam. I'm not happy with it, probably because I'm still trying to wrap my brain around everything. Thank you for doing what you did. I'm not my grandfather. I don't always do what needs doing. But this is definitely one of those times for me to step up."

"For what it's worth," Miriam says, "I am sorry. For both of us. When I met you and said you looked just like him I wasn't joking. And now, even more so. It's . . . it's hard to be here. Talking to you." She looks at Gabriela, who squeezes her shoulder. "If you want to talk more, though, I'll be here for a while."

"He won't," Gabriela says. She gives me a meaningful glance and I nod my head. Not the time, not the place. "You should go home. If anything comes up, I'll call you."

"Thank you." Miriam stands, tears in her eyes not quite falling. "Goodbye, Eric." She closes the door quietly on her way out.

"You're an asshole," Gabriela says.

"Since when is this news? I'll make you a deal, I'll put away the victim card if you stash the guilt card. Shit needs doing. Deal?"

"Deal. You're still an asshole."

"Stones and glass houses, chica. By the way, you might want to put a leash on that rakshasi of yours."

"Oh, god. She try to eat you or fuck you?"

"Neither, though I got the sense she wanted to do both. If she tried, I don't think a squirt bottle and yelling 'bad kitty!' would do it."

"That'd just turn her on. So, what did she do exactly?"

"She told me about Vibhi."

"Ah," she says. "She tried to kill him and he sunk the island under the ocean."

"You seem surprisingly okay with it," I say.

"I wouldn't go so far as to say I'm okay with it," she says. "I want to get this shit with the bottle handled as quickly as possible. When those two finally run into each other again I really don't want it to be here."

"She tell you about San Francisco?"

"Yes. Part of our deal is that I keep an eye out for Vibhi. So, if, you know, you bump into a pissed-off rakshasa who can look like pretty much anybody, let me know if he doesn't kill you first."

"Did she happen to mention her particular role in Hindu mythology?"

Gabriela's eyes go wary. "She did not."

"You might want to ask her about that. I think you'll find it . . . interesting."

"Interesting like it's neat trivia, or interesting like marrying into an ancient pantheon and becoming a part-time death god?"

"The latter."

"Fuck."

"Welcome to my world. So, back to the shit that needs doing. Everything all squared away here? All the little monsters tucked in their beds?"

"No," she says. "I mean, you're still up. We lost a few more residents. They just didn't want to be here anymore. I think a few more are considering."

"Because they no longer feel safe, or they no longer trust you?"

"I don't know," she says. "This place was never de-signed to be a lifetime home and they all know it. Some of these people live two, three hundred years. We've only been open a few years and already we're having to turn some away."

"That's gotta be rough," I say.

"Oh, they're all survivors. They'll be fine."

"I meant for you."

She frowns at that. Doesn't like it at all. "I'm fine, too."

"Okay. Just seems you've put a lot of emotional investment into this and having your charges leave has to be difficult."

"Easier than when you burned my hotel down," she says.

"That was not me and you know it. Anyway, I'm not here to talk about burning your hotel down or horny cats. Let's see the bottle." She goes through a door at the back of her office and a couple minutes later comes out with Darius's bottle. She sets it on the desk between us.

"That's it, all right." I recognize the wards and locks I put onto it five hundred-years . . . the wards and locks that Mictlantecuhtli put onto it. I pick it up and look it over.

"I'm gonna try to shore up some of these spells," I say. Whether they fail in a week or a month or five hundred years, it can't hurt to tighten them up a bit and plug any holes.

"I was hoping you might have an idea of how we could trap him in something else."

"How about let's see if I can do this and keep us all from making a terrible mistake and being torn to shreds by an angry djinn?"

I check each strand of the intertwined spells. She's right about the degradation. Last time I saw it I could tell it was happening, but it was minimal. Looked like it'd be good for a few hundred more years.

That was optimistic to say the least. The breakdown has advanced like a wildfire. Some of the spells are completely useless, fortunately not the main ones, but their loss weakens the structure overall. I spend a good half hour turning it this way and that, following glowing strands that only I can see. Finally, I put it back down.

"Well?" she says. "Can you fix them? Strengthen them? Something?" I'm thinking, saying nothing, doing math in my head and cataloging all the different places I might be able to shore something up. There aren't a lot of them.

"You want the bad news or the worse news?"

"Let's go with bad," she says.

"You're wrong about the timeline. They're not failing in a week, they're failing in about two days."

"That's the bad news?"

"Yep."

"What's the worse news?"

"I can't do a goddamn thing to fix it. The bottle's booby-trapped."

Chapter 16

Spite.

Long time back, I find myself handcuffed to this corpse, forced to drag it through the Arizona desert in the middle of summer. We've all been there. It's not just the smell, the heat, the lack of water, the exhaustion. It's the fucking ghost of the mage who I killed hounding me every second to move faster because he needed to get his body to Scottsdale before he was nothing but shredded sinew and bone.

I'd tell him to fuck off except for the goddamn geas he'd cast on me right before he died. I'm a kid. Not even twenty-five. I don't know how to counter that shit. So I stay cuffed to the sonofabitch halfway to Scottsdale before I manage to steal a car and shove his corpse into the passenger seat next to me.

We run into state police a little before we hit the city. Talk about awkward. I spell them into thinking that the guy's body is my napping grandfather and I'm just trying to get him home. Sympathetic sounds all around. Fuckers still give me a speeding ticket.

The second we hit Scottsdale the geas lifts. Guy's too stupid to word it right. I got this ghost screaming an address into my ear, his stinking, oozing corpse sitting next to me, and suddenly no need to do a goddamn thing for either of them. So I slip the cuff off, stick it to the driver's side outside door handle and drag that sonofabitch across the blacktop all the way to his destination.

By the time we get there he's nothing by stripped meat and bone, barely recognizable as a mammal, much less human, leaving a five-mile-long trail of blood and viscera all the way down the street.

The guy's ghost is losing his shit the entire time. Would not shut up. I uncuff the body, do a little necromancy and lock his ass in place as a Haunt tethered to his own corpse. I drag his skeletal ass a little bit further up to the porch and dump him on the doorstep.

Then I piss on the corpse, ring the doorbell, and drive away.

That, my friends, is spite.

And that is fucking amateur hour compared to the kind of spite that a pissed-off djinn can toss around.

"A booby-trap?"

I'm parsing everything I've just seen and wondering why I hadn't seen it before when it's so glaring now. Of course—because it was covered up by everything else. Now that Mictlantecuhtli's spells are degrading they're like a blinking red DANGER signs.

"Yeah. More than one. I don't know if you can see it, but one of them's spent. Pretty sure that's the one that turned Mictlantecuhtli to jade." She leans in to get a closer look.

"Nothing," she says. I take her hand in mine.

"How about now?"

"Oh. Yeah. Sort of a gray band floating around the rim of the bottle?"

"Right, and these ones here are still active. They've wrapped around some of the locking spells and taken them over like kudzu. Somebody tries to strengthen them they'll go off. Not sure what it's supposed to do. I think this one stretches you out like a rug and slowly kills you over a few hundred years. This one's just disintegration, but it doesn't do anything to you. It targets any living relatives slowly and painfully and leaves you alive. I don't know the other glyphs."

"Jesus," Gabriela says, pulling back quickly.

"Thinking this was Darius's plan B," I say. "Pretty sure I see a plan C, D, E, and F on there, too. If the jade spell didn't get Mictlantecuhtli, that or one of the others would. Since he's the only one who could do anything to these spells, nobody else would trigger the trap."

"Except you," she says.

"Yeah, well, I don't plan on doing that."

"And there's nothing you can do to tighten those locks up?"

"Duct tape?" I say.

"I don't think that'll work," Gabriela says, "though we'll file it for later. Where does that leave us?"

"Two days to find a solution or the cork pops with or without my help."

"Any ideas?" she says.

"Who else has a stake in this?" I say.

"Besides everybody?"

"I was thinking the Doll— Ya know, I can't call him that, it's just too fucking stupid. It makes him sound like a Batman villain."

"Don't look at me. I'm not the one who gave him the name," she says.

"Geppetto. We're calling him Geppetto. Dollmaker. Jesus. So, what did Geppetto want the bottle for?"

"Open it himself?" she says.

"But he can't do that without me. So, why's he trying to kill me?"

"Maybe he just wants to kill you because he doesn't like you," she says.

"Nobody likes me. He extra-special-doesn't-like-me. Why?"

"Because you can open the bottle?"

"Okay, what if Geppetto wants to make sure it stays closed, and sees me as a threat to that?" I say.

"And he wants the bottle so he can keep it safe."

"Right," I say. "And if that's the case, maybe he has a plan to keep it shut up."

"Or he just doesn't know the wards are disintegrating and figures burying it will solve the problem. We need to find this guy," Gabriela says. She stands up and starts toward the door.

"The hell are you doing?" I say.

"I thought I just said. We need to find this guy."

"No, you're not. You said it yourself, you go out there and you might as well paint a target on the back of your head."

"So, I'm supposed to do nothing?"

"You can take that huge brain of yours and try to figure out how we get out of this," I say.

"Are you flirting with me?"

"Appealing to your narcissism. That bottle's opening and I can't do a goddamn thing about it. I'm expendable. You're not."

"You can't stop me, you know," she says.

"Jesus, Gabriela, I'm not trying to. I'm trying to get you to figure out a way out of this dumpster fire."

"Take Pallavi with you," she says.

"Oh, hell no."

"You're going to need someone to watch your ass."

"Kind of what I'm worried about," I say. "I don't need her. I have leverage." I pull out the spirit bottle half-filled with the kid's soul. "I don't think he's going to try anything so long as I've got this with me."

"So, what, you're just gonna drive around and hope it points you in the right direction?" she says.

"Kinda, yeah."

"And that went so well the last time. How about we do this the smart way?" When the business with

Quetzalcoatl went down we went looking for his helper. Ended up driving all over the goddamn place. He made it hard enough that we didn't realize it was a trap until way too late.

"Smart's not really my style," I say.

"Oh, shut up and follow me." She picks up the bottle and peers at it, the soul sloshing inside like the fluid in a glow stick.

———

Gabriela has a scryer in the building. One of her homeless supernaturals, an aswang from the Philippines named Mariel. A Filipino woman with long black hair, friendly eyes, a nice smile. She looks completely human, so long as she doesn't open her mouth or the second set of eyelids. The five-foot-long tongue curled into a ball just in front of her throat, razor-sharp teeth that fit together like a bear trap, and glowing red eyes are kind of a giveaway.

In one hand she holds the spirit bottle hanging in its little macramé cage. In the other she has an iPad open to the map application. The bottle is pulling away from her hand toward the south.

She runs her finger along the streets on the iPad, and the bottle shifts where it pulls. It's a neat little bit of magic. She's substituting the map for the actual location of the bottle. I really hope this guy's not on the other side of the toxic zone. That's gonna take forever to get to.

She pans the map south-west past the 10 Freeway across the border to the toxic zone, down Flower until— Shit. Geppetto isn't on the other side of the toxic zone. He's in the fucking middle of it.

The bottle starts wobbling in circles like a top. She zooms in the map, and soon the bottle is hanging stock still straight down.

"Is that—holy shit, that's the USC campus."

"Doheny Library," Gabriela says. Then I remember. "You went to school there."

"Undergrad," she says, quiet. Voice barely above a whisper and filled with something like nostalgia and something like rage. "Managed to convince my professors to let me do my grad work there. I was visiting some of them a few days before Vernon went up."

"Did they—"

"Make it? No. They were dead by the next morning. Everything blew toward the west. A shift in the wind and it would have come up this way, and we wouldn't be having this conversation."

"I'm sorry." For her loss, for their deaths. Thousands upon thousands of people who would be alive if I hadn't pissed off Quetzalcoatl and brought him straight here.

"I know," she says.

The aswang looks to Gabriela, who nods and says, "That's it, Mariel. Thanks. I really appreciate the help." She nods in return and hands the bottle back to me.

"It's in the toxic zone," I say. "What can you tell me about it?"

"It's toxic," she says. "The Vernon blast released a lot of heavy metals into the air, poisonous gas, rocket fuel, solvents, all sorts of shit. It's in the soil, the water. For some reason it's not dissipating and moving out of the area. One of those good news/bad news things. It's not moving out into any other neighborhoods, but nobody's entirely sure how to get rid of it."

"For five years?" I died only a few months after Vernon. A lot of government types kept saying that clean-up efforts would start any day. They waited for winds, rain, heavier-than-air gasses settling. I never paid much attention to it, and then I had bigger things to worry about.

"Yeah. Which has a lot of the mages in town a little nervous. Unnatural occurrences are easy to write off, but this is getting attention at higher levels than any-body's comfortable with. Most of the dead are still in there. Fire and Rescue, National Guard, Marines, they've all tried to get deep into it, and they all start dropping like flies before they get more than a few blocks in."

"Even with Hazmat suits?"

"Even inside airtight troop transports. They've tried flying helicopters in, lowering people from above. I don't know everything, but I've heard a few people calling it our Chernobyl."

"And mages? Somebody had to have gone in."

"Yeah," Gabriela says, "though a few kicked be-fore we all figured out it wasn't natural magic. It's clear somebody's been behind it, but mostly nobody really cares, or they're too afraid to look too closely. There is a lot of power going into that. If it's the Doll-maker keeping it going, then this is gonna be even uglier than I thought it might."

"Geppetto," I say. "We're calling him Geppetto. I need a gasmask."

"No. Have you not heard a fucking word I said? Half the shit in there will eat your skin off."

"I'll keep up a shield spell."

"Uh-huh. And what are you going to breathe?"

"I'll get an oxygen tank."

"Let me make sure I got this," Gabriela says. "You want to go up against the Doll—Geppetto, while maintaining a shield spell, breathing out of an oxygen tank that if it goes empty you're dead in about four minutes, and have a conversation that will likely turn into a fight because, so far, the guy has only tried to kill you."

"Okay," I say, conceding the point and trying to salvage what little pride I have left. "Put that way it doesn't sound like a workable plan, but it's, you know, evolving."

"You're an idiot," she says.

"I prefer to think of it as impulsive."

"There's a better way to do this," she says.

"I am open to suggestions."

"Good thing I have some then. Come on. Let's walk."

I follow her down the hall from her office out of the administrative area and into the shelter proper. Besides the locker rooms and showers, there are large dorms with beds more like Japanese coffin hotels than bunk beds. Curtains, individual lights, power, fans. The place is deluxe, but it's still a homeless shelter, and no matter how much you clean the place it's got a funk that's less an odor and more a feeling. Hopelessness, mostly. Despair. Mourning.

People go to homeless shelters when there's no option left. Gabriela's tried to anticipate the needs of as many of her charges as she can. There are the dorms, private rooms for those who can't cohabitate with others for one reason or another. Areas for parents with children, abused women, drug rehab.

I cannot even imagine how much money this all cost to build, much less run. Wherever Gabriela's getting the funding for it, I doubt it's all legal. Tish thinks Gabriela's gone legit, but I hope she's wrong. Legit just means more eyes looking at your books. More paper trails, digital transactions. Better to launder dirty money through legit businesses than actually run legit businesses.

We stop at a plain door with an intercom and a camera to one side. Gabriela punches the button and says, "It's me, Sam. Gotta grab a couple of things."

"One second," Sam says. I can hear typing on the other side. "What's the password?"

"Uvula," Gabriela says. The door buzzes and unlocks.

"Uvula?"

"We change it up every day, sometimes two or three times a day. I really don't want anybody getting in here." We step into a storeroom with a front desk covered by three-inch plexiglass from floor to ceiling. A sort of airlock about three feet square is built into the plexiglass at the floor. A thick-set Latino man—Sam, I presume—sits behind it.

"Miz Cortez," he says. "What can I do for you?"

"I need the travel packages."

"How many?"

"Two."

"One second." Sam disappears into the back and shows up again with a box. He puts it into the airlock, hits a couple of buttons, and the box opens on our side. Gabriela pulls it out and closes the door.

"Thanks, Sam."

"Happy to help."

"What in the hell do you keep back there?" I say as we leave.

"Trinkets," she says. "Odds and ends. Most of them can kill you."

"I got a place like that," I say. "Few of 'em, actually." When all this is over I should check on those. The inventory's in the ledger in my messenger bag, but it's a crapshoot whether we'd find anything useful in it. I remember her telling me once that she had a warehouse or two filled with magical crap. We should compare notes. "With all that security, why isn't the bottle in there, too?"

"My room's more secure than that is."

"I don't remember seeing a guy behind plexiglass in your office."

"You'll only see him when he kills you." She hands me a heavy zip-lock bag holding a plastic bracelet, three crystal talismans, and an earpiece for a radio. One of the talismans is on a necklace, another on a ring, and the third isn't attached to anything.

"I take it these will keep me from dying in the wasteland?"

"The crystals, yes. They're redundant. You keep all three on you so if you lose one you don't asphyxiate or dissolve in five seconds or die in five days from cancer. The bracelet's a heavy duty Don't-Look-At-Me spell. Saves on the Sharpies."

"The earpiece?"

"You can key it to others so if you get separated from whoever you're with you can still communicate. It's thought-triggered, so you don't have to talk and give yourself away if needed."

"They're cool and all, but why do you have these?"

"Just because most mages won't go in there doesn't mean I won't go in there. I've had teams of people go in looking for, fuck, clues, answers, anything. I put these together to let them get in there without dying. Lot of trial and error. Lost some good folks."

"I'm guessing it's not just the chemicals and shit in the air you have to worry about in there."

"You know how places like that are. The magic gets just as toxic as the air is. We've run into some pretty nasty nightmare shit walking the streets."

"I'll keep it in mind. Who's the other package for?"

"Who the hell do you think?"

"Oh, no. No, don't even. We already talked about it."

"No, you talked about it. I didn't agree to a goddamn thing. I'm going with you and that's that. Or you can stay here and I go talk to the—"

"Don't say it."

"Dollmaker. We're out of ideas and out of time. If you go alone he's just going to try to kill you again. We go together, we have a better chance of actually staying alive and having a civilized conversation."

"Goddammit."

"If you want, we can have Joe come with us."

"Can he be trusted?"

"Yes."

"Even though he's never told you about that rock in his chest?"

A moment's hesitation. Then, "Yes."

"All right. How do we do this?"

———

Zombie Joe pulls up outside the shelter in a monster black Hummer with oversized tires and a lightbar on the roof with blazing halogens. Gabriela takes shotgun with, appropriately, a shotgun. I sit in the back with a Mini-14. We both have pistols, Joe's got at least one gun that I know of and I suspect two or three more hidden on him somewhere. Between the three of us we have enough ammunition and hardware to take out some Latin American countries.

"Little overkill, don't you think?" I say when I get into the beast of a car.

"Bulletproof glass, run-flat tires, armored body," Joe says. "I think it's a little light, myself."

"We likely to run into bullets?"

"Haven't so far," Gabriela says. "Haven't seen any survivors, either."

"Lots of bodies, though," Joe says. "Heard you made this mess."

"Joe," Gabriela says, warning in her voice.

"No, he's right," I say. "You drill down enough, you'll find me at the bottom of it." I can tell he's trying to goad me, but that's the wrong way to do it. He can't say anything about this that I haven't screamed at myself a thousand times already.

"You know what the death toll was?" he says. I can feel Gabriela tense. I am not in the mood for a dick-waggling contest.

"Which one?" I say. "Over a hundred thousand the night of the fires. About eight hundred just from the Vernon blast alone and another, what, five thousand from all the crap in the air before morning? Before I died, I think it was up to half a million county-wide. Couple hundred thousand in L.A. proper. I felt a lot of 'em. Like getting punched in the nuts a few thousand times an hour. I spent the night trying to stop it. Could have been a lot worse. How about you? What were you doing?"

"Gambling in Vegas," he says. "Made a couple thousand bucks on poker. I tend to unnerve the other players."

"Ya don't say." I can think of a lot of people who should never be raised from the dead, and this guy is definitely in the top hundred.

"Yeah. It was all over the radio out there. Fucked traffic out toward L.A. for almost a week and a half and even after that it was a mess."

"Sounds real inconvenient."

"Enh," Joe says. "I just hunkered down for a bit. They tried to arrange some relief effort out there, I think. Heard about it, but mostly I just hung out in the casinos."

"You're all heart," I say. "Speaking of which, how long does one of those hearts Gabriela gets for you last?"

"Couple weeks," he says. There's a dangerous tension in his voice. "I know a guy runs a mortuary in Vegas who could keep me supplied. But it never got that bad."

We head down Figueroa, pass by cement barriers that were put up before we hit the 10 Freeway. Most of them have been torn down. Probably by people thinking it's a good place to go looting. That's like those guys who try to rob houses that are tented for fumigation. They're not the brightest.

I can already see why everybody calls it the toxic zone. Within a block the air outside is green. More than half the streetlights are out and there are cars parked along the street, and some in the middle of it that Joe either drives around or, more often, simply over. It gets worse the further in we go. I can feel the magic of Gabriela's and my talismans working, which might be a problem. If I can feel the spells, what's to say Geppetto won't be able to?

"Huh," I say. "Couple weeks? And here I thought it was all about that stone in your chest."

Silence.

"Yeah," Gabriela says. "When we get back, Joe, I think we should have a conversation. But until then, how about we all talk about something else? Like what we're going to do when we get to campus."

"You said the place was the Doheny Library?" I say. "Any way we could get to it quietly? Like not driving a Sherman tank down the street?"

"You wanna walk, be my guest," Joe says. "I can let you out right here."

"Joe, enough," Gabriela says. "And you too, Eric. Jesus. It's like a fucking high school locker room in here."

"Hey, I showered," I say.

"And I don't sweat," says Joe.

"I'm gonna kill you both you don't—"

And then the gunfire starts.

Chapter 17

"I thought you said nobody was in here?" I yell over the sound of bullets pinging against the car door, embedding into the bulletproof windows.

"Clearly, I was wrong," Gabriela yells back. While we're arguing Joe stops the car, puts on the parking brake, and calmly steps out into the gunfire.

"The fuck is he doing?" I say.

"Ruining more of his clothes. Get ready to step out and start shooting." Even inside the car I can hear the meaty thwack of bullets punching into him, through him. He shrugs them off like they're a minor inconvenience at best. The man is a juggernaut. He pulls his pistol from his shoulder holster and returns fire. He takes the time to consider every shot, firing into the shadows and green haze.

Then a round hits him square in the forehead. The back of his skull explodes into fragments of blood, bone, and meat. Even then he doesn't fall over. A moment later the missing parts of his skull stitch themselves back together. It's like watching one of those high-speed films of mushrooms growing they show you in science class.

He hasn't stopped firing this whole time, though his aim gets a little erratic when he takes the headshot. A moment later he's grown his head back and it's like nothing ever happened except for the spray of blood and skull shrapnel behind him and covering the back of his clothes.

"That was disgusting," I say.

"You should see him when he starts rotting," Gabriela says.

"I really need to get a look at that stone in his chest."

"Later. Come on." We both get out at the same time using the car as cover. It's hard to see through the darkness and fog, but I can see a few silhouettes running from cover to cover. Joe hits one and instead of falling down it explodes in a spray of moist clay.

"Fighting our way through this isn't going to work. He'll just make more clay soldiers and keep sending them until one of them gets a lucky shot."

"Do you have a better idea?" Gabriela says.

"Actually, yeah." I hand her the Mini-14, fish out the spirit bottle, and put up a shield. I step out from behind the car, bullets punching into my shield, but none getting through. I raise the bottle high overhead.

"I hope nobody accidentally shoots me and makes me drop this bottle of somebody's soul. It might shatter and boy, wouldn't that just suck?" All of the clay mannequins stop shooting. Joe, of course, doesn't, which doesn't seem fair, but then I've never been a huge fan of fair. I do yell at him to stop only because I can't hear myself think.

"We're just here to talk," I say. "So, how about we have ourselves a nice little chat and nobody shoots anybody." One by one the mannequins crumble. Like with the kid, as each one disintegrates the remainder becomes more and more lifelike. Soon there's only one left, an older black man with a thin layer of gray hair on his head and a scraggly gray beard. It's so detailed that I'm not sure I would be able to tell the difference even in bright sunlight.

"All right," he says. "Let's talk."

"Nuh-uh," I say. "We want to talk to the guy in charge."

"I am the guy in charge."

"No, you're a puppet of the guy in charge," I say. "I want to talk to the real you, not some cheap knock-off."

"If you think I'm—" I toss the bottle from one hand to the other and make a show of almost dropping it. "Okay. Okay, fine. Yes. You know how to get to Doheny Library?"

"Yes," Gabriela says.

"All right. I'll see you on the second floor when you get here, right outside the library proper." The mannequin disintegrates.

"Where the hell is he getting all this clay?" Joe says.

"Probably just conjures it," I say. "Oh, nice trick with the head popping thing. Useful."

"It comes in handy."

"Can we still drive the car?" Gabriela says.

"Yeah," Joe says. "Take a lot more than magic clay bullets to take it down."

"Then let's get the hell out of here," she says. "I'd rather not be out in the open longer than I need to."

The rest of the drive to campus is quiet but grim. As we go deeper we start to see the bodies. They're surprisingly well preserved. I guess nothing lives in this toxic soup—no coyotes, dogs, bugs, bacteria.

I'm not sure if it's better for the families of the deceased if they get this shit cleared out or worse. Everybody talks about closure. Closure is reliving the same shit that you're trying to get closure on in the first place. Ripping open old wounds and letting them fester all over again.

There's a sort of relief in not knowing what happened to your husband, your daughter, your cat. You can make up whatever bullshit story you want to tell yourself. Trust me, they won't mind. They're dead.

But you suddenly pull hundreds of corpses that have barely begun to decompose and you not only get to relive their death, but now your beautiful story of them being in a better place falls to shit because, hey, here they are, like they just died yesterday.

Closure is bullshit.

There are surprisingly few ghosts. I would have expected wall-to-wall Echoes at the very least, but besides a few Wanderers a couple blocks away I don't see anything. Something on the other side caused this. There are things that will drive ghosts away, but this is bigger. Echoes and Haunts can't go anywhere. Whatever it is prevented them from being created in the first place. That's not a pleasant thought.

Joe pulls the Hummer onto the USC campus, jumping curbs, tearing across sidewalks. It's not like anybody's going to give him a ticket. Gabriela gives him directions and he parks right in front of the entrance to the library.

"Something's wrong," Gabriela says.

"Yeah, we're parked on a lawn sitting in the middle of a fucking tomb," I say. "Wait. Why is there a lawn?" We have not seen a single living thing this whole drive, but now here's a lawn of well-tended, healthy, green grass.

"It cuts off over there," Gabriela says. "Looks like it goes in a circle. A big one."

I was expecting Geppetto to be living in sewers or maintenance tunnels. But no, he's gone and created himself a little bubble of life in here. The only times I've seen this sort of thing were in the more powerful mage families where they go whole hog and create little bubble spaces that look like normal houses from the street, but once you cross a barrier it's a whole different world that they've created to spec for themselves. It's maybe not on par with those places, some of them are their own pocket universes, but this is heavy duty magic here.

"I just had a terrifying thought," I say.

"You and I have slightly different ideas about terrifying," says Gabriela.

"Oh, I think you'll agree with me. You feel any active spells? Any siphoning of the local pool? Anything?"

"No. What the fuck is this place?" she says.

"Let's go ask the man in charge."

Getting out of the car is its own revelation. Though the sky is that sickly green it is everywhere else, the air isn't. There's no poison fog, no acrid smell. Instead I can smell flowers.

"Is that jasmine?" I say.

"Smells like it," Gabriela says. "Joe?"

"Don't look at me. All I smell these days is fresh meat."

Interesting. "By fresh meat you mean—"

"People," he says. "Two or three hiding behind those trees. Somebody on the roof. Whole gaggle inside the building."

"You don't look like the sort of guy who drops gaggle into the middle of a sentence."

"Got one of those word-a-day calendars." He pulls a pack of cigarettes out of his jacket pocket, shakes one out, lights it with a disposable Bic. He catches me about to open my mouth and says, "Trust me, whatever you're about to say I've already heard it."

"Joe, can you stay with the car?" Gabriela says. "Our earpieces are keyed to each other's so we should be able to stay in communication, but with this much power anything might happen."

"Roger that," he says. "Hardware?"

"I say we leave it," I says. "I doubt it's going to do much here. And walking in with a bunch of guns isn't going to endear us to the locals." I hand him the Mini-14 and Gabriela gives him her shotgun. He places them onto the hood in easy reach. We both keep our pistols, though.

"Have fun, you two," he says, and leans against the car. His body goes still. Like a statue still. I wonder how often he forgets how to act human, how to interact with other people. I almost feel for the guy.

I've never been in the Doheny Library, but I got to tell you, this place could give cathedrals a run for their money. Everything is marble. I mean fucking everything. Floors, stairs, bannisters, walls, arched ceilings. Mission-style chandeliers hang from a ceiling made up of deep-set panels carved into geometric designs.

Every sound echoes. Every step we take is like a gunshot. There's no reason to be quiet. Whoever's here already knows we're here.

"Where did you find that guy?" I say, bringing my voice down to a whisper. The place has a weird reverence to it, a towering sanctuary of knowledge.

"Joe? I tried to have him surveilled. He beat the crap out of the boys I sent to cover him and demanded that they take him to see me. I don't think he killed any of them. Might have kneecapped one or two."

"Very direct."

"Yeah, Joe and subtlety aren't well acquainted. Anyway, Sandro Giavetti was in town and he had this stone, kind of like an opal. I think there used to be three or four others. You might have heard about it."

"No shit. Yeah, I've run across one. Some asshole thinking he can get immortality if he could just figure out how the damn thing worked. I take it Giavetti was doing the same?"

"And then some. Joe got caught in the middle. The raised corpse of a dead friend strangled him to death."

"Jesus. Whoever took him down must have been huge."

"Way he tells it the guy was a mountain. Anyway, he wakes up in an old sanitarium in the Santa Monica Mountains. Place was knee-deep in corpses of people Giavetti had already tried to raise. Joe's the only one who stuck."

"I have a feeling he regretted it."

"Yeah. Joe's kinda messed up."

"I meant Giavetti."

The stairs take us to a wide hall with a checkout counter, old card catalog rooms converted to miniature museum spaces to one side, a short hall leading to the reading room to the other. An open doorway behind the counter leads to whatever secret library chambers doors like that lead to.

A man and woman at the desk. She looks like she just got back from Burning Man. Blond hair in cornrows with beads woven into the strands, skin deeply tanned, tank top and shorts. Tattoos flow out from under her clothes down her arms and legs. I haven't met anyone quite as inked as I am, but she's close.

She sits cross-legged on the counter with a shotgun casually resting on the tops of her knees. Her energy is easy, calm, relaxed. I smell patchouli and pot and can only assume it's coming from her. I should see if she's got any extra. I could use a decent high.

The guy, on the other hand, is a different story. Where she's relaxed and chill, he's just about vibrating. Stocky guy, Indian maybe? Pakistani? He's wearing a button-down Oxford with the sleeves cuffed tight against his wrists, blue slacks, loafers. I didn't know people still wore loafers.

Wild eyes that don't quite track. Fear. Or he's on speed. Who knows? The important thing is that he's got a Glock pointed at us. The shaking of his hands has me ready to throw up a shield just in case.

"Your trigger discipline sucks," Gabriela says. It's like popping a bubble. The guy's energy shifts from scary dangerous to confused and bewildered.

"Right?" the woman says. "I keep telling him. Plus he flinches every time he pulls the trigger and stove-pipes the brass half the time. Hi, I'm Amanda. And my colleague here is Ramesh. You can put the gun down, Ramesh. Trust me, it won't do you any good."

He lowers the gun slowly, places it on the counter behind him. He's still shaking. "You are not my colleague," he says, fear and anger pulling at each other. He has a New England accent. Not quite posh and upper crust, but you can tell he's been raised with East Coast money. "You're all—" He cuts himself off and looks at the floor.

"Freaks, Ramesh. The word you're looking for is freaks. Though you occasionally call us abominations. Mister Carter here has a close and personal relationship with the dead, and Miz Cortez—or do you prefer La Bruja?"

"Gabriela's fine."

Amanda nods and continues on. "Gabriela is particularly adept at folk magic. More of a generalist, but a very good one."

"And you?" I say. "What do you do?"

"Oh, I like to party," she says. She holds her hand out and a couple of pills appear in her palm. "You need something, I can probably whip it up."

"How are you for Percocet?" I say.

"Hell, that's easy." She closes her hand and when she opens it there are half a dozen white pills in her palm. She closes her hand again, and when she re-opens it, they're gone.

"If I take a bullet later I might want to hit you up," I say. For years I was popping painkillers like they were Tic Tacs. Because, well, I had a lot of pain to kill. Whether that made me an addict or not seems to be a moot point now. This body hasn't broken anything, yet.

"I'm surprised to see anyone here," Gabriela says. "This place is a wasteland."

"Exactly," Amanda says. "Why else would we be here?"

"I'm a prisoner," Ramesh says. "You have to save me."

"Ramesh is not a prisoner," Amanda says. "Ramesh is a very freaked out TA who we're trying to keep alive despite his best efforts. We let him go out there, he dies."

"I will expose you all," he says. "I'll go to the police. The news. Reporters. I'll call my senator."

"And not necessarily from all the shit in the air, either," Amanda says. Yeah, no shit. Guys like him are the reasons mages are A) so secretive and B) so bloodthirsty. We don't like people threatening to go on national TV and "expose" us. Sure, he'd be seen as a crackpot, except to a handful the people he won't. And those are the ones we really don't want sniffing around.

"Why not just kill him?" I say. Ramesh steps back like I've slapped him. "Oh, come off it. You know they had to be thinking that at some point. Clearly they either like you, though I have no idea why, or they're worried about you."

"We don't kill him because we don't do that sort of thing," Amanda says.

"Don't you threaten me," Ramesh says. "I'll kill you for that." He reaches for the gun and his muscles freeze up. Whether it's Amanda or Gabriela who does it I can't say, but he is not happy.

"As I said," Amanda says. "We don't do that sort of thing."

"Based on how somebody's been trying to kill me since I woke up the other day, I'm gonna have to say I don't really buy that."

"It's complicated. Professor Holt can explain it better than I can."

"Holt?" Gabriela says. "I know that name. Philosophy professor, wasn't he?"

"Is," Amanda says. "Every quarter he tries to get at least one class that's all mages. Ethics of magic, what really are higher planes of existence, a search for meaning in a world with wizardry."

"There isn't any," I say.

"Leave it to the necromancer to be all gloom and doom," Amanda says. "You listen to the Cure a lot, don't you?"

"Okay, so everyone, most everyone, here is a mage from his class, right?" Gabriela says.

"Yeah. And a lot of others. He's turned into kind of a guru around here."

"That still doesn't explain why you're all still here. Somebody in this lot needs to know a teleportation spell, or something to keep you safe leaving the zone."

"We leave all the time," Amanda says. "Like I said—"

"Professor Holt can explain it better than you can," I finish.

"Exactly." She hops off the counter, gently pats Ramesh on the shoulder, and leads us into the reading room.

"What's Ramesh's deal?" I say.

"We picked him up wandering the zone about five months ago. We're not sure what he is, but he's definitely not human. That's why we're hanging onto him. Didn't even have a name, know where he was. But he acts like we're all servants and he's freaked out when we do magic around him."

"Keep a close eye on him," Gabriela says. "Where did you get that he's a TA named Ramesh?"

"Made it up," Amanda says. "Wouldn't stop screaming that he didn't know who he was until we told him. So, Ramesh the TA."

"Well, keep pushing that," Gabriela says. "Let us know if anything changes with him."

"Why?" Amanda says.

"Aw, shit," I say. "You don't think he's—"

"If he's who I think he is," Gabriela says, "it's in all our best interests that he not remember that. At least not for a little while."

"You're not going to tell me who he is, are you?" says Amanda.

"Safer this way," I say. Less chance of Pallavi finding out her worst enemy might be hanging out in the same city. "You might even want to tell him he's delusional and keep him on some heavy-duty sedatives. And for god's sake why does he have a gun?"

"It's not real," Amanda says. "I'll keep this whole 'mystery identity' in mind, but I'll have to check with Arthur."

"Arthur?"

"Sorry, Professor Holt."

The reading room is all checkerboard, marble floors. Tables, chairs, bookshelves. Half a dozen people are sitting scattered around the room like they're students. Why would there be students on an abandoned college campus?

"Tell me these people aren't taking classes," I say.

"Sort of. We're a collective of those who want to study our magic in solitude. None of us is a prisoner. Some of us let our families know we're okay, others have chosen to let them believe they're dead. We leave to get supplies, and sometimes one of us leaves and doesn't come back."

"The hell can you learn here that you can't learn out there?" Gabriela says.

"Restraint, Miz Cortez." The voice is like sandblasted velvet. Holt, the old man whose mannequins keep trying to kill me, steps into the room from a side door with a load of botany books in his arms. "Not every problem can be solved by fire and sword, you know."

"Professor," Gabriela says.

"I've heard a lot about you," he says, setting the books on a table to shake her hand. "Not all of it's good."

"I'm surprised any of it is good," she says.

"And Eric Carter." I've never heard a man's voice turn to ice so quickly. "A pity we had to meet under these, or any, circumstances."

"Is that a fancy way of saying you wish you'd killed me already?"

"Yes."

"I can work with that," I say.

Chapter 18

"Amanda," Holt says. "Be a dear and take these to Wells. She's doing potions work, and it would probably be a good idea if she knew what she was tossing into her brews before she poisons someone."

Amanda takes the books, gives me a wink and says, "See you around." She turns her attention to Holt and her face changes into something a lot less chipper. "Won't I, Arthur?"

Holt waves her away. "Of course. Provided talks go well."

"And if they don't you'll, what, kill us?" I say.

"I'll kick you off campus and not tell her until you're gone. She's your advocate, Mister Carter. The only one you have here, in fact. Satisfactory?"

"That works," Amanda says and leaves us.

Once she's out of earshot Holt says, "If I have to, I'll wait until you're safely away from my home and then I'll kill you, regardless of how Amanda or her grandfather feel about it."

"Her grandfather?" Gabriela says.

"Attila Werther," he says. "When the head of one of the most powerful mage families in the city demands something, one does try to accommodate." I watch Amanda walking away and . . . maybe she looks like Werther's granddaughter? I never met her. I only saw photos.

"Werther's granddaughter is dead," I say. "She was gunned down while dancing at a warehouse party. I saw the photos and video. Her head popped like a swollen scrote after a bad vasectomy."

"Oh, right," Gabriela says.

"What do you mean, 'Oh, right'?" I say. "You knew about this?"

"Yeah. You don't think the scion of the Werther family is going to die from a bullet, do you? She survived and went into hiding. Her grandfather's idea. Tried to smoke out the killer."

"You're fucking kidding me."

"She was here with me," Holt says. "Which is why she was here when Vernon exploded."

"You know you can't keep this place running indefinitely, right?" Gabriela says. "You've had a good run. I mean, shit, five years? I don't even know how you pulled that off. But five years of nobody even being able to set foot in here has got to people talking."

"How has nobody shut you down yet?" I say.

"Friends in high places," he says. "We're not going to be here for much longer for exactly those reasons. So far we've been able to explain it away with doctored weather data, but not everyone's buying it, of course. I have students looking for ways to remove the toxins completely and I'm in touch with mages around the world helping us with the spells. We don't want this crap blowing over the rest of L.A. and killing even more people. We're close. Half the battle in restoring this place is making it habitable.

"Now, can we get to the business at hand? May I have my son's soul, please?" He puts out his hand.

"Just like that?" I say. "No, I think we have a few more things to iron out before we get that far."

His scowl deepens the lines in his face until he looks a little like a gargoyle. "Then let's find a good place to talk."

———

He leads us to a little cafe that his class has been using as a kitchen. A few students are in there studying textbooks that no college I know of would have except in their rare book department, if they even knew they existed.

"It's like fucking Hogwarts in here," I say.

"Are you calling me Dumbledore?" Holt says.

"I was thinking more Voldemort, actually." We take a seat at a table in the back, Gabriela and I making sure we have clear sight lines and our backs aren't to any windows.

"You wanted to talk," Holt says. "So, talk."

"First of all, this is the real you? Not a mannequin? If I shoot you, you'll die?"

"Yes, this is the real me, and no, because I'm not stupid enough to let you in here without protecting myself."

Gabriela and I stumble over each other's words. "Why are you trying to kill me?" from me, and "Why do you want Darius's bottle so badly?" from her.

"One at a time, please."

"I'm not raising my hand to ask a question," I say.

"What are you planning to do with Darius's bottle?" Gabriela says.

"Hide it," he says. "Bury it in a place nobody would even think of looking for it. Drop it into an offshore oil well, let it take a ride on the next Mars Rover. Whatever keeps it from being found." He looks me in the eye and points at me. "And I'm trying to kill you because you want to open it."

"I think when you point at somebody like that

you're supposed to say, 'J'accuse,' or something," I say. "Where the hell are you getting the idea that I want to open it?"

"Why else would you come back?"

"I—What? You think I brought myself back? Do you not get how this works? You know that death is usually a one-way ticket, right?"

"You're a necromancer," he says.

"And up until the other day I was a dead necromancer. I didn't even have a body. Hell, I wasn't even me."

"He got the idea because he jumps to conclusions based on prejudice and incomplete information," Amanda says as she enters the door. "It's kind of a habit."

"Amanda—" Holt says.

"No, Arthur. All I did was tell you Carter was back and I thought it might have something to do with the bottle. The rest is all you. I tried to tell you several times, but you refused to listen."

"Professor Holt," Gabriela says, "Eric didn't bring himself back from the dead. I did. He doesn't want to open the bottle either."

"Yeah, that's her idea. I want to lock that fucker up tighter than a nun's asshole. She wants to pop the cork."

Holt stares at her. "Do you understand how dangerous that abomination is?" Whenever anyone says the word "abomination" the hairs on the back of my neck pop up and start to take notice. I wonder if that's where Ramesh is getting it.

"Yes," I say, "and because in a couple days, with or without my help, those wards are going to disintegrate. And if we can't figure out somewhere else to put him before that happens, he's going to get free. I don't know what he's going to do, but he's been stuck in there for the last eight thousand years and I bet he's got a shit list a mile long of people he'd love to pay a visit."

"How is that possible?" Holt says, confused. I

know that lost look. You think you know all the angles. You think you know exactly what's going on, and then BAM, you get a truth bullet right in the forehead and you know just how wrong you fucking are.

"Darius put some spells on the bottle that we think have degraded the original wards," Gabriela says.

"Booby traps," I say. "Really nasty ones. I can take the wards off the bottle just fine, but if I try to do anything else to them, like tightening them up, adding anything, whatever, things are gonna go to shit fast."

"Which is why we're here," Gabriela says. "We thought since you seem to be so interested in this problem that maybe you knew about the failing wards and had a plan in place to take care of it. Like another bottle, anything."

Holt slumps in his seat. "This isn't possible," he says. "How could I be so stupid? So blind?"

"You're angry," Amanda says, voice gentle. "All this is not his fault."

"Have you tried therapy? Maybe some Zoloft? A good anti-psychotic? Maybe just pull your head out of your ass?" I say, my voice oh-so-not-gentle.

"Eric," Gabriela says. "Cut him some slack."

"No," I say. "Fuck him. I killed three of his people yesterday who came for me. Only one of them was a mage. The other two were normals who drew the short straw. And he watched them safe through the eyes of his little mannequin. That doesn't get you slack."

"They weren't supposed to die," Holt says.

"Oh, but it was okay for them to kill me."

"You were already dead," he says. He slams his palms on the tabletop. "You were dead and you were supposed to stay dead. Those men— I made a mistake, and I take full responsibility for that. I regret each and every one of those deaths."

"Nice rationalization," I say. "That help you sleep at night?"

"Not particularly," he says. "What's your rationalization for the thousands you murdered?"

"You mean the ones Quetzalcoatl murdered? You're getting your gods mixed up, Professor."

"Why don't we all take a step back," Gabriela says, her voice calm, reasonable. "We came here to talk to you about the bottle. And also to give back something you lost."

"Had stolen," Holt says. By this time the cafe's empty except for the four of us. The handful of students who were in there have all packed up and left.

"You know the kid's terrified of you, right?" I say.

"What?"

"The kid. The one who attacked me. He was doing it to impress you. And when he got his ass handed to him he didn't give you up. And not out of loyalty. He was scared of what you would do to him."

"That's not true," Holt says, but there's doubt in his voice.

"He thought I was going to eat his soul, and he still wouldn't give you up. Out of fear. So tell me, Professor, why's the boy so scared of you?"

"Eric," Gabriela says. "Now is not the time."

"He's my son," Holt says. "I—I might run him a little harder than some of the other students, but—"

"Everybody on this campus is at least eighteen, twenty years old? How old's your boy? Thirteen? Fourteen? Sure sounded like it."

"Eric—"

"No. That kid's terrified of his father. I've heard that sort of tone in a kid's voice, only they were all ghosts who were scared of what their parents would do to them until they went and did it. I'm not handing him over to somebody who's just going to turn around and give him a beating."

Holt closes his eyes. I can feel the rage coming off of him, but a sadness, too. "I just want him to be okay."

It's a true statement, I can tell that. But his idea of okay may not be the kid's, and his idea of motivation probably involves a lot of yelling. Maybe some hitting, too.

"If I give this back to you," I say, "what are you going to do to him? Are you gonna punish him for pushing himself too hard? For getting stuck in this situation? For doing it to make you proud? You gonna 'teach him a lesson'?"

"No. I would never— You've heard the phrase 'tough love'?" Holt says. "That's what I was taught. And what I've been trying to teach Jordan. I think I've gone harder on him since his mother died." I have a sinking feeling in the pit of my stomach. I know where this is going. And it's nowhere good.

"She died in the Vernon blast," I say.

"She did," Holt says. "She was a regulatory inspector for the EPA. She'd been at some chemical plant finishing some paperwork and was heading over here to pick up Jordan and me."

It would be nice if this really wasn't all my fault. But everything, the blast, the fires, Quetzalcoatl's attack, and yes, Holt's wife, comes down to me. I take out the spirit bottle and place it in front of him.

"Take it to him and open it up. The closer the better. Maybe even make him drink it."

Holt takes it. "If you're expecting thanks for giving me back my boy after you kidnapped him, don't. This doesn't change anything between us."

"Didn't think it would," I say. "But I'm going to ask for one thing and demand another. Could you please cut down on the murder attempts until after we get this bottle problem solved?"

"Agreed," he says. "Reluctantly, but agreed. The other?"

"If you so much as lay a finger on that kid I will come for your fucking head. You. No one else. There won't be any collateral damage because I'll make sure you're in a place nobody can get to and then I'll make you hurt. For a really, really long time. Are we clear?"

"Are you threatening me?"

"No," I say. "I'm not a fan of threats, but I really do try to keep my promises. Are. We. Clear?"

"We are."

"You had no other plans? Ideas?" Gabriela says, pulling the train back onto the tracks. "Anything?"

Holt shakes his head. "I didn't even want anyone here to touch it but me. We've got a couple hundred mages here. Some teachers, mostly students. If they got their hands on it, they'd tinker with it. So, get rid of the bottle, get rid of the only person who could open it. Temptation gone."

Or they'd kill each other trying to get it for themselves. The possibility of power can drive even the most well-meaning people to do horrible things.

"That's like not putting the Tree of Knowledge in Eden in the first place. There's always something else to be tempted by," Gabriela says. "Even if the bottle did stay sealed up, somebody would have found it eventually. It might not be for a couple hundred years, but somebody would still find it. And Darius would keep trying to find another way to get out."

"I'm getting that," he says.

"So, we're pretty much right where we started," Gabriela says.

"I dunno. I think the Professor not trying to murder me for a couple of days is an improvement."

"Debatable," Gabriela says. "We need to go. Thanks for your time, Professor Holt. If you think of anything, let us know."

———

"Quite the little Harry Potter setup he's got going on here," I say as we're heading back to the car, Amanda on our heels. "I'm surprised you didn't hear about it."

"Life's moved on," Gabriela says. "I'm not in the loop anymore. But Amanda here seems to be."

"I try to be," Amanda says, coming across the lawn to us.

"Did you know he didn't have a plan?" Gabriela asks.

"He kept telling us he did. But wouldn't say what it was, like it was some state secret. I wasn't buying it. It felt too much like that flowchart, you know? Get bottle, lots of question marks, profit. So, what's your plan?"

"We don't have one either. We were hoping he had one," I say.

"What does your grandfather think of all this?" I say. "And come to think of it, why are you all chummy with us? Last time I saw him he wasn't exactly hostile, but damn near."

"Arthur told you?" Amanda says. "Kind of surprised. Keeps telling me I'm nobody special when I'm in here. I figured he'd keep that to himself. Arthur's kind of a weird guy. Losing his wife really fucked him up. He hasn't left campus since it happened except to hit the Natural History Museum down the street near the beginning. There was some artifact they had that he used to create the shield around this part of the school."

"And he's kept his kid in here with him the whole time?" Gabriela says.

"Yep. We don't see him much. Mostly he keeps him in Widney."

"Where?" I say.

"Widney Alumni House over on Figueroa," Gabriela says. "Just across the lawn from the library. First building built for the school. So he basically hides the kid in the attic like it's a Brontë novel."

"Better than a V. C. Andrews novel," I say. "So, you're about to tell us about your grandfather."

"First, he's not my grandfather," Amanda says, "he's my dad. But it's easier to let people believe that because he looks the part. He's about two hundred years old. The rest of the Werthers live in Europe waiting for him to die so they can swoop in and take everything. But they'd have to kill me first, since I'm the heir. It's complicated. I move around a lot.

"As to the bottle, he thinks that if Darius gets out, we're all fucked. He's got a list of all the known things that Darius has done under different masters. It's a long list, and an ugly one. Small things to huge."

"But that doesn't mean he's going to actually do anything," Gabriela says.

"Except for the bit where a captured djinn can be commanded, but they have to agree to do it. Darius didn't have to do any of those things. He wanted to."

"Well, I'm sold," I say. "We gotta come up with something."

"What about the spirit jar that you had Quetzal-coatl trapped in?" Gabriela says.

"I found some others, but I don't think they'll work," I say. "The one that looked the most promising turned out to actually be Darius's bottle. But we can check. Ledger's back at the hotel."

"Which hotel are you staying at?" Amanda says.

"All over, but I have a room at the Ambassador." They both stare at me.

"The Ambassador," Amanda says. "The hotel that got torn down so they could make a school?"

"The very one," I say. "It's a ghost. I've got a deal with it for a room up on the fourth floor."

"The hotel is a ghost? The whole thing?"

"Yeah, it's a trip."

"Why didn't I know about this?" Gabriela says.

"Probably because I didn't tell you. Come on, Gabriela, what we don't know of each other could fill the Grand Canyon."

"Fair. I would like to see it, though."

"I'm not sure how it would react," I say. "But one way to find out."

"Much as I'd love to join," Amanda says, "and I would really love to join, I'm going to go see how Arthur and his son are doing." She waves at us and peels off into another direction. Ahead of us Joe still stands stock still at the Hummer.

"School," Gabriela says. "The Ambassador was torn down and they built a school?"

"Yeah. It's a fucking crime against nature."

"Is this the same school you died at?"

"Unless you hauled me to some other school while I was still breathing, yeah."

"That was a rough time," she says.

"How do you think I felt about it?"

"I was thinking after," she says. "We have to go there to get into the hotel?"

"They're superimposed, yeah. One right on top of the other. That a problem?"

"Why would you say that?"

"You said—ya know, never mind. Shall we?"

"I'm driving," Gabriela says.

Chapter 19

Gabriela stays in the car with Joe as I get out and head over to a basketball court that's just outside the school gate, but still on the Ambassador's grounds. A lot easier than trying to run through a sea of Wanderers to get through a warded school gate.

I flip to the other side, and instead of the howling void and dim shades of blacks and blues, I'm on a nicely paved side road leading to a shed. Probably where it keeps all of the tools for the yard work. Does it do yard work? It certainly doesn't need to, but I have a feeling that it does anyway.

One of these days I should ask it why. Why recreate this? Or is it not all a recreation? Maybe some of this is original work, and it's all a ghost equivalent of a journal. Another time, maybe.

From here I can see the hotel proper. People are driving up, handing their cars over to valets and strolling leisurely into the hotel. They're dressed to the nines. Elegant dresses, smart tuxedos. Every one of them could be a movie star, there are no ugly people here. There are also nothing but white people. I hadn't really noticed that before. If it's a recreation of its glory days I can see why it would do that. The place was built in 1921 and closed down in '89. Very few people who came here wouldn't be white, and then mostly for the Cocoanut Grove nightclub. Still, it feels a little jarring.

"Excuse me," I say. I know the hotel can hear me. Everything I can see is part of it.

"Yes, sir," the bellhop says behind me. I've gotten used to it doing shit like that so I'm not surprised. I just calmly turn around so I can see him. "Is there anything I can do for you?"

I'm about to ask about Gabriela but then I remember Hank. "I ran into Hank outside the hotel. Are you all right? Did he break out? Did you let him go?"

"He was released. I received a telephone call from his lawyer, name of Darius. He explained that I was holding his client against his will. As that was the case, I said truthfully that I was, and hung up on him."

"Darius faked being an attorney?"

"I think he believed I might be more easily fooled, being a ghost and all," the bellhop says. "When he called back he asked for me to release him, and so we negotiated." Negotiated? What does the ghost of a hotel want? I look around for some clue. The people, the cars, all the activity. Then it comes to me.

"Memories," I say. "He offered you memories." Ghosts hunger for life, anything that will remind them what it was like to be alive. They'll tear chunks off your soul for a light snack. But a ghost like the Ambassador doesn't need that. It remembers what it is just fine. The non-stop puppet shows make sense now. It tells itself stories so it doesn't forget who it is.

"Quite so, sir. New memories help me have a better understanding of the world outside, and without them things can get a little stale. He made an offer, and I have to say he came through on his end of the deal."

Of course. What happens when it's played the same story over and over and over again? Or the same variant. Or using the same characters. After a while it's going to need new material. It's going to need memories.

The pit of my stomach turns as I realize what probably happened. I've run into a thing or two that ate memories. The way they got them involved tearing a soul apart and eating the pieces.

"How did he deliver them?"

"They all arrived through a door. One every minute or so. Most of them were very surprised and didn't struggle, so it didn't take long. Quite a few of them were looking at thin, glass bricks they held in their hands and didn't notice anything. Do you know what those are?"

"Smartphones," I say. "Little computers." I'm really having a hard time with this. There are questions I need to ask that I don't want to ask.

"I will remember that should I run into them again. Smartphones. Little computers. Imagine that."

"How—" I so don't want to know this. "How many souls did you negotiate for?"

"Five hundred. I know how easy it is to be taken in by confidence men. I made sure to count. But don't you worry, sir. Five hundred on the nose."

I can see just how it happened. Darius creates five hundred doors across as far as he can reach. Doors people don't notice, or mistake for other doors. He puts the doors in their path and they're so preoccupied they never notice. Then, before they can be in his domain for more than a blink of an eye, he opens another door right in front of them. Right to where the hotel is waiting for them.

I knew that the ghost of the Ambassador hotel was not a benign thing. No ghost is. They're hungry. Always hungry. Always eating whatever they can find.

But where a lot of ghosts are hunters, even if they're bad hunters, the Ambassador is a spider at the center of a giant web, waiting for the stray fool who might come by and make a decent snack. Ghosts mostly, I

assume. Would explain why no Wanderers ever cross
onto the Ambassador's land.

When my grandfather negotiated the room here,
he paid in blood. The Ambassador didn't say whose
blood, and I didn't want to know. But it would have
had to be a lot of it because the hotel has told me that
the room is my family's for decades to come.

"My grandfather," I say. "How did he pay for the
room?"

"Much the same way," the bellhop says. "I got a lot
of memories, but I needed the life more. Things were
beginning to fade. To be honest, he saved me. I'll always be grateful for that."

"That must have taken a lot of souls."

"Oh, thousands," the bellhop says. "Over the course
of a couple of years. I could never figure out how to
remove all the shells, though."

Shells? Oh, Jesus. "You mean the bodies?"

"Quite so. They don't decompose over here very
well, you know."

"No, they don't." That's because all of the things that
cause decomposition have all their energy sucked out.
The very environment will do it. Over time a corpse
will disintegrate, but there's usually not much left once
a ghost gets hold of one—it turns into a feeding frenzy.
Any ghosts that can take a bite will. But here it's just
the hotel. The Ambassador is the one and only predator in these waters.

Most of the bodies could very well be intact. Which
means—

"Where are they?" I say.

"Just nearby," the bellhop says, and points to the
shed behind me. It's a big building, but it would never
hold a hundred corpses, much less five hundred. But
this isn't regular space. "Would you like to see?"

No. No, I wouldn't. I so very much fucking would
not like to see the five hundred corpses that you just

fed on and possibly all the thousands of corpses that my grandfather got for you like he was some sort of serial killer's victim broker.

"I would," I say, instead.

We walk over to the shed, which opens just before we get there. I can see well enough inside from out here. The inside is far larger than the outside suggests. Two, maybe three times as much volume. There's a lip of cement that goes around the inside of the building, past which there is a pit.

A very large, very full pit. I cannot count the number of bodies just on the top. They're fresh. No smell of rot. Men, women, some children in there. Those on the top layer are all dressed in modern clothes. Some still clutch their phones. Dead eyes grayed over and staring at nothing. Others, because the space is so cavernous that five hundred bodies aren't going to cover the whole thing, look to be wearing clothes more from the fifties.

And there are the bodies under the bodies. And under those bodies, and down and down and down. The sheer immensity of this is mind-boggling. And my grandfather brought them all here. Miriam told me he had a problem with necromancers after fighting some real horror shows in the war. Was she telling the truth? This does not look like the work of someone who's afraid of a little necromancy.

"How long have you been aware?" I say. "Conscious, I mean."

"Some time in the late thirties, I believe," the bellhop says. "I was constructed in 1921, and it wasn't long after that." There are a lot older buildings, more famous buildings in L.A. than the Ambassador. So, why did it become conscious and not, say, the Bradbury Building?

"My grandfather came to you, what, late forties? After the war?"

"Definitely after the war. I think the fifties. I was tied to the earthbound hotel until it was torn down, even though it had stopped being used a long time before then."

"Can you feel the bodies? I mean, sense them?"

"Sometimes. Like I imagine having a pebble in one's shoe would feel. It doesn't hurt, it's barely noticeable. I think there's something I should do with all of them, but I don't really know what. It's not too much of a problem. Space here isn't really an issue, but sometimes it annoys."

"I can see how it would feel that way." Annoys. If anything can get across how alien the Ambassador is, it's that. All those corpses left over from all those devoured souls and isn't it just a travesty that there's no one to clean them up?

I push out any lingering horror out of my mind and plaster a smile on my face. "Well, I'm glad you got what you needed from Darius. Got the better end of the bargain, I'd say. Hank was an asshole."

"Too true. Was there anything else you needed, sir?"

To run away and never come back? I never trusted the hotel completely, but I started to think of it as a person, and not the ghost that it is. I was beginning to forget that regardless of what deals have been made with it, it's a predator. I will never forget that again.

"As a matter of fact," I say. "I have a friend I'd like to bring across."

"Family?" the bellhop says. "The stipulation is quite clear that only the Carter family and partners of members of the Carter family are allowed entrance."

That's awfully specific. Grandpa didn't want anybody else coming in. Makes sense. He locked away a treasure everyone was trying to get hold of. How better than to set an enormous ghost as a guardian.

"Yes," I say. "She's my partner. We're together."

Glad I asked. Who knows what the hell might have happened if the Ambassador tried to eat Gabriela's soul. I honestly don't know who I'd put money on.

"Then by all means, sir." He flips one gloved hand over and presents me with a key identical to the one I have to get into the room. "Very happy to accommodate guests in any way that we can. I take it the lady will be entering at this spot when you bring her?"

"Uh, yeah. Here will be fine. Maybe a little further away from the shed, though."

"Excellent," the bellhop says. "I'll have a car waiting nearby to take you to the hotel when you return." I'm so shaken that I almost forget to tip the bellhop. I give him a fifty. If I don't play my part in his puppet show, will he start to think differently about me? Will I be food?

I flip over to the other side, shaken, sick. I hold myself up against a basketball pole. Gabriela is sitting a few feet away on a bench, Joe's still in the Hummer. She hurries over to me.

"You don't look too good," she says. "What happened?"

I tell her about Darius's deal with the Ambassador. What it did, how it did it. If Darius is willing to sacrifice five hundred strangers just to get the likes of Hank released, how far would he go for something really important?

"I get the feeling there's more going on here," she says.

"There's a mass grave over there where the Ambassador has put the five hundred bodies that were left over. He showed it to me."

"Ugh. How did it smell?"

"It didn't. They're not rotting. Nothing lives over there very long, not even bacteria, and I guess stomach acid doesn't work very well, or calcium leeches, fuck,

I don't know. Point is they're sitting there, as are the thousands of bodies that they were dumped on top of. Bodies of people my grandfather lured over there and fed to the Ambassador to secure that hotel room."

Gabriela doesn't say anything as she processes this. "If we go over, are we in danger?"

"We shouldn't be. You're on the invite list now, and if it's one thing the Ambassador seems to do is keep its word. I don't know why it never occurred to me that the hotel was like this. Of course it's like this. It's a ghost. Every ghost is like this. It's just smarter and larger than any other ghost I've run into." I lower myself to the ground and sit against the basketball pole.

"It's an ugly world, Eric. You know this."

"I do. It just didn't occur to me that maybe my grandfather had led thousands of people to their permanent deaths all so he could get a fucking hotel room. That pit is huge. I don't know how far it goes down. All those corpses piled up like chicken wings at a sports bar during the Super Bowl. It's just a little more than I was expecting. Gimme a second. I'll be fine."

"What do you want to do?"

"Need to go back, get into the room. There's got to be something in that ledger that can help."

"You're okay to go in there?"

"Yeah. I'm just—" I'm about to say "annoyed," but after the Ambassador's talk about being annoyed at the corpses in the shed, I think the word's in the same league as "moist" now. I don't even want to think it. "I'm pissed off at myself. I swim with sharks. I started to forget that with the Ambassador." I stand up, brush dirt off my pants. Take a deep breath. "You know, you don't have to come."

"And miss the Hotel of Horrors? Come on, I lived in a murder hotel with a bunch of vampires. This is like a two-for-one special. I'll feel right at home."

"All right. Let's go. And remember, as far as the hotel's concerned, we're together."

"Does this mean we're going steady?" she says.

"So long as you'll go to the prom with me."

"I better have one hell of a corsage."

"You okay if it's made of rat bones and bullet casings?"

"I wouldn't have it any other way." She slides her arm through the crook of my elbow and I slide us both over to the other side.

"Holy shit," Gabriela says. "This is all the hotel?"

"Far as you can see." The hotel is lit up like it always is. There's an addition to the front of the hotel, a pair of searchlights scanning the sky like we're at some gala premier.

"This is amazing."

"And bloodthirsty."

"Come on, Eric, beautiful and dangerous is nothing new." She's right. It is beautiful. The place is a glowing jewel. Even though I know what it is and where we are it's still easy to believe that we're at the real hotel, that it's some time just after the War and all the beautiful people want to celebrate.

"Even has the Cocoanut Grove," she says. "Ever been?"

"No. Been invited a couple times."

"By the hotel?"

"By one of the hotel's . . . actors." I point to my ear and she nods. Anything we say here the Ambassador is going to hear. Antagonizing the hotel by calling the actors puppets out loud might not be the greatest idea.

"Got it. Should check it out some time. So, where's the room?"

"Hello, madam," the bellhop says behind us. We turn and he's holding open the backseat door of a white Rolls Royce. "It's a bit of a walk to the hotel proper. I've arranged for transportation."

"That's very kind of you," Gabriela says, not missing a beat. "Thank you very much." Without batting an eye she slides into the back seat of the car.

"Appreciate the pick-up," I say.

"Can't leave guests simply stranded out here," the bellhop says. "I have a reputation to uphold."

The drive is short. Honestly, we could have walked it easily enough, but if the hotel wants to drive us, the hotel can drive us.

"What's the occasion for the searchlights, if you don't mind my asking?" she says.

"You, of course," the bellhop says. "It's not often that I get to welcome a new addition to the Carter fold. Welcome, Miss—I'm so sorry, I didn't catch your name." Shit. I told it she was my partner. What if it thinks she's my wife? What it will it do if we don't share the same name? Does it hold on to values from the sixties? Does it care?

"Gabriela Cortez," she says. "I'm honored."

"Think nothing of it, Miss. If anyone should be honored, it should be me. I know Mister Carter doesn't like to make a fuss, but I'll take any excuse to pull out all the stops."

The car pulls up to the hotel and another identical bellhop opens the door for us. Gabriela freezes in surprise for a nanosecond and then rolls with it. I get out of the car after her, and my surprise lasts just a touch longer.

Hotel guests, staff, reporters snapping photos are all gathered around the entrance with a red carpet leading up the steps. Gabriela slaps a smile on her face and waves to the crowd and they eat it up like she's a fucking Disney princess, jeans and the t-shirt that says JUST FUCKING DIE ALREADY notwithstanding. The applause is like thunder.

I follow, try to keep a smile on my face, stomach turning just a little bit as I recognize half a dozen faces in the crowd. I just saw them, in fact, lying in a pit piled together like trash bags in a dumpster.

"Is there anything we can do for you, sir, ma'am?" the bellhop says once we reach the lobby.

"I am exhausted," Gabriela says. "So much attention has me absolutely giddy. Eric, honey, I think I'd like to just go straight to the room and have a lie down."

"It has been a long day," I say. "I think we're good for now. But thanks." I tip the bellhop a couple hundred dollar bills.

"Thank you so much, sir. Have a pleasant stay." It turns around and walks away.

"We're on the fourth floor," I say. The elevator closest to us opens with a ding. And there's another identical bellhop standing at the lever. I don't remember it having a lever before. I wonder if the hotel changes its design based on what era it wants it to be.

"Fourth floor. Right away, sir." We step in and head up. I've never had this much attention from the hotel before. I can't tell if this is a good thing or a bad thing. After the revelation of the consumed souls I don't know what to think right now.

Finally the bellhop leaves us to go to the room. I start to hand Gabriela the key that the bellhop gave me for her but stop. This is a physical key. I felt it on the living side. That shouldn't be possible. Nothing here should be real, or at least not physical. So how did it come over with me?

"Problem?" I tell her what I'm thinking as I give her the key. "Mysteries within mysteries, I guess. Shall we?"

"Do the honors," I say. Gabriela opens the door, and once we're inside it takes everything I've got not to slam it closed and pile the furniture up against it.

Chapter 20

"Jesus fucking Christ," Gabriela says, falling into one of the leather club chairs. "Did you get the feeling that was a test? I sure as hell felt like it was a test."

"Yeah," I say. "But for what?"

"We're alive, so I guess we passed?" She looks around the suite. "Your grandfather built this place? This is one sweet dimensional pocket. He liked the forties, I see."

"Kind of ironic, really, considering how much the war fucked him up."

"Maybe trying to heal?"

"Maybe. But if that's the case he did a pretty shitty job of it if all those corpses are any indication. He didn't build this all on his own. I don't know who helped him. Seems like a lot of effort for a bachelor pad, or even a safe house."

"What I want to know is do you have any booze in this place?" she says. "I think you said something about a rain check on that drink? After that, I really need a drink."

"As a matter of fact, I do. Don't ask me where it comes from, but it's real, it's good, and it will get you just as shitfaced as anything on the other side. What's your poison?"

"Oh, something that fits the era. Can you make a gimlet?"

"Let me check." I open the liquor cabinet. And what do you know: "I got gin. I got limes. I don't remember there being limes in here before." I grab a shaker, get ice from the always-filled ice bucket, and start pouring.

"Maybe you've just never made a gimlet before." I pour her drink into a highball and hand it to her.

"I tend to stick with rye straight out of the bottle. Sometimes I'll use a funnel, or maybe a straw." I pour some rye into a tumbler and sit down on the loveseat across from her. "But you'll see I'm using a glass. Because I am classy as fuck."

"To being classy as fuck," she says and we clink our glasses together.

"Did you actually say you were 'giddy' out there?" I say.

"I did. It seemed the right thing to say."

"That sounded really weird coming out of you," I say. "So did calling me honey. Please don't do that again."

"I have hidden depths." She takes a sip of her drink. "And no promises. Huh. This isn't bad. If this necromancy thing doesn't work out you could always moonlight as a bartender."

"I'd just spit in people's drinks if they pissed me off."

"See, you're a natural."

Neither of us talk for a long time. It's nice to take in the quiet. No sounds of traffic, no shrieking of the panicked dead, nothing grabbing my attention as Mictlantecuhtli looking for guidance among the dead, nobody trying to shoot me. For a few minutes I can just stop moving.

"I think this is the first time we've had a drink together when neither one of us was bleeding," Gabriela says. "That's pretty fucked up."

"Are we re-examining our life choices now? Regrets? 'Cause I got myself a looong list."

"I don't know," she says. "Every time I turn around there's some new fucking tragedy happening. There are more supernatural homeless than I can help. Way more human homeless. The mages do fuck-all about it. The government does fuck-all about it. Nobody wants homeless in their neighborhood, human or not. Why am I even doing this anymore? Maybe we should let Darius out. Let him go hog wild, burn everything to the ground."

"I know what your problem is," I say.

"If you say I need to get laid, I will shoot you."

"I'm not going anywhere near that. The problem is you give too many fucks. Wait. That came out wrong. You care too much."

She laughs. "What's that you keep telling me?" she says. "Stones and glass houses?"

"What? I'm a heartless bastard. Everyone knows that."

"You're a bastard, that's for sure."

"What are we doing wrong?" I say. "I mean, we can't be the only people who give a fuck about what's going to happen when Darius gets out. Can we?"

"Pour me another," she says, handing me her glass. "Just gin and ice. Or just gin. Or a little ice and a lot of gin. Fuck, I don't care. Here's what I think. There are two kinds of people." I give her a new glass and she starts in on it right away.

"What, people who care and people who don't?" I refill my glass of rye, maybe put a little too much into it, and throw it back like it's a shot. Miraculously, I don't choke. I fill the glass again.

"Nope," she says. "People who don't know, and

people who don't want to deal with it. The people
who don't know, well, they don't know. How fucked
up is everything? They haven't a clue. They don't even
know that there's a thing that can be fucked up in the
first place. The world's really fucking complicated.
They're not stupid, just ignorant."

"Yeah, but there are still a lot of stupid people out
there," I say.

"Okay, ignorant and sometimes—most times stupid."

"And the people who don't want to deal with it?"
I say.

"Sometimes they're stupid and ignorant, too. But
the ones that really matter are the ones catching the
last plane out before the revolutionaries storm the air-
port. They're the ones who build bunkers and hope the
barbarians can't breach their gates. They're the ones
who expect, who know, that people like us are going to
fix the problem."

"That's three types of people," I say.

"What?" she says. "Oh. Right. Three types. Gimme
a refill."

"You sure about that?" I say as I take her glass.

"I'm a very functional drunk," she says. "You should
have another, too. Oh, never mind." I've already poured
for both of us and given her glass back.

"The ones who don't want to deal with it aren't
waiting for people like us to clean up the problem," I
say. "They're looking for people who have their shit
together to clean up the problem. I don't know about
you, but I don't think there's a goddamn thing I hav-
en't tried to fix that didn't fuck something else worse
than before. If those people were smart, they wouldn't
let me anywhere near a goddamn problem."

"Oh, come on," she says. "You're not that bad."

"Name one thing."

"There's . . . I mean." She snaps her fingers. "You

didn't let me die when the crazy sicaria stabbed me in that factory."

"But I let her get away," I say.

"I'm alive, she's dead. I call that a win."

"And what happened because she got away?"

"Okay, yeah, Vernon exploding was bad. Fine. You want to be a shit magnet, be a shit magnet."

"Thank you," I say. "What the hell are we doing here, again?"

"I'm thinking of riding out the apocalypse if the booze keeps coming."

"Ah, right. Finding some way out of this shitshow." I stand up and immediately sit down again. "I probably should have eaten something today. I think I might be drunk."

"I got a spell can fix that."

"I wasn't complaining," I say, "just commenting. How are you doing?"

"Same," she says. "Where's this magic ledger of yours?"

"Rolltop desk." She stands, centers herself with that look on her face you see on drunks when they're trying not to act drunk.

Gabriela slides open the desk and pulls out the ledger. Two rings, each with a different colored stone, one red and one blue, fall out of the desk along with it. "What are these?" she says, picking up one of the rings.

"Remember that portal, teleportation, whatever-you-call-it ring I used to get to the top of the building in Skid Row?"

"Yeah. Handy."

"There's more than one. They're both mated to each other. Besides teleporting to wherever, whoever has one can open a portal to where the other one is. That's how Hank got in here. I managed to snag his ring when he was beating the crap out of me in the hallway outside, flipped over to the living side and stranded him here."

"And then died," she says.

"Well, yeah, that too."

"I'm taking one of these," she says. "I like the red one."

"Knock yourself out," I say.

"What's the range?"

"Not sure, but I think not very far. I was able to go from the bottom floor to the top of the building, but I doubt I could use it to get past traffic down the 405."

"You haven't tried?"

"When? I've been dead this whole time."

"Point." She tosses me the second ring. I slide it into my pocket. Feels weird not having a ring on my finger, but I can tell it'll feel even weirder if it's not my wedding ring.

She sets the ledger down on the coffee table, sits next to me on the loveseat, and opens it up. It bursts open like a flower blooming. "Okay, what the hell?"

"There are more pages inside than there should be," I say. "I think it grows to accommodate anything new that gets written down."

"There are a lot of entries here. Is there an index?"

"Wouldn't that be handy?" I say. "No. And the organization is weird. I have no idea if everything in the book is actually everything in the warehouses."

"Warehouses, plural?"

"Well, storage units. Might as well be warehouses. I've only been in one of them, but there's at least one more. Plus property scattered across the city. My parents owned a lot of shit."

"You're landed gentry," she says. "Should I call you m'lord?"

"It sounds better than 'hey, asshole,'" I say.

"M'lord Asshole. Has a nice ring to it." She flips

through pages and I can see the dawning realization of just how big a mess this thing is.

"This thing is a librarian's nightmare," she says. "Some of these items sound just plain stupid. An umbrella that changes color and style? That's it? That's all it does? And what about this one. 'Boxer's mouth guard—1923—One punch will instantly shatter the teeth of whoever is unfortunate enough to use it.' Who the hell would use it?"

"There's a lot of that kind of thing in there. Magical? Absolutely? Useless? The best ones don't even tell you what they do. Here." I flip a few pages until I find an entry from the 1920s and point it out.

"'Bird cage, brass: Do not open'," Gabriela says. "That's it?"

"Yep."

"Why?"

"You really want to find out?"

"Yes," she says.

"Me too. I just haven't had time to go looking for it. The spirit bottle entries are useless, by the way. I only found two that I thought might be able to trap Quetzalcoatl, and one of them turned out to be Darius's bottle."

"What was the other one?"

"Nuclear powered," I say. "Techno mages."

"I dated one of those in college. Tried to make a flying car."

"What is it with those guys and flying cars?"

"Right? Anyway, he drove it off a cliff. It didn't work."

"Sorry to hear it."

"We were about to break up anyway." She flips through pages, quickly scanning the entries.

"What's this one? Vorpal Razor?" She reads the entry. "Oh. That would come in handy."

"I've seen that one." Supposed to cut through anything and especially good at slicing off heads. "I'm afraid to go near it. First time I nicked my arm to get some blood I'd probably lop my hand off."

"Yeah, that would be a problem. Plus shaving with it would require a pretty steady hand," she admits. She flips through a chunk of pages. "This is going to take hours."

"Probably. How about you take one side, I take the other, and when we're done we flip the page?" It's a process that works surprisingly well. At least insofar as we quickly determine that it's fucking useless.

"How far are we through this thing?" she says.

"I'd say about two percent."

"Fuck it. I'm done. Move over."

"Why?"

"Need more room. Or not. I don't really care."

She leans against me, pulls her feet up onto the loveseat, shoves me further to the side. A moment later, she begins to snore. This is worse than a cat sleeping on your lap. At least the cat can't lob a fire-ball at you if you wake it up.

———

I wake up lying on the loveseat with no idea what time it is. I don't feel nearly as hungover as I would expect. I sit up, wipe sleep from my eyes. Gabriela sits on a chair over at the window, curtains open, a blanket over her shoulders. The orange sky through the window makes the room look like sunset and the shoggoths are shambling or whatever it is you call what shoggoths do.

"I smell coffee," I say.

"It's in the kitchen," she says. "Found it already there in a percolator. And you have milk and sugar and warm blueberry muffins under a kitchen towel on the counter and I'm going to kill you and live here now as a hermit."

"Hey, you brought me back me to life, you're stuck with me," I say. I stagger toward the kitchen and she hands me her mug.

"The fuck is this?"

"Refill," she says. "Please. Little milk, two sugars." I'm too tired to argue with her so I go in, pour myself a cup of coffee and refill her mug. I overdo it on the sugar. Because I'm petty like that.

"I thought this was a pocket universe," she says. She sips the coffee, but if she notices the eight sugar cubes I put in she doesn't say anything. Probably the magic in here fixed it for her. My petty vengeance thwarted by a hotel room.

"I don't think so. Not like the way Darius's bottle is. I think it's more of a bridge between two, I dunno, planets, realities?"

"I've heard of things like this. Not bridges, but more like pits. An opening in one reality and the rest of it dug into another reality. The interaction of both is what keeps the structure stable. As long as you don't breach it from the inside it's fine."

"What happens if you do?"

"The whole thing collapses. Folds in on itself. Ceases to exist." There's something about this that's poking at the back of my brain. Something about a bottle. Not Darius's, but something else.

"How is this different from Darius's bottle?" I say.

"I think it's a similar principal, but it's not connected to other realities. I think it's more surrounded by them. We can't see them, but they're there and that's what's holding the whole thing together." That would explain why nobody's ever been able to break it, and how Darius has never been able to break out.

"Wait a minute," I say. "If this place is breached, it collapses, right?"

"Yeah."

"So why is there a window here?"

"That's what I don't understand," she says. "Whoever built this had to know how it worked. Why put in something as brittle as glass inside?" Brittle glass. Strong on the outside. Weak on the inside.

"Oh, you sneaky motherfucker," I say.

"Sorry?"

"You know how I was saying this seemed like a lot of effort to go through for a safe house? It's not a safe house."

"Then what is it?"

"A trap."

Chapter 21

"It won't work," Gabriela says after I tell her my idea.

"Why not? You said the whole thing would collapse."

I could never figure out what exactly my grandfather had in mind when he had this place built. He kept Darius's bottle in it, which I thought might just have been enhanced security. Under normal circumstances, the room is safer than any vault. But I think he had other ideas.

"First off, the bottle is its own universe held together with other universes. As long as it's sealed, this place collapsing won't destroy it. I honestly don't know what it would do. It could just as easily end up in our reality as pop into the other one, but I think Darius would be just fine. Might piss him off, though."

"Not convinced that's a deal breaker," I say.

"How about this then? Who's going to break the window?"

"Timed detonator?"

"You're going to trust this to a timer? All right, let's say we do this. The bottle's got to be opened. You're the only one who can open the bottle. You would have to open it, break the glass, and get out before Darius can do anything."

"I could do that," I say, trying to sound convincing.

"No, you couldn't. You know why? Because that door right there needs to be locked and barred or he's just going to waltz on out of here before you can so much as blink. And if it's not closed, I don't know if it would work at all. Will it just throw everything in here out into our world like toothpaste squeezed out of a tube?"

"The portal rings. I open the bottle, break the glass, and port to a safe place outside the room." If someone can port in, then I should be able to port out.

"Say it even works once you've got everything sealed up. Then you use the ring and open a door you have to walk through. What makes you think Darius won't just tag along and step through before everything goes to shit?"

"So we lock me in the room, too. It's the only way it would work. I open the bottle, break the glass, problem solved."

"What part of 'will cease to exist' isn't getting through?"

"I get it. I won't just be dead, I'll be dead-dead. But come on, I'm not even really me, am I? I'm a chunk of soul carved off a death god and shoved into the body of a mass murderer who just happens to be a good fit."

"No."

"Holt said it himself. I'm supposed to be dead. Hell, if more people knew I was alive, I'd have squads of mages running me down in the street. Even Letitia knows it, for fuck sake. The world's better off without me in it."

"I brought you back to—"

"To do this exact thing. The point was to get rid of Darius before he gets out. We're not going to find anything else that he's going to fit in, much less keep him locked up."

"We might."

"Not in the time we have."

"Goddammit, Eric. You are such a pain in the ass."

"It's my brand."

"And an idiot."

"Also my brand."

"Fuck it," she says, reaches up, pulls my face to hers and kisses me. It's a nice kiss. Goes on for a while. When we part she looks at me with the kind of horror like she's just accidentally set off a bomb.

"Uh—"

"Oh my god," she says. "I—I didn't mean—that was a mistake," she says. "Shit. Can we ignore that?" She stands up and starts to pace the room. "I don't know what the hell just happened. Shit."

"This is why you brought me back," I say. She stops pacing. But doesn't say a word, like not talking about it means it never happened.

"This is . . . I don't know what this is," I say. "But I don't think we have time for it? Right now? Later, maybe?"

"Or never," she says. "Never works. I will never bring this up."

"It's okay. We're okay." Are we? She tore me in half just to dump a chunk of my soul into my grandfather's body to do something with Darius's bottle. Was that the only reason? Yeah. Of course it was. And even if it wasn't I'm still pissed off at her for what she did.

But goddamn, that was a nice kiss.

"Right," she says. "Yes. Okay. Where were we?"

"I'm the only one who can open that bottle. And when that bottle opens this place needs to be locked up tight. So I need to be in here to break the glass."

"Yes," she says. "And it's still a stupid idea. We don't know enough about this place to bet everything we have on it."

"Yeah, but the guy to ask is kinda dead."

"Is he?" Gabriela says.

"If he isn't then he's gonna be real pissed that I'm walking around in his body."

"I don't mean your grandfather."

———

"Well, this is a pleasant surprise," Amanda says when she picks up the phone. Gabriela and I are parked outside the shelter, each making our respective phone calls. "News about the bottle? Or did you just want to talk to me?"

"Bottle," I say. "Sorry. What I really need is to talk to your dad."

"Aww," Amanda says. "Yeah, I can set something up, but he can be kind of a pill when it comes to, you know, people."

"I'd noticed that. How'd you avoid going that route?"

"Oh, I've just got a carefully crafted shell hiding the fact that I'm a complete sociopath."

"I thought we all did that," I say.

"Yes, but I'm good at it. When do you need to talk to him?"

"As soon as possible. I need to know if he ever worked with my grandfather sometime in the late forties, early fifties."

"He's certainly old enough. Let me check and I'll call you right back."

"Thanks."

"No problem. And by the way, you owe me one," she says.

"Happily," I say, and hang up the phone.

"Thanks, Miriam," Gabriela says and ends her own call. "Miriam's on her way over. Be here in half an hour or so. You sure you want to talk to her about this?"

"No. I'd like to think that whatever the hell my

grandfather did was something she wouldn't know anything about, but she's not stupid. If he was feeding the Ambassador thousands of people, she had to know about it." I just hope she didn't help him.

"Any luck with Werther?"

"Amanda's setting up a meeting."

The phone rings. Amanda. That was faster than I'd expected. "Dad says yes," she says. "He says that if you'd taken much longer to figure it out he would have had to come find you. I don't know what the hell that means. Can you swing by the house? He really wants to talk to you."

"Now?" I say. Gabriela nods. "I can do that. I'll head right over. Oh, hey, can I get Arthur's number? I need to talk to him."

"Not sure he wants to talk to you."

"It has to do with the bottle."

"That, he'll want to talk to you about." I take down the number on a stray fast food receipt and hand it to Gabriela.

"Much appreciated," I say.

"I'll let you into the estate when you get here," she says, and hangs up.

"Why do you want to talk to the Dollma—"

"Arthur. Or Holt. Hell, even Geppetto if you want. Whichever. I've been thinking about the problem of being in the room when it collapses. I have an idea I'd like to run by you."

It takes me about ten minutes to explain the whole thing, and Gabriela punches holes all through it until we have what sounds like something that might be doable.

"I'll call him," Gabriela says. "Hopefully, he says yes, and he can move fast on it."

"What about Miriam?"

"I'll talk to her after I call Arthur," she says. "Might

be better if I'm the one to have the conversation with her anyway. You do look like her dead boyfriend, you know."

"Good point," I say. "I'll let you know what I find out from Werther."

"Be careful," she says, opening the car door and getting out. She watches as I pull away from the curb, a troubled look on her face.

———

Mages for the most part love to flaunt their power. But how do you do that so the normals don't notice it? Simple. You never let them see it. Attila Werther's place is an almost typical Hollywood Hills estate. Vine-covered fence, electric gate at the front.

But get past the gate and things are a little different.

"You know how to get to the house?" Amanda says.

"I've been here before. You're not coming?"

"He said it'd be better if I weren't around for the meeting, which usually means there will be some fuckery I won't want to know about lest it damage my hero worship of the best father a girl could have."

"This happen a lot?"

"Since I was like ten. At this point I know where most of the bodies are buried. There's not much he could have done that would offend my delicate sensibilities."

"You must have been a nightmare to raise."

"You don't know the half of it. I'll be here when you get back. Provided he doesn't just kill you on the spot."

"That's reassuring."

"Just setting expectations. Oh, one more thing, dad's been in kind of a whimsical mood lately."

"Whimsical?"

"You'll see what I mean. Just don't let it fool you, okay?"

"Deal." I step through the gate and everything goes all Willy Wonka. The sky is bright green with pink cotton candy clouds, the road to the house is paved with cobblestones made of giant circular mints. The trees on either side look more or less like trees but the bark looks like Kit Kat bars and the leaves are all fruit leather. Whimsical indeed.

A bright pink golf cart drives out of a side road and stops in front of me. No driver. Because of course. I get in and the cart takes me to the house, past a chocolate river. The house is a Victorian with a widow's walk, peaked tower roofs, and tiles that at first I think are wood and then realize that no, they're gingerbread. It's a fucking gingerbread house. Maybe I should have been dropping breadcrumbs on my way up here.

The door opens as I get close. I pause for a second, weighing whether I really want to do this—whimsical doesn't mean safe—and then go inside. Last time, the place was all black and white marble with all the coziness of an embalming room.

Now it looks a lot more human and lived-in. A tiled foyer gives way to a carpeted hallway. I pass a grandfather clock made out of gingerbread, icing, and giant candy canes, a marzipan-covered bureau with framed photos of Amanda at various ages. It looks almost normal except for the whole gingerbread-house witch vibe, and the fact that the hallway ends in a single room and I haven't seen any other doors in the place. It's like a reverse Tardis, way smaller on the inside.

Werther's there, an older, distinguished-looking man who appears to be in his early sixties, which he so isn't. He's wearing a sweater, slacks, and slippers and sitting in a comfortable chair, a slight smile on his face. The room is painted in greens and browns and

smells of the wood burning in the fireplace and a hint
of leather.

"Glad you could make it, Eric," he says. "Please,
have a seat." A chair appears behind me and I sit down.
That's when the shadows recede and I see everyone
else.

"I didn't know this was a party," I say. There are
four other people in a rough half-circle with Werther
in the middle. The two to Werther's right look like
brother and sister. Their faces have a Polynesian cast,
and their hair is long and black, pulled back into po-
nytails. The man is built like a linebacker, the woman
like she does Olympic-level volleyball. They're very
well dressed.

The two to his left are an older black woman, gray-
ing hair and a regal stance, red dress and pearls,
and a much younger man, barely a boy, sitting sullen
and slouched next to her wearing one of those prep
school uniforms, blue blazer and slacks and no imag-
ination.

"Show some fucking respect," the boy says, sitting
up and puffing himself out trying to be all manly. The
woman next to him slaps him hard enough across the
face that even I wince.

"Pardon young Lucas," the woman says. Her voice
has a slight French lilt to it. "He is impulsive."

"No problem . . . Miz Rochambeau, isn't it? Lisette
Rochambeau?" I've never met any of the Rochambeaus, but I have heard of them.

"It is," she says and nods her head slightly. The boy
is staring at me with a rage he isn't even trying to
hide. Jesus, kid, I'm not the one who slapped you.

"And you're the 'Aumākuas," I say to the others.
"Leilani and . . . Duke, isn't it? The twins." I've heard
some interesting things about the 'Aumākuas. Strictly
speaking, 'aumākuas are Hawaiian family gods that
take the forms of animals: owl, shark, sea turtle, and

so on. I don't know if the family just took the name or
if there's a more complicated connection. Never had
to really think about it. With my recent god issues I
might learn a thing or two from them I could use.

"You're wearing sharkskin?" I say. "Really? Little
on the nose there, don't you think?"

Like the Rochambeaus, the 'Aumākuas are one of
the hoity-toity big magic families. And I don't mean
mage families that are big. These are the types of people who manipulate stock markets, weather, time.

The man, Duke, laughs loud. "Told you he'd notice." He has a deep voice, the sort of pidgin accent
you can only really get through a lifetime of living in
Hawai'i. I've heard he uses it to make people under-
estimate him.

"My brother has the sense of humor of a twelve-
year-old," Leilani says. No trace of an accent there.
They might be twins, but she prefers to throw people
off their guard by her sheer presence. Of the two of
them, she's the one I'd hate to tangle with more.

"You've all met?" Werther says.

"I only know y'all by reputation," I say. "Curious
what the three most powerful mage families in Los
Angeles are doing here."

"Four," Werther says. "Four families."

"You can't be lumping me in that category," I say.
"Everybody in my family with any real power is dead."

"I told you, Mother," Lucas says. "I don't know
why we're even talking to him."

"Lisette, was it really necessary to bring your son?"
Werther says.

"He needs to learn sometime, Attila," she says.

"Maybe so," says Duke. "But did you have to do it
on our time?"

"Okay, time out," I say. "What the hell is going on?
Werther, if you're trying to kill me again can you just
get it over with? I got shit to do."

"Apologies, Mister Carter. We tend to bicker from time to time."

"Last I heard y'all were trying to murder each other."

"We've set aside our various disagreements in favor of a more important task," Lisette says. "But, yes, we have been known to do that, too."

"She means the bottle," says Duke.

"Why do we even care?" Lucas says. "So a djinn gets out of a bottle. The world is filled with djinn. Trapped, free, roaming temple ruins. I've killed djinn in the desert, hunted ghouls in the swamps, aswang in the Philippines, I'm not scared of fucking Aladdin."

"Can I slap him this time?" I say.

"I would rather you didn't," Lisette says. "I have so very few joys in life, after all." She turns her gaze to her son. He immediately shrinks into himself and shuts up.

"If it helps any, kid, that's a good question," I say. "Here's what I know. Darius is eight thousand years old. He helped Hernando Cortes enslave the Aztecs and managed to murder almost the entire Aztec pantheon of gods."

"Darius is a type of djinn known as a Marid," Werther says. "They're the ones you hear about the most and are the most powerful. They're the wish granters. You don't see Marid on Earth very often. Darius is the only one I know of. All the others have gone."

"Destroyed?" I ask, without much hope.

"No. They just decided to go home. They live in an alternate plane. Islamic folklore calls it Al-Ghaib, but that's about as vague as saying 'Heaven.' It's the Unseen realm. The djinn aren't very forthcoming about their origins, so folklore is most of what we have."

"What's so special about a Marid?" Lucas says. "A djinn is a djinn."

Werther turns a cold eye toward the boy. "The combined power of all the mages in this room probably couldn't kill a Marid."

"Oh," Lucas says.

"The only saving grace we have is that Darius has been stuck in his bottle his entire time here on Earth."

"I wouldn't call it stuck, exactly," I say. "He's plenty good at letting people in and out of there, even if he can't get out himself."

"In comparison to his past, he might as well be," Werther says. "He's thought to have contributed to some political scandals, influencing some mass murders, but for the most part he's been fairly quiet since the battle in Mictlan.

"But before the Aztecs he'd already been linked with a number of massacres throughout the ancient world: Carthage in 146 BCE with Scipio Africanus, the Bar Kokhba revolt that killed over five hundred thousand Jews from 132 to 136."

"He helped some Roman generals with a genocide?" Lucas says. "That's it? That doesn't sound that bad."

"You sure raised yourself a winner there, Lisette," I say. The woman gives me a haughty sniff.

"You keep to yours, Mister Carter, and I'll keep to mine."

"Darius also set off Mount Vesuvius in 79 AD," Werther says, "burying Pompeii, Herculaneum, Oplontis and Stabiae. Also the Crete earthquake in 365, the Minoan eruption, and the Cymbrian flood. He can be directly linked to several hundred thousand deaths, genocides that history has only barely remembered. Then there is, as with the Aztecs, substantial evidence that he has destroyed whole pantheons and planes of existence."

"So can we all agree that this is a bad thing? Or does the kid get slapped again?" I say.

"What do you plan to do with the bottle?" Duke says. "If you can get control of the djinn—"

"You've never met Darius, have you?"

"That won't be a concern," Werther says. "It's not

as simple as rubbing a lamp or saying, 'Open sesame.' There are rituals that have to be performed to hand off from one owner to the next. And since the last owner is dead and hasn't been replaced in five hundred years, Darius is a free agent."

"Still doesn't answer my question," Duke says.

"I'm either going to open it or do nothing and let it open itself. Which one I do is going to depend on what I hear from Mister Werther here."

"The hotel room," Werther says. "I take it you've figured out that it was designed specifically to destroy the djinn. I, and ancestors of the Rochambeau and 'Aumākua families, worked with Robert Carter to build it."

"Who murdered all the people?" I say. Everybody on either side of Werther makes surprised noises, but Werther doesn't.

"Oh, y'all didn't know? This 'trap' is only there because a deal was struck with a ghost using thousands of souls. The bodies are still there. In a pit on the ghost side of things. I've seen them."

"I killed them," Werther says. "Robert was complicit only insomuch as the Ambassador and he had an understanding. It's not quite what you might think."

"Really? 'Cause I think you're a fucking mass murderer and the only reason I'm not walking out that door is because I need to know about the room."

"It wasn't thousands of people," Werther says. "It was one person thousands of times over."

"Come again?"

"It was part of my research for the spell to make the room. We needed to tap into multiple realities, and we discovered alternates of our own. Only ours seemed to have a Darius, however.

"We had one person who existed throughout all of these different realities. They were different from each other, but the same person nonetheless. Men, women, different ethnicities. But they all knew the stakes, and they all volunteered. So, we brought them over from each of these realities and they sacrificed themselves to the ghost."

"Fuck, brau," Duke says. "Das cold."

"I don't see how that's any different," I say. "You still killed them all and fed their souls to the Ambassador."

"That's rich coming from you, necromancer," Leilani says.

"If you're gonna bring up the fires, I'd like to point out that I'm not the one who set them all off. I kept them from getting worse."

"My daughter—" Lisette starts, rage growing on her face, but Werther cuts her off.

"We are not here to discuss the fires," Werther says. "No, Eric, what I did was not murder. No one was forced, they all knew the stakes not just to our reality, but to all of theirs as well."

"I find it hard to believe you could even find that many people," I say, "even if they are all the same person. And all of them 'volunteered'? How the hell do you even know what they were thinking?"

"Because they were all me," Werther says. "So before you start throwing hypocritical, self-righteous accusations as if your own hands are free of blood, maybe find out the truth instead of jumping to conclusions and whining like a little brat about it." His face is going red from anger. Okay, I found one of his buttons. Good to know in case I ever need to press it again.

No sound but the crackling of the fire, the ticking of the clock. Then I say, "All right, fine. I'm the asshole here. Now tell me how the room works."

Chapter 22

The room works exactly how Gabriela thought it would work. Pierce part of it from the inside and the whole thing collapses, destroying everything inside it. Unless it's Darius's bottle and still sealed because the forces holding it are pretty much the same forces keeping the room in one piece.

"Why don't you just wait until the wards degrade completely and he comes out and then break the window?" Lucas says.

His mom looks to be about to slap him again, before I say, "I was wondering that, too."

"There's unsealed and there's open and they're not the same thing," Werther says. "Unseal it and Darius can come and go at will, and destroying the room is just going to drive him back inside. The bottle's stopper has to be removed."

"So somebody needs to be in there to remove the wards, pop the cork, and break the glass."

"And let Darius out," Lisette says. "Or am I misunderstanding the nature of this trap?"

"No, that's right," Werther says. "Darius easily has enough power to hold the bottle together if the stopper is pulled. He won't bat an eye. If anything he'll wait until everything's collapsed and then start creating his own reality in the void."

"If we get this wrong he'll create a new universe?" I say.

"He'll certainly be able to. And he'll definitely be able to cross over to ours, or any other."

"This is a really shitty trap," I say.

"We hadn't worked out all the bugs," Werther says, defensive. "That's why we kept the bottle in there. We were hoping that we'd come up with an actual plan eventually."

"What can we do?" Leilani says.

"Nothing. Unless you want to be destroyed by a collapsing mini-universe," Werther says. "I invited all of you here because your families were involved in the room's creation, and should know about it."

"So, if it goes south we can all feel bad about it?" Duke says.

"If it goes south you probably won't have time to feel bad about it," I say. "So, what you're saying is that I'm fucked either way."

"Pretty much, yes," Werther says. "Sorry, son. I really wish there was another way. But getting you out of there before it collapses without letting Darius out isn't possible. Robert and I did the math, and the math hasn't changed."

"You could lock the bottle in the room, can't you? And just leave it alone? He'd be trapped in there," Lucas says. He's shifted from sullen teenager to geeky science kid.

"Same problem," I say. "He'll figure out what's going on pretty quick. Then he can just crack the glass, pop back into the bottle and wait until he can say, 'Let there be light.'"

"I think we have one choice here," Lisette says. "Eric must sacrifice himself to destroy Darius before he can escape and doom us all." Everyone is nodding except Werther. Probably because Werther knows me well enough to anticipate my answer.

"Fuck all of you," I say. "Look, in case you weren't aware, I'm a petty, vindictive asshole. Which means that if I'm going down, I'm taking all you fucks with me."

"Even the whole world?" Werther says.

"Sure, why not. I'll cease to exist, so what do I care?"

"You wouldn't," Lisette says.

"Oh, yeah, he would," Duke says.

"You'd let us all die?" Lucas says. He sits back in his chair like I just slapped him harder than his momma did.

"You especially," I say.

"Then there's no reason we should let you live," Lisette says.

"Knock yourself out," I say. "But what does killing me get you? I know what it gets me, a free one-way ticket out of here for my soul. So go ahead. You can bask in the knowledge that at least you gave me a quick exit while Darius is consuming everything that was ever you."

"Lisette, enough," Werther says. "He's right and you know it. All we can do is try to shore up our own defenses and be ready for a major attack by Darius. He's going to come after us first. We can hurt him if anyone can."

"That's going to take time," Leilani says, her brother nodding along.

"We got a lot of territory to cover," Duke says, "and family we gotta get safe."

"Then best get started," Werther says. "Thank you all for coming. I'll continue to work the problem."

"I still want to kill you," Lisette says to me.

"How about we see if we can survive the potential end of the universe before the killing starts," I say.

"I'll have my satisfaction," she says, then she and Lucas disappear from their chairs.

"Brau, I get where you're comin' from," Duke says. "I'd say the same thing in your shoes. I know what it means and I know what it'll do. But I'm asking you to not walk away from it. I'm asking for myself and my family and all our people."

"If I can come up with a better idea, I will," I say.

"All I can ask. Laki maika'i, brau."

"I hope that doesn't mean 'go fuck yourself' in Hawaiian," I say.

"We survive this, I'll translate it. Aloha." Duke disappears from his chair.

"Sorry about that," Leilani says. "I don't know why he talks like that. We haven't lived there for years. Oh, and it means 'good luck.' Sort of. And for what it's worth, I hope you come up with a better plan. I'd really like to not die." A moment later she's gone, too, leaving only Werther and me in the room.

"Interesting group you dug up," I say.

"Much as I would like to say I did it out of the kindness of my heart, they're the only people close enough and powerful enough who might have a chance of taking on Darius."

"Surprised they give a fuck. Where were they when Quetzalcoatl showed up? Or when the fires started? Did they even try to help? Or did they shove their heads up their asses more tightly and hope for the best?"

"A lot of them left town," he says. "Even before Quetzalcoatl came on the scene. They knew he was coming. We all did."

"And you didn't do a fucking thing about it," I say. "Did you know it was Q's pet assassin that was murdering everybody?"

"I did."

"And you tried to kill me anyway."

"You don't understand this, son," Werther says, "and I doubt you ever will. Another facet of Robert's personality that seems to have jumped a generation and landed on you. There are politics with us. There have to be. Do you want to know what a wizard war looks like? It looks like plagues, famines, earthquakes. It looks like Chernobyl going critical. It looks like failed levees in New Orleans."

"And you, what, control yourselves? Is that what your politics do? Keep yourselves and each other on a leash so fucking tight you can't be bothered to think about regular people? About normal people?"

"How many 'normal people' did you kill on your way to Mictlan to murder your gods?" Werther says. "Quite the body count from what I heard. You cut through people like a scythe through wheat. How many of them were collateral damage? Do you tell yourself that they were bad people? That they deserved to die? Or do you just lock it up in that box of hypocrisy you stand on?"

"You don't know—"

"Yes, I do," Werther says. "It's vengeance, and it's anger, and above everything else, it's wounded pride. That pair from Mictlan caught you like a fish on a hook. You, a mage. A necromancer. A man with the power to control life and death itself. How fucking dare they. If you think I haven't been there, then you're an idiot."

"Ya got me," I say. "I am a walking, talking barrel of denial. But at least I'm trying to do something about it. What do you do?"

"We keep our hands out of each other's pies," he says. "You think we all do nothing because we're so high and mighty that we simply don't care. Sure, some of us are like that. A terrifying number, in fact. But there are some of us who go to great lengths to keep the peace so that hundreds of thousands of innocent people don't die. Can you imagine that? Killing hundreds of thousands of people? Oh, of course. You don't have to imagine it, do you?"

"Have you ever considered being a motivational speaker?" I say. "Your pep talks are superb."

"I worked on that one for days," he says, his smile never reaching his eyes. "So how are you going to get out of this?"

"Excuse me?"

"Darius," Werther says. "How are you going to get rid of him, and not die? You have a plan."

"You fucking people," I say. "Every time it's the same goddamn thing. You know how many mages out there honestly think I've got some master foolproof plot to take over the world, like I'm a Bond villain? I've got an army of the dead, you know. At least that's what everybody tells me. Not sure where I'd keep them. Refrigerators are expensive. And now you. The hell makes you think I have a plan?"

"Because you're Robert's grandson and you don't just look like him. The two of you aren't that different."

"Yeah, did he set fire to most of L.A. by pissing off a god, too?"

"His fuck-ups were never quite so epic, no. But he always managed to get himself out of scrapes at the last minute."

"You do remember that bit that I've been dead for the last five years, right? I think that officially qualifies as not getting out of a scrape at the last minute."

"You've been a god, Eric," Werther says. "For the last five years you've been ruling Mictlan."

"That's the other guy. I'm the leftover scraps. Look, just because I was related to some kind of magic badass doesn't mean I have a plan," I say. "Right now, all

I've got is letting Darius out and taking a hammer to the window. I'm not real fond of that one. We done here? Or you want to tell me stories about ol' grandad before I die? Again."

"No," Werther says. "None of them have happy endings."

"I guess he and I really do have a lot in common."

———

The golf cart is waiting for me when I step out of the house. It would be interesting to see what else Werther's done with this place, but I'd probably get eaten by some magical chocolate fruit tree, so I hop into the golf cart and let it take me back to the gate.

The fact that the big families could put their differences aside and avoid killing each other long enough to talk about Darius should have everybody fucking terrified. What Werther says isn't wrong. Political games, occasional backstabbings, a murder here and there between mages are a small price to pay to avoid an all-out war. Doesn't mean I'm not pissed off that none of those fuckers will step up to the plate.

The higher up the food chain you go, the less the people care. It's not a mage thing, it's a human thing. Power and wealth are all ways to keep someone insulated from the rest of the world. We're all scared little children afraid of the monster under the bed.

He called me a hypocrite. Am I? Fuck yes. I'm running. Always fucking running. I ran away from friends and family, then I went and did it again. It didn't take much for me to be okay with taking Mictlantecuhtli's place. Could I have refused? Maybe. Point is I didn't.

Well, I can't run away from this. If Darius gets free I don't know where I'll be on his shit list, but it'll be high enough it won't take him long to get to me no matter where I go.

Funny. The only solution to keep from running away from the fight is to run away from everything else. I break that window and I'm still in the room, I'm gone. As gone as it is possible to be.

I have a chance. A glimmer of an idea. I don't know if it'll work. I don't know if I want to risk it. But if I'm going to try it, it'll have to be soon. We're running out of road and there's a cliff at the end.

The golf cart stops at the gate, which opens as I approach, then closes smoothly behind once I'm through. Amanda's gone, but she's left a note drawn in the dust of my windshield that says CALL ME. There's a couple of hearts drawn over the words.

"Now isn't that just fucking adorable?"

"Hello, Hank," I say, turning to see the demon nearby. He does something with his wrist, a slight shake, and everything goes slightly off. I can feel the spell—some kind of shield, maybe? I'm not entirely sure.

"How ya doin', meat?" he says.

"Meat? That's a new one. I would have expected a better class of insult after that German Expressionism. Or at least something in German. What can I do for you?"

"Just here to kill you again," he says. "Gonna make it stick this time."

"Bold words," I say. "You know where we are, don't you?"

Hank's got a cruel face. Never really noticed that before. He always looked like a schlubby, mid-forties suburban husband to me, somebody with a dad bod who lost the fight with baldness and beer a long time back. But there's a glint in his eye, a certain angle to his grin. I already know he's a mean motherfucker, but I hadn't quite noticed he looks like one.

"Old man Werther's place," he says. "Yeah, I know it. But that's okay. Nobody in there is gonna notice anything out here." He raises his left hand to show me what he was fiddling with on his wrist, a bracelet made of teeth.

"Raiding grandma's dentures again? Hank, that's low even for you."

"We might as well not even exist as far as the rest of the world's concerned." He's right. Now that I'm looking I can see a faint shimmer in the air around us in a dome. Outside it birds are frozen mid-flight, a leaf fallen from a tree hangs in the air, almost but not quite hitting the ground.

"Nice. How long does it last?"

"Long enough to kill you." He moves like lightning and he's on me before I can put up a shield, but I block his hook with my arm, narrowly avoiding a slash to the face from the five-inch claws he just grew out of his fingers. The magic in my tattoos takes the brunt of the force, but my arm goes numb from the impact all the same.

I throw a push spell with the force of a jackhammer knocking him down and sliding him a good ten feet. "Bit of a policy shift, isn't it? I thought Darius wanted me alive to pop his cork."

"Nah, old news." Hank gets up, brushes dust off his pants, and comes for me again. This time he's smart about it. I'm expecting him to come at me directly and I throw my shield up to intercept, but he skates around me and before I can redirect the spell he's got his arm around my neck in a stranglehold and squeezes.

"Darius doesn't need you anymore," he says. "Turns out all those locks keeping him inside are falling apart faster than he thought they would." Shit. If Darius has figured that out then the whole collapsing-universe trap is a wash.

I spread my shield out around me, but instead of trying to push him away from me, which would likely take my head off, I form it into foot-long spikes of energy that punch through his chest and abdomen.

Hank yells and throws me. I hit the car's windshield hard. The glass spiderwebs under the impact. Hank pulls me off and throws me again before I can get my bearings. I hit the driveway hard and roll, almost but not quite to the edge of the spell hiding us. If I can just get a hand out . . .

But no, Hank grabs me by the ankle and drags me back. I slam my hand into the ground and shove enough magic into it to cause a mini-earthquake around us. Hank falls on his ass, letting go of my foot.

I throw out a lightning spell. Arcs of electricity dance along his skin, but all that seems to do is piss him off more. I try to get another spell off, but before I can form the magic around my thoughts he's on me again and kicks me in the side hard. My eyes go blurry with the pain.

"Yeah?" I say, spitting blood out of my mouth. "How long did he say it would be? Couple hundred years? Couple months?"

"He figures a few weeks. He's willing to wait it out." I roll away from his next kick and manage to get my feet under me enough that I can sort of shove my ass backward across the cement. I could pop over to the ghost side, but I don't know that I'm going to stay conscious much longer. Passing out over there would be a really bad idea.

I try to get my hand around to the Browning at my back but somehow my coat's gotten torn in such a way that my hand snags on the cloth. It's just enough to throw me off balance so I fall onto the side he just kicked. I let out a yell like a fucking howler monkey and almost pass out then and there.

The Browning falls out of its holster and skids a few feet away from me. I reach for it and my hand lands on something even better.

"Hey," I say. "You remember when I said I was gonna kill you?" I say.

"Haven't laughed that hard in decades," Hank says.

I roll to the side, away from another one of those mule kicks. I get enough concentration to throw a push spell at him. It shoves him back about three feet or so. He laughs at me. To be fair, it was a pretty paltry effort, but I just wanted a little more distance between us.

"Hope you like surprises."

I trigger the portal ring in my hand, creating a hole beneath him that leads—I don't know, I didn't really have a place in mind. The important thing is that Hank has dropped most of the way through when I turn it off.

The portal disappears, slicing Hank in a clean line at an angle that goes from just under his neck to the top of his right shoulder. The only thing left on the pavement is his head and part of his right arm. The arm bursts into flame and turns into ash in the space of a heartbeat.

"Not bad," I say. "All things considered." The portal ring must have fallen out of my pocket at the same time I lost the gun. If my hand had been an inch to one side or the other I never would have found it.

I hear a pop at the gate, Werther teleporting from inside his house. Now that the bracelet keeping us hidden from prying eyes and passing minutes is gone, I bet every alarm on the other side of that gate just went off.

"What the hell happened?" He looks around at the car, the ashes, me bleeding on his driveway, Hank's head blinking its eyes. Thing with demons is if they still have a head, they'll grow a whole new body. Like vampires that way. Big pain in the ass.

"You play golf?" I say.

"I— Occasionally. What—"

I cast a shield into a sphere around Hank's head

and squeeze. I hear a pop as it compresses, everything squeezing together to form a solid lump. I let the shield go and Hank's head, crushed to the size of a golf ball, rolls smoking to rest in front of me.

"Dammit," I say, "I can never get the dimples right," and finally pass out.

Chapter 23

I bolt awake, heart racing. I sit up on Werther's driveway, the old man kneeling at my side. I can feel the fading magic of a spell as he holds Hank's diamond-dense head in his hand and turns it over and over.

"I wonder how far it would fly," he says. "How are you feeling?"

"Like I haven't just been beaten to shit by a pissed-off demon."

"Yes, well, that's the least I could do, seeing as it's just outside my front yard. I see someone left you a message on your windshield. Who wants you to call them?"

"No idea," I say because even hinting to an extremely powerful mage that his daughter has given me her phone number, no matter the circumstances, strikes me as a very bad idea.

"Hmm," he says. "So what was that all about?"

I pull out my phone and dial Gabriela. "One second and I won't have to repeat myself."

"Hey," Gabriela says. "Uh, the other night—"

"I got you on speaker," I say. "Attila Werther's with me."

"Oh. Okay, what's up?"

"Darius knows that the wards are failing faster

than they were supposed to. He just sent his demon boy toy over here to take me out. He doesn't need me to open it anymore."

"But why kill you?" Werther says. "He could just ignore you until he's out?"

"Probably because he thinks you've got enough of Mictlantecuhtli in you that you could still be a threat," Gabriela says. "Even if you trigger those traps on the bottle, that doesn't guarantee you can't lock him back up even tighter than before."

"Whatever the reason, we need to get that bottle into the room as soon as possible," I say. "Where are you? Can you get there?"

"I'm back at the shelter," she says. "I can cross over, but not as easily as you can. It'll take me a few minutes."

"Okay, just be sure you do it on the hotel grounds. If you can get into the school it'll be easier, but the basketball court should be fine." I glance at Werther. "Just, uh, don't look in the shed."

"See, that's like telling a toddler not to push the big red button. You're sure the Ambassador won't eat me?"

"You're vetted through me, so it shouldn't be an issue. But act fast. I'll meet you there."

"No," she says. "You need to go see Holt. He said yes."

"You trust him?"

"I trust Amanda and his son. Holt's been having some heart-to-hearts with his kid. Apparently the kid was aware of everything during his ride along with you. He remembers you sticking up for him, and some of the other shit you pulled. I think you might actually have a fan."

"Jesus. Best nip that in the bud."

"Or don't," she says. "Might be good for you."

"Okay, so moving on," I say. "You get the bottle into the room. I'll go hit the campus. I have to make a stop first, but it's close enough it shouldn't take me too long."

"Don't get killed," she says. "We need to talk."

"If you ever want to strike terror into a man's heart, those four words will do it. You don't get killed either. I don't know if Darius can speed up the process by pushing on the stopper or something."

"I got it covered. Call me when you're at Holt's."

"Excuse me," Werther says, "Miz Cortez, this is Attila Werther. Before you hang up, I would like to invite you over for lunch once all this messiness is finished. I have some things I would like to discuss with you."

Silence.

"Miz Cortez?"

"Sure. We can do lunch. I'll talk to y'all later." She hangs up.

"Is she afraid of me, do you think?" Werther says.

"With all due respect, everyone finds you fucking terrifying."

"Good. Glad to see I haven't lost the touch, then. So, you do have a plan."

"It's the same plan," I say. "With a few modifications. But I need to get moving." I look over at the car with the busted windshield, the dented hood. Somehow one of the tires blew out. I didn't think I hit the car that hard.

"Where do you need to go?"

"You know the Forum in Inglewood?" I say.

"Ah, Mister MacFee, yes. I'm sorry for your loss. He was a good man." I blink at him, not sure what to say. "Please give Casey my condolences. Close your eyes and hold your breath."

I'm about to ask what he's talking about when I'm suddenly hit with a bone-deep cold. I snap my eyes shut and don't breathe as the chill gets worse and worse, then suddenly stops.

I open my eyes and I'm standing in front of Mac-Fee's booth, the noise and bustle of the swap meet all around me. There's frost on my jacket, a little hanging from my eyelids. I'm shivering.

"Where the fuck did you come from?" Casey's staring at me from just outside the tent.

"Oh, you know, here and there."

"Now's not a really great time if you need anything," she says.

"I know. And I am really, really sorry. But this is kind of an emergency."

"Okay. But please, make it quick. I—I'm having trouble looking at you right now."

"Thank you. I understand."

"Do you?"

"More than you know."

"All right, come on back. Just—just take whatever you need. We'll settle up later. And so you know, this isn't anger or hate or anything. I'm grateful for what you did. It's just all really, really raw right now."

"I'll be in and out as fast as I can."

"Wait," she says. "You need to know this." Her eyes are wet, threatening to spill over. "Talked to his doc. He said he'd have hung on another month or so, but the pain would be so bad he'd be sedated to the point he wouldn't know what was going on, where he was, who any of his family were. I don't know about the rest of our family, but I couldn't watch him suffer like that. So, thank you."

'You're welcome' seems like such the wrong thing to say, so I just give her a nod and her space, and head into the tent to grab what I need.

———

The drive into the toxic zone is less full of gunfire than the last time. I make sure I have all three of Gabriela's talismans in place before I head in. I consider trying the portal ring, but I don't know the area well enough to be comfortable doing that, or its actual range. Not to mention stepping unannounced out of a hole in space in the middle of USC Hogwarts is a good way to get fireballed.

Nobody seems to care when I drive up, though. Makes sense. If you can get here, you belong here. I park in the library's actual lot this time and head in. I don't get ten feet before I see Amanda waiting for me at the base of the stairs.

"I expected you half an hour ago," she says. "And you never called." She gives me a pouty face that is so ridiculous I can't help but laugh.

"Sorry, but I got bushwhacked in your dad's driveway by a pissed-off demon who killed me once already. Things kind of cascaded from there."

"I heard. You okay?"

"Your dad fixed me up. Kinda weird, actually. Usually I'm stitching myself up with dental floss or digging bullets out of myself with forceps." The look of horror on her face is priceless. "Hey, you haven't lived until you've had to carve a busted-off claw from a Jersey Devil out of your own chest with a straight razor."

"I don't know if that's badass or just really fucking stupid."

"With me it's better to assume stupid. Badass, I most definitely am not. Holt around?"

"Yeah. He's up in one of the study rooms. He and Jordan are prepping the spell."

"How are they doing?"

"Holt's . . . ashamed of how his relationship with Jordan has gone. And Jordan . . . I think Jordan's grown up a little. He's pushing back on his dad more. He'd never done that before. I don't know how long it'll last, but I think it's a positive step. I think you might be a role model that his dad might not be comfortable with."

"Jesus, I'm not comfortable with it. Kid'll get himself killed. He needs to have a conversation about me with my ex, Vivian. That'll fix him right up."

"Isn't she a little biased?"

"If she is, it's only toward the truth."

"I'll see what I can arrange. Come on, I'll show you where they are."

We walk through the library. It's hushed as it should be, but there's a tension in the air. It takes a second to realize I don't hear pages turning, but when I glance to the side I see plenty of heads turned.

"Why are they looking at me?"

"Because they know who you are now. You have something of a reputation."

"Yeah," I say. "Mothers tell their kids to go to sleep or I'll come eat their souls or some shit. Tell me they don't think I've got an army of the undead lying around."

"I've heard that one from a few people. Some think you're a monster."

"Like in the boogeyman-under-the-bed type monster, or the Heinrich Himmler type monster?"

"Bit of both."

"Then I'll watch my back."

"I wouldn't worry too much about that. They're all too fucking scared of you to try anything."

The study room has been cleared of all furniture except for a table and a podium on which rests an old, heavy book. Holt's there looking kind of nauseous, along with a kid who I assume is Jordan, who's looking at me a little wide-eyed. He looks a lot like his dad. Holt in miniature.

"Sorry about the soul thing," I say to him. I put out my hand. "No hard feelings?" He grabs it and shakes it like a terrier with a rat.

"That was awesome," he says.

"Uh, okay." I pull my hand out of his and turn to Holt. "And you?"

"I'm still angry," he says. "But I understand what we're up against."

"So you won't screw me over?"

"Not as far as anyone will be able to prove."

"I've had worse offers," I say. "Let's do it."

———

Three hours later I'm standing in a men's bathroom stall at Union Station Downtown. The sound of trains being announced filters through the walls. I've closed off the entrance with a maintenance sign and locked the door, so we should be fine for as long as this takes, unless it all ends up with me dead and a freed djinn.

Been a long time since I've been here, which sounds odd when you're talking about a toilet stall, but maybe not so odd when it's one of the first places you found a door to Darius's little world.

"God, do all men's restrooms stink this bad?" Gabriela says. She's wearing a paramedic's uniform, a Sharpied Post-It on her chest that says SAVING A LIFE GET OUT OF MY WAY.

"I hear women's restrooms are just as bad."

"They don't smell quite this strongly of homeless desperation."

"Then I'd argue that you haven't been in the women's restroom here at Union Station."

"I run a homeless shelter for humans and supernaturals alike, Eric. Trust me, it's never as bad as this. You ready?"

"Ready. Interesting word. I don't think I've ever been ready for anything."

"Are you getting philosophical on me?"

"I'm just thinking that as soon as I think I know what the hell is going on, the universe pulls the rug out from under me."

"Sure that's the universe's fault?"

"No, but it's nice to have something to blame it

on." I pull a fat red marker out of my bag and draw runes and sigils that I memorized decades ago on the wall over the toilet. A lot of Arabic in there, Aramaic, even some Linear B. I don't understand most of it. I just know that it works.

"Open sesame," I say, and push at it with a little magic. The wall ripples like water with a stone thrown in. The wall and the toilet disappear, and in their place is a red leather door with brass tacks, like you'd see at only the best dive bars.

"He's upgraded this one," I say. "Used to be it'd sort of fade away into a black pit. I almost didn't walk into it the first time."

"Not all the doors are his doors," Gabriela says. "I'll be here when you come out."

"Much obliged. Appreciate if you don't let my head hit the floor."

"No promises. That new face of yours needs a few more bruises."

"Give it time," I say, and step through the door.

Chapter 24

Jazz. It's always jazz these days. I remember a time when Darius liked something a little more aggressive. A little more violent. Years ago, when I thought we were friends, he had a thing for CBGB in New York. Tried to make his little world look like it, but never had quite enough information.

So I took a trip to New York and took a fuck-ton of reference photos. Everything from the entrance to the color of the stained tile under the back of the toilet. I was drunk most of the time and almost lost my camera in a fight, but I got what I needed and gave him the photos.

Next day he had punks in a mosh pit, screaming along with a band on stage that may or may not have been real. Come to think of it, maybe the punks weren't real either.

But when I got back to L.A. he'd gone and turned it into a smoky jazz club. Leather chairs, big mirrored bar that he'd stand behind and survey his domain. Sometimes the music would be swing, with wartime sailors and soldiers and their dames kickin' it to some Benny Goodman, other times it was the sixties with Stan Getz doing cuts from his Big Band Bossa Nova album.

At first it was nice. And then I learned to trust him less and less and now I just fucking hate smoky jazz clubs with leather club chairs and complicated cocktails.

And here we are again. The place is in full swing. I imagine the Ambassador could learn a thing or two from him on how to do the Cocoanut Grove. Hell, maybe that was part of their deal to let Hank go.

But I don't see Darius. He's always standing behind the bar, or at a tall table near the wall listening to the music. But he's nowhere to be seen. I stop a waitress as she passes by. She's dressed like one of those old-time cigarette girls. Little bellboy box cap, red jacket, bustier and fishnet stockings.

"Hey, you seen Darius around?"

"Oh, Mister Carter," she says when she notices me.

"You know who I am?"

"Darius had all the waitstaff memorize your face. He wasn't sure where you'd pop up. He's in his office. He's been waiting for you."

"I don't think I've ever been in his office," I say.

"Behind the bar. Benny'll let you in." She points at the bartender, a skinny white kid who looks barely out of puberty.

"Thanks. Appreciate it. Hey, before you go, can I ask you a question?"

"Sure."

"Are you real?"

She laughs. "Sometimes hard to tell here, isn't it? Yeah, I'm real. Met Darius when he let me in while I was dreaming. Then he let me in for real. He's good people. Helped me out of a jam a time or two."

"Helped you out?"

"Yeah. That's why I'm here. Said he had a VIP coming by and he'd like it if I could do some waitressing for him."

Oh no. Oh, that fucking bastard. I'm getting a sick

feeling in the pit of my stomach. "Anybody else here you know? Like, from the real world?"

"Gosh, everybody, I think. First time I've seen it like that, actually. Benny's real, and the other waitresses. Most folks are ones he invited for a big party. You got some pretty important people here tonight. There are still people coming in. Always weird being in here. It never seems to get larger, but it always has enough space for everybody."

I look around the room. She's right. There are noticeably more people in here than when I arrived. "They're all real," I say. "How many you reckon he's got in here?"

"Couple hundred at least," she says. "At least when I got here. Might be twice that by now. He's even put in a bunch of new bars. See?" Dotted around the club are bars just like the one I'm next to, all tended by, as far as I can tell, real people.

The fakes, the ones that Darius populates his domain with to make it look fuller, are kind of like the Ambassador's. They're not part of him like the hotel's puppets, but they always fit a particular look. They're all beautiful. Old, young, men, women, they're all beautiful people. Flawless skin, perfectly proportioned, eyes crystal clear and not a blemish on their bodies.

None of these people are like that. Oh, there are good looking people in here. A lot of them, in fact, but they're all normal. Even in the low light I can see people at the tables next to mine with acne scars, too much makeup, crooked teeth. These people are people.

And they're insurance. Because he knows something's going down, and he doesn't trust me. Why would he? I wouldn't in his shoes. And I knew he wouldn't. But I didn't realize he'd put a bunch of human shields between the two of us.

"Thanks," I say. I'm about to ask her name and stop myself. I don't want to know her name. I can't know her name. She's the waitress, and nameless, and if I try real hard maybe I can make her faceless in my memories.

The kid at the bar—Benny his name is Benny and you will never forget it and you will hate yourself and you will throw it on the stacks of people who you are trying to forget and can never forget because they won't ever let you—sees me and lifts up the counter so I can step behind the bar.

"The door's in the wall just behind the mirror, sir," he says. After I go through and close it, everything goes utterly silent, the music, the voices, the clink of glasses and pouring of drinks.

Short hallway, thick, green carpet, soothing lighting pointing me to the office at the end where Darius sits behind a grand mahogany desk puffing on a cigar with two cocktails: one for him and one, presumably, for me.

"Eric!" he says, jumping out of his seat and reaching over to shake my hand. "My boy, I've been expecting you. Sit, sit. Lord but it is good to see you. How are you doing? You look fantastic. I poured you a Manhattan, I hope you don't mind. Would you like a cigar?"

"I'm good, thanks. You seem awfully . . . effusive."

"Oh, my boy, I am. Seeing you here brings joy to my heart."

"You know Hank's dead, right?"

"Oh, yes. Heard about it hours ago. Nicely done. I honestly didn't think he'd have much luck taking you out, and I am truly glad he didn't."

"You did order him to kill me, right?"

"Oh, yes. Of course I did. I don't need you to let me out. I can get out all on my own. Can you feel it? I bet you can. It's anticipation. That sense in the air that things are about to happen. I haven't felt that in such a long time."

"So why are you glad I'm here?"

"Because I like you, my boy. Without you, none of this would have been possible. A Mictlantecuhtli trapped in jade was useless to me. So was one that wasn't. I'd never have gotten the old one to try anything. But you, you might. You became him. You're the only one, the only one, who could loosen these bonds."

"Not exactly what I heard from Hank," I say. I take a sip of the Manhattan. As usual, it's perfect.

"Oh, that the wards are failing? That's old news. Hell, I told you that myself some time ago. But I think you knew, or somebody knew, that they were failing a lot faster than anybody expected them to."

"Guilty. Nobody consulted me on it, of course," I say. "I was doing just fine in Mictlan. Gotta say, I'm not all that keen on being human again."

"That is a tragedy. And I am so very sorry it's happened. I know I'm not the one who brought you back, but I'm the reason for it."

"You got a timeframe on those wards?" I say.

"Not yet, but I can feel them weakening more and more every second. Do you?"

"I do. Another couple of days, I think. But I'm not sure you're going to like the result."

"A trap, eh? Hmm. I expected something like that. So let me guess, you've come here to offer me a way to avoid the trap and escape unscathed, is that right?"

"Oh, fuck no," I say. "I'm not gonna blow smoke up your ass. I came here to kill you. Yes, there are traps. And yes, I am offering you a way to get out."

"You've always been so refreshingly forthcoming with me, Eric. I do appreciate that. So, assuming I take your offer, what's your plan?"

"It was going to be to let you out and set off those traps I was just talking about. Figure if I fucked it up, there were backups in place, and it'd be a lot easier to take you down if you walked out on your own. But—"

"Ah, but. You met some of my guests," he says.

"You're a cruel motherfucker, Darius. I know what you did to free Hank. You got, what, four hundred people out there? Five?"

"Oh, I think I'm up to a couple thousand at this point. Most of them in their dreams, but they're here, nonetheless. I have a hook in their souls. Anything were to happen to me, I'd hate to think what would happen to them."

"We're on the same page there," I say. "So here's my new deal. No song, no dance. I let you out with some conditions."

"And what might those conditions be?"

"All those people out there, they gotta go back to where you found them. I know what you're doing. They're hostages who think they're at the world's greatest party. I should have expected you'd pull something like that, and I'm honestly a little pissed off at myself that I didn't see it coming."

"That the only one?"

"That's the only one I think I might have a hope of you keeping, but here are the others. Leave me alone. Leave most of the world alone. I know you're gonna go fuck up a lot of people, a lot of places. I expect the natural disaster quotient to jack up considerably. But leave me out of it. I give a rat's ass who else you kill, but I'd like enough of the world left that I can still drive around in a convertible and eat bad fast food."

"Really," he says. "Then why let these people go? Don't care about anyone else? Sounds like you care about these good souls."

I have to think about that for a second. I decide to tell him the truth. "I thought I was okay once I was in Mictlan. I had other things to keep me occupied, and let's be honest, a death god's not supposed to have a problem with death, right? But I know that whether I set those fires or not, I'm at the root of over a hundred thousand corpses. I don't want that again. I can't have that on my conscience. And these people? They won't just die. Their souls will cease to exist. That's a real death. I've got too much of that shit already."

"And the rest of the world?" he says. He leans forward and steeples his fingers in front of him. "What about the rest of the world? Who knows what I'll do when I get out of here. Maybe I'll kill millions. Maybe I won't do anything at all. But say I do. Say I'm the monster everybody seems to think I am. What about those people?"

"Do you know what pisses me off more than anything else about coming back to life?" I say. "The world was better off without me in it. I would love to save everyone, but so far all I ever do is make things worse. But this. Give me this. Let those people go. Let me at least pretend that I've done something right for once in my life. Promise me that. Promise me that and I will let you out, no tricks, no traps."

"And if I say no?"

"Then when the wards fail you'll see what the combined brainpower and magic of every mage in California can come up with to make sure you don't exist."

"Ouch. Every mage in California? Most of you can't even stop bickering and killing each other long enough to have a conversation. Every mage. Please."

"The ones who count. Werther, Rochambeau, 'Aumākua. Couple other families I'm not familiar with. They're from up around San Francisco."

"That is some impressive firepower," he says. "My, what it must have cost those people in pride to band together. I'm almost tempted to see what they come up with. But not tempted enough. You got yourself a deal."

"You'll let everybody in here go?"

"Absolutely. They go home and you let me out, no strings."

"No strings," I say.

"I think you're lying," he says. "I think you got a trick up your sleeve."

"Maybe," I say. "Probably. But I'm just me. The hell am I gonna do to you? Offer stands. Let these people go and I let you out, or else wait for the wards to fail and get hammered on by the best of the best. I'm sure whatever they've got planned, it'll be quick. They'll want to get back to killing each other as soon as possible."

"All right, Eric," he says. "I don't trust you. But I'll accept your terms. How do we do this?"

"Pop open a door back to where I came from and I'll get going on the rituals."

"That door goes to a bathroom in Union Station, you know."

"I know. I can still smell it. But that's where I've got the bottle. And that's where I'm going to open it."

"You fuck me on this, you know I'll turn you inside out and make your suffering last an eternity."

"Wouldn't doubt it for a second."

"Then here's your door." A red leather door appears next to me.

"I'll see you on the other side, Darius."

"I better."

I open the door and step through.

Chapter 25

There's a dizzying sensation as I get to the other side. I catch a glimpse of Gabriela that's gone so fast I'm not sure I saw it at all, and then I'm in my room at the Ambassador.

I check myself. All my pieces here? Fingers? Toes? Everything feels fine. I try a minor spell, levitate a lamp. Yeah, everything seems to be working as expected.

I do a final check of everything. Front door's locked, stoppered up as effectively as Darius's bottle is. Same spells and everything. Nothing's getting out of this room. But there is something getting in. I have a hole in it that's like Darius's doors. One way only. No matter how hard he tries he's not getting out that way. And neither am I.

I maneuver my butt on the couch just so, pull out the Browning, make sure there's a round chambered. It's angry, that gun. Angry at me. How dare I. I can feel its hatred of me coming off in waves.

"Oh, shut up," I say. "You knew this day was coming a long time ago. It's this or you get melted into evil magical paperweights." Sullen mental silence. Fucking Nazi gun. I'll be glad to be rid of it.

Everything checks, everything's hooked up, ready to go. I've already undone most of the wards on the bottle. Just need to undo one more.

"It's show time, folks," I say, and let the genie out of the bottle.

The bottle's stopper explodes, taking part of the neck with it, sending out a powder of disintegrated glass. A plume of purple smoke, and then there he is: Darius standing before me, clothed in golden robes.

He stretches, takes a deep breath. "Free. So, so long. And now I'm free."

"Not to ruin a moment," I say, "but purple smoke? Really? I don't know if that's like your thing or you were just fucking around, but it feels kind of cliché, you know."

"Eric! My boy! It is so good to see you." He frowns when he sees the gun, frowns deeper when he really starts to look around himself. "This doesn't look like a bathroom stall in Union Station. Where are we?"

"We are in a room that my grandfather left for me in the ghost of the torn-down Ambassador hotel," I say. "Nice place. I'm not crazy about all the decor, but it suits. This is where Hank popped up to grab the bottle. He killed me, but at least he didn't get the bottle. Don't tell me he never told you about it."

"A room inside a ghost, you say?"

"Well, it's really more of a bridge connecting two different realities, held together by forces I don't have the math to describe. That door goes to my reality, and that window behind you goes to . . . I have no idea where. But it looks fascinating, doesn't it? I like the orange sky."

"What the hell is this, Eric?" he says. "We had a deal."

"And you didn't uphold your end of the bargain." I hold up a hand when he starts to protest. "Those people aren't back safe and sound. The bottle might be open, and it might never be able to be closed again, but that universe sitting inside it is still there, isn't it?"

"What makes you think I didn't let them go?"

"Because I know you, you fuck," I say. "I know you didn't let them go, you weren't going to let them go, and you're not going to let them go now. I wish you would have. I wish you were somebody who could keep your word, but no, you're really not. And I hate it. I hate that they're caught in the middle. I hate that you put them in the middle. I hate that you've put me in the position of determining not only whether they live or die, but what happens to their souls."

"What's your play here, son?" A throne of gold appears behind him, pushing the table with the bottle back a few feet. "You think this place will hold me? I can feel the edges, the magic. This is nothing compared to where I was. Give me a little bit, I'll bust out of here, and you and all your friends will be in a world of hurt."

"Oh, it won't hold you," I say. "Not supposed to. You actually gave me the idea when you went on about how fragile my emotional and mental state is. How easy it is to shatter once somebody got under my skin. I hate to admit you're right, but you are. At heart I'm just a big softy. What was it you called it? A demon bottle? Devil something?"

"A Devil's Flask."

"Right. Devil's Flask. One little pinprick from the inside and the whole thing collapses. It's a good trick. I looked it up on YouTube. And thanks for the whole magic-of-perception thing. You were right there, too. Stage magic is fascinating. Perception, redirection. Given me a lot to think about."

"I see. And this room is a Devil's Flask? This is the trap you've laid for me?"

"It is," I say. "Probably shouldn't have broken your

bottle like you did. Might have saved you." I raise up the Browning and fire at the window. The gunshot reverberates through the room, deafening. I shift my weight on the couch as the brass flies out of the pistol. I start to count down.

Laughter. Deep, hysterical laughter. "That's your play?" Darius says. He inspects the bullet. "You thought I couldn't catch this? Or was I supposed to, and it's got some magic on it I can't detect?"

"Just a bullet," I say. "Nothing special. I knew you'd catch it. I just didn't want you to notice me moving off this pressure plate dead man switch I've been sitting on this whole time."

"What?"

"Go big or go home, motherfucker."

The window explodes as the fifty kilograms of C4 packed around it, hidden by the curtains, go off, shattering the glass and the wall, shredding the furniture, and ripping into me. Shrapnel punches into my face, my body. I've never felt this much pain.

But it's a flash in the pan compared to the pain I feel as the room collapses. I feel my body and soul twisted, all those people Darius didn't let go dying, every single one. Their souls shredded like confetti. All I can hear is Darius's screaming and I can't join in because I don't have vocal cords or lungs and a moment later I don't have ears to hear as the universe collapses around us.

———

"Fuck," I say. Eyes popped open, heart racing. "Fuck, fuck, fuck. Jesus fucking fuck fuck. Holy fuck that hurt."

"I told you it'd be just like the real thing," Holt says. "Some of my best work, to be honest."

I sit up in the gurney in a hospital room. Blood pressure monitors beep, defibrillator ready to go, an

IV-line snaking into my arm. Gabriela is next to me in her paramedic uniform, half a dozen of her people dressed the same. Amanda's there, Holt, his kid, even Werther.

"Toto, we're home," I say. "Which one of you gets to be Auntie Em? You have any problem getting me out of the bathroom?"

"Even in context that doesn't sound good," Gabriela says. "Yeah. No problems. How are you feeling?"

"Shaken. I'm missing something." I look at Holt. "That's what it's like for you? Losing a chunk of your soul?"

"I usually don't, but yeah. It doesn't take much. If I'd been really pissed off at you I could have stuck the whole thing in there. Oddly enough, it'll grow back, though I honestly didn't expect you to have one at all."

"Funny," I say.

"The bottle?" Amanda says.

"Oh, it's good and busted. The room definitely collapsed, but I need confirmation from the Ambassador." My phone rings. The number is just a string of zeroes. "And that would be it now."

"The ghost has a phone?" Holt says.

"One in every room, apparently. Don't ask me how it's connecting to the rest of the network."

I put the phone on speaker. "Mister Carter," the ghost says.

"Ambassador. How are we doing?"

"Your room has, as you expected, disconnected from your door. It's gone. I'm so sorry, though I understand the necessity. You and your lady friend are, of course, always welcome. Your grandfather merely rented the door. You are still guests in perpetuity and I would be happy to have you stay in one of the luxury suites."

"I would be honored to take you up on that," I say. "Might be a little while."

"Any time, sir. My doors are always open." The phone disconnects.

"It's over?" Gabriela says.

"It's over."

"You need to get some rest," Holt says. "Piloting one of my simulacra can take a lot out of you."

"I'm glad you didn't die," Jordan says.

"Me too, kid."

"All right, everybody out," Gabriela says. "Go on, git." She ushers everyone out through the door. I catch a glimpse of the hall outside. I'm not in a hospital, this is her shelter. She closes the door once everyone's gone.

She sits in a swivel chair and rolls it over to the bed. "You okay?"

"I'm fantastic," I say.

"Tell me the truth," she says.

I close my eyes. "I felt them all die," I say. "I knew it was going to happen, and I let it, and I felt them all die. And they didn't just die. They screamed and howled as the world disintegrated around them and their souls shredded apart like a trailer park in a tornado. All of them. They're all gone." I can feel every single one of them like a punch in the stomach.

"Who?"

"Darius had a couple thousand people in his club that night to use as human shields," I say. "He said he'd let them go, and I knew he wouldn't."

"Oh, fuck."

"He counted on me not being such a bastard. Proved him wrong, didn't I? I mean, what's a couple thousand compared to a hundred thousand in the fires? What's that phrase? The butcher's bill? I'm running a butcher's tab. I have to admit, Holt does do good work. I felt every single one of them."

"There is a difference," she says. "I know you don't want to hear this, and I know it won't help, probably the opposite, but you need to hear it. You did not kill those people in the fires."

"I know, I—"

"But you did kill those people in the bottle."

"Great pep talk, coach," I say.

"If anyone is on your butcher's tab," she says, "it's them. It's not your fault, you didn't put them there, but you did kill them and you knew it was going to happen. I know it hurts. I know it's agonizing. You'll never forget it, just like you've never forgotten anyone else you've killed, whether you knew their names or not."

She puts her hand over mine. After a minute she says, "Move over."

"Gabriela, I—"

"Shut up and move over." Her eyes are wet, same as mine. I move over and she climbs onto the gurney, wraps her arms and legs around me.

"There's a price to pay for doing what needs to be done," she says, her voice barely a whisper. "They paid it. You paid it. You'll pay it again. We'll both keep paying it. We can think of ourselves however we want, we can make other people think we're hardasses. But like it or not, we're human. Even you, Eric. Even me."

"Hey, about that talk—" I say.

"Later. I'm not going anywhere," she says. "And I hope you aren't, either."

We don't talk after that, just hold on to each other. I've only been alive for, what, two days now? Two days and I'm so tired. Eventually, I sleep.

———

The kid in the botanica, can't be more than twenty, ushers me behind the curtains and into the empty chapel. They've rebuilt since the fires, made it nice and posh. They still get the occasional gawker, or Good

Christian Soldier who throws a brick through the window, or a guy trying to make a reality tv show about them.

"I'll leave you alone with her," he says, and slips back out through the curtain.

The chapel to Santa Muerte is like most chapels. Provided those chapels are in the back room of a storefront in a strip mall next to a nail salon. There are pews, a podium, candles. The twice-life-size skeleton in a wedding dress dominates the room over to the side. She's on a stone stand covered in offerings. Roses, tequila, cigars, a couple bricks of cocaine. I sit in the pew in front of her and think back to the one I killed, and the one who rose from her ashes.

I feel jangly and cracked. Where does a former death god go to look for solace? I'd like to think this would be the place, but I know it isn't. After today, I don't think I'll ever come back here.

I snip the end off a cigar, a nice Romeo y Julieta I picked up on my way over, and light it with a spell. I'd use Huitzilopochtli's lighter, but I don't really want to burn the whole place down. I crack open a bottle of tequila, good stuff, not that Jose Cuervo crap sitting on the altar, and pour drinks into two red Solo cups.

Have a smoke, relax a little, wait. It doesn't take long. I don't see Tabitha or even feel her presence until she picks up her cup, sips the tequila. "Is it over?" she says.

"Is it ever really?" I say. "Yes, it's over. Darius is gone. Gone gone. I trapped him in an alternate universe and collapsed it around him and got to witness the whole thing and feel every single moment of it and did I mention he'd trapped a couple thousand people in his bottle thinking I wouldn't do anything while they were there, but I did it, anyway, and I felt all their deaths and souls disintegrate, too. So, how was your day?"

She sips her tequila. "I'm sorry."

I toss mine back and pour another. "Me, too. I don't suppose—"

"No," she says. "I wish I could, but even he can't make it so you can come back. Did you find who did it?"

"Gabriela of all people."

"That bitch."

"I understand her reasoning. Don't like it, but I understand it."

"She should learn to keep her mitts off of other people's stuff."

I laugh. "Seriously? You have enough of me, you can't spare a chunk to help bring down your greatest enemy?"

"I'm very possessive," she says. "What was it you'd said? Don't like it, but I understand it."

"You didn't answer my question. How are you doing?"

"Would it be terrible to say I was doing well?" she says. "Like really well?"

"No. You feel what you feel. I can't really get jealous of myself, can I? Stings a bit, though."

"I'm not going to see you again, am I?" she says.

"I thought that was supposed to be my line. I don't know. I have to admit I hope not. This is nice, sitting here with you. But it won't last, and truth be told, I don't think it's good for me to see you again. Not like this, at least. Like we're on some kind of equal footing."

"What if I want to see you?" she says.

"You just have to look over and you'll see me. Everything you need of me is right there. And he won't leave your side for anything."

"And if he isn't everything?"

"Isn't he?"

She takes the cigar from me and blows out a couple of smoke rings. Of course, Santa Muerte knows how to blow smoke rings. "I don't know. He's different.

Not bad, but different. Different enough to notice. And you're not like him."

"I don't know what I'm like," I say. "I don't even know who I am. Or what I am, for that matter. Am I really Eric Carter? Am I any different? Am I a better man? Worse? I'm wearing my grandfather's skin. Am I part him, or is he part me? What the hell am I?"

"I think you're just you," she says. "That's all anyone can be, right?"

"Life advice from the death goddess. You should pen a column for the New Yorker," I say. "You know he loves you, right?"

"Does he? He's never said."

"He won't. Because he's an idiot. But trust me, he loves you. And he's happy. He's where he wants to be. Where he needs to be. It's given him a purpose he's never had before."

"I'm sorry, Eric. I didn't want any of this to happen."

"Is what it is."

"This is goodbye?" she says.

"I think so."

She takes my hand and slips something into it. "Something to remember me by." I look down into my hand and there's my wedding ring. Gold, calaveras carved all along it. It would feel weird to wear it. I don't know if I ever will. I slip it into my pocket. I look up to thank her and she's gone.

I stay a few more minutes to finish my cigar, and then I leave it all behind, too.

Joe Sunday's dead...

...he just hasn't stopped moving yet.

Sunday's a thug, an enforcer, a leg-breaker for hire. When his boss sends him to kill a mysterious new business partner, his target strikes back in ways Sunday could never have imagined. Murdered, brought back to a twisted half-life, Sunday finds himself stuck in the middle of a race to find an ancient stone with the power to grant immortality. With it, he might live forever. Without it, he's just another rotting extra in a George Romero flick.

Everyone's got a stake: a psycho Nazi wizard, a nympho-demon bartender, a too-powerful witch who just wants to help her homeless vampires, and the one woman who might have all the answers — if only Sunday can figure out what her angle is.

Before the week is out he's going to find out just what lengths people will go to for immortality. And just how long somebody can hold a grudge.

City of the Lost
by Stephen Blackmoore
978-0-7564-0702-5

DAW 209

Tad Williams

The Last King of Osten Ard

"Building upon the revered history of *Memory, Sorrow, and Thorn*, Williams has outdone himself by penning a 700-plus page novel that is virtually un-put-down-able.... Williams' grand-scale storytelling mastery is on full display here. Not just utterly readable—an instant fantasy classic." —*Kirkus Reviews* (starred)

"Tad Williams is a master storyteller, and the Osten Ard books are his masterpiece. Williams' return to Osten Ard is every bit as compelling, deep, and fully rendered as the first trilogy, and he continues to write with the experience and polish of an author at the top of his game." —Brandon Sanderson

"What got me the most about this new one, the thing that felt the best, was not the book's considerable literary merits but its power to muffle the outside world for the time it took me to read it." —Tor.com

The Witchwood Crown: 978-0-7564-1061-2
Empire of Grass: 978-0-7564-1062-9

To Order Call: 1-800-788-6262
www.dawbooks.com

DAW 52

Patrick Rothfuss
The Slow Regard of Silent Things

Deep below the University, there is a dark place. Few people know of it: a broken web of ancient passageways and abandoned rooms. A young woman lives there, tucked among the sprawling tunnels of the Underthing, snug in the heart of this forgotten place.

Her name is Auri, and she is full of mysteries...

The Slow Regard of Silent Things is a brief, bittersweet glimpse of Auri's life, a small adventure all her own. At once joyous and haunting, this story offers a chance to see the world through Auri's eyes. And it gives the reader a chance to learn things that only Auri knows....

"*The Slow Regard of Silent Things* is a microcosm of everything fantasy is about.... When an author has built an entire world, they naturally want to tell a story that fills all its corners. And that's fine: I wouldn't trade that massive scale for anything. But I'm also eternally glad that, even just this once, one of our greatest working writers dared to tell a tale this small."   —Tor.com

Hardcover: 978-0-7564-1043-8
Paperback: 978-0-7564-1132-9

To Order Call: 1-800-788-6262
www.dawbooks.com

DAW 103